The Scaevola Conspiracy

A Crime Thriller

By

Timo Bozsolik-Torres

ISBN: 978-1-914933-67-7

i2i

PUBLISHING

www.i2ipublishing.co.uk
i2i Publishing, Manchester.

Dedication

To my wife Cindy
and my kids the pumpkin and the peanut.

For making my life a breeze and supporting all my crazy
ideas.

Chapter One

The diner smelled of stale filter coffee, fried onions and bacon, mixed with sweat and the scent of cleaning product from the freshly polished linoleum floor. The table in his booth was sticky; sugar granules congregated around the metal napkin box on its centre. What a place to decide the future of such an ingenious invention. But it provided anonymity. A disconnected island in the ocean of our hyperconnected world.

Resisting the waitress' efforts to tempt him with food, the young CEO sipped his coffee and observed the darkness outside. It reminded him that he no longer had a social life. Managing a startup was hard work, especially after his breakthrough, technology that could change life as we know it.

Despite his best efforts to keep a lid on their achievements, news of their success had leaked to the public over the last few weeks. Reporters drowned him with interview requests, other companies with acquisition offers. All he wanted was to concentrate on research, but now was the time for a decision. He was running out of funding and needed a home for his discovery, an application in the real world. And much as he hated it, that meant meeting investors and listening to their visions about the future of his work.

Which had led him to this table. He'd agreed to meet this particular outfit on such short notice out of courtesy. When one of the largest, most innovative tech companies in the world requested an urgent meeting, he at least had to show up and hear what they had to say. He didn't plan on accepting their offer, however high it may be — they'd optimize for the bottom line, not humanity.

'Your technology's very impressive,' the man on the opposite side of the table said. 'We've been tracking your progress for a while now, and we're excited to see you're finally ready.'

The proposal started as expected. Acquisition, generous payouts for all early investors, enough shares to make every employee an instant millionaire, and the promise of virtually unlimited funds for his research.

What followed was beyond his wildest imagination. With every offer came demands, the CEO had expected as much, but what they wanted was nothing short of insane. They sure had found an application for his technology, in some brutally twisted way maybe the perfect application. And it was nothing short of evil.

No. This couldn't be true.

'Sorry,' he said, looking at his watch. 'It's way too late for pranks. With all due respect, I've had a long day. This isn't funny. Whoever's hiding in the kitchen, come out already. I'll buy you a beer for trying.'

The man on the opposite side didn't laugh, didn't flinch. He gave no reaction at all.

The CEO checked his surroundings. If he hadn't been so exhausted and in such a bad mood, he'd have laughed. The whole situation was such a cliché.

'I can assure you this is no joke,' the company spokesperson said. 'Here, this is my business card. Go ahead and verify I'm for real.'

Reluctantly, the CEO took it and typed on his phone. His counterpart waited patiently. It seemed he'd gone through these motions many times before.

'OK. So you're legit,' he said after three minutes of research. 'Is this your way of making sure new acquisitions share your weird sense of humour?'

'I'm one hundred per cent serious. I'm speaking for our CEO and on behalf of the entire company.'

Could this be real?

'Think about it,' the representative said. 'You'll become insanely rich and secure the future of your company. But more importantly, you'll make history. The world will remember your name.'

The world will remember my name.

Reading people was one of the qualities that made him a successful leader. He wanted this to be a joke, he really did. But at the same time, he knew the person on the other end of the table was absolutely sincere. There was an aura around him, something shady and mysterious. Fanatical even.

'I don't know if there's a protocol for these meetings,' the CEO said. 'Maybe I should tell you I'll think about it, even if I don't intend to. Then I could give you a call back tomorrow and decline politely to make sure our business relationship stays friendly, yadda yadda yadda. But what you just told me is nothing short of insane.'

He chose his next words carefully. Madness was best addressed with a firm response. 'If this is your plan, then you're out of your mind. Which means I'm out. Obviously. And because you might actually have the means to go through with it, I'll go to the media tomorrow and tell them your company is employing a lunatic in a senior position. They always love a good story from crazy town, so I'm sure they'll write a nice little piece about it. Then, there'll be consequences. For your company and for you personally.'

The CEO's hands were shaking, so he kept them hidden under the table. He'd threatened an executive from one of the most prestigious companies in the country and meant every single word of it.

The other man took his time. He was European, maybe French, and built more like a soldier than an acquisition liaison. Yet he was well-dressed and mannered. His face had no discernible expression at all. No signs of distress.

'Let me tell you something,' he said, finally. 'I've done this several times now. I've heard enthusiasm, scepticism and threats. In the end, your answer doesn't matter. If you decline, we'll simply change our strategy. But we always get what we want, one way or another. Do yourself a favour, and let's do this the easy way.'

The CEO chuckled, a mad chuckle of resignation and disbelief. 'You're nuts. We're done here.'

'Then you leave me no choice. Have a good night.' The man stood up, paid their bill and left the restaurant. At least he had manners.

Bewildered, the CEO took a couple of minutes to finish his coffee and check his emails. Maybe it was a prank after all. Maybe his British friends, with their famous dry humour, had set him up. He'd find out soon enough. It was late, and his tiredness ran too deep to think about it now.

Back outside, fumbling for his keys in the dark parking lot, he noticed a movement in the shadows. He turned towards the sound.

Too late.

The bullet struck his chest before he heard the soft thump of the silencer. A second bullet hit him, right next to the first. He stumbled backwards, unable to run, unable to scream. Pain flushed through his body.

The CEO hit the ground hard. He couldn't move his arms and legs. Was that due to shock or had his body mechanics already gone? It didn't matter. Nothing mattered anymore. He was dying, right then and there.

His eyes and his brain worked for a few more moments. The shooter came closer and checked on his target. The same man who'd sat opposite him in the restaurant a few minutes ago. The same expression of indifference.

It was no prank.

He felt his body being dragged away, towards the trunk of a car.

Then the world disappeared.

Chapter Two

Four Months Later

Lukasz concentrated on keeping his knees from bouncing as he watched another employee badge in. For years, he'd been looking forward to the day when he'd walk through that door, working for the most prestigious tech company on the planet. Today, this dream had become reality.

He went over the facts he'd memorized: specifications for all of Swoop's flagship products; how many employees worked in engineering, sales and all the other support roles; the core values of the company; and pretty much every known detail about their famous founder. As always, he'd come prepared. Much depended on him surviving in this new environment.

What he didn't know was which team he was about to join. These days, all the fuss, the big wave everybody wanted to ride, was machine learning. The space was full of pretenders who repeated the same buzzwords over and over, but Lukasz was a true data scientist, freshly out of university and ready to apply his knowledge. At Swoop, he had the chance to change the world as well as to provide for his parents, who'd never admit it but desperately needed money. When the offer came, he signed without even asking where he'd be placed. But now he couldn't wait to find out. His dream was to work on *Personal Secretary*, a revolutionary feature at the forefront of new technology. Breaking barriers, working with the best of the best—now he was the one using the buzzwords.

The huge lobby housed nothing less than a rainforest. Not a stylised version with fake flowers here and there, but an actual proper jungle. Plants concealed the walls and grass covered the floor. A tropical tree spanned several floors; lianas dangled from its massive branches and dipped into an artificial river leading to the base of a Mayan pyramid. It reminded him more of a theme park than an office building.

The scenery had several built-in TV screens, their frames painted in rusty colours. One of them showed a Swoop-specific collection of the latest news, selected in real-time by an artificial intelligence algorithm from TV channels all over the world.

'...which is why we at Whitefeed are pleased to become the newest member of the Swoop family,' a young Asian woman said. 'Especially after losing our beloved CEO to such a random act of violence. I'm sure he'd be proud of us. Today, we're sealing our partnership with Swoop to make sure his ground-breaking research will be preserved and applied in practice.'

The show didn't disclose the exact nature of that application, but Whitefeed's Wikipedia page revealed they specialised in brain wave technology—a way to connect people's thoughts directly to machines. The opportunities were endless.

At nine o'clock, the other Noops—new Swoop employees—trickled in, and a tall, middle-aged man with a blond ponytail appeared. His worn badge read Shawn, no last name. The haircut in his security photo screamed nineties, a long-term employee. He hadn't aged all that much, hence he probably wasn't in the engineering gene pool.

They entered a meeting room organised in a classic U-shape; Lukasz counted eighteen men and five women. All appeared within a couple of years of his age, twenty-four. Most of them were tall, lean, handsome and had great hair. In other words, they didn't look like any of the other software engineers he'd met before.

'Welcome to the first day of your new life,' Shawn swept his arms up, a magician announcing his greatest trick. 'I can't tell you how happy I am to have the privilege to lead you through the first days of this new era. I'm the sales director for North America and I've been with Swoop for thirteen wonderful years.'

The most overly enthusiastic person Lukasz had ever met, he talked at length about how great the company was, how lucky they were to be a part of it, and the bright future that lay ahead of them. Lukasz developed an immediate grudge.

Twenty minutes into the introduction, a girl entered the room. Lukasz was baffled. Who showed up late on their first day of work? She was dressed all in black and had dark green hair with washed-out pink tips — a cliché nerd girl, at the same time impossible to put in any drawer.

'Hey there, I assume you're another Noop?' said Shawn.

'A what?' the girl asked.

'A Noop. You know, new at Swoop.'

She rolled her eyes. 'That's literally the fucking dumbest word I've ever heard. Whoever invented it should be fired and banned from making up any more words, ever.'

Suppressed chuckles came from around the room. If Lukasz wasn't so polite, and it hadn't been his first day, he'd have laughed too.

Shawn looked at her for a couple of seconds and then moved on. 'Terrific. Have a seat. We were about to go around the table to introduce ourselves. I'd like you all to share how you felt when you found out you got hired by the greatest company in the world.'

'Oh cool, are we holding hands while we're sharing? We could sit on the floor and sing "Kumbaya, My Lord",' the girl said.

Half of the room giggled, the other half kept their faces blank. Lukasz made a mental note, he'd just identified the engineering and the sales halves of the room.

Shawn stared at the girl in shock, clearly unsure how to process this comment. Finally, he snapped back into his normal mode of operation. 'OK, I'll start. I was walking my dog, Bennie, in Central Park back home in New York City when my phone rang, and I received the offer. I was so incredibly happy that I cried in front of everybody. I sat down on a bench and spent a whole hour staring at the sky, dreaming of the impact I'd have on the world. But mostly, I was just crying.'

Around Lukasz, the sales half of the room had wide dreamy smiles, the engineers looked as puzzled as he was. The girl in black's mouth dropped wide open.

Shawn rambled on for a few more minutes. When he was done, he asked the girl to share her story. They were going clockwise, putting Lukasz in the last third of the circle.

Fifteen people … he had fifteen stories to prepare his own spiel.

The girl flashed a tired smile and shrugged. 'Fine. My name's Ada and I'm from downtown San Francisco. My parents were into computer science, so I thought I'd continue the family tradition. I used to be a tech blogger, at least until a couple of weeks ago. I mostly wrote about security, privacy and stuff. And now I'm here. End of story.'

'Oh, come on. Even you must be happy to be here. Tell us how you found out,' said someone from the sales camp.

'Nope, definitely don't want to talk about it. Not everybody's a fucking walking smiley face.'

Shawn entered damage-control mode. 'Alright. Sharing isn't for everyone. Let's move on.'

Next up was a person named Clark, no last name either. Black, with short hair, tall, and extremely passionate about his favourite activity – golf, of all things. Lukasz quickly identified him as an extrovert. Unusual, for an engineer.

One by one, people around the table told their stories. Most of them made a point of obnoxiously mentioning their interests and hobbies. Their tales were ridiculous clichés of perfect lives – four serious mountaineers, two who'd made an attempt at Mount Everest, although neither had succeeded; two guitarists, a drummer and a singer, all playing in rock bands on the experimental end of the spectrum; a marathon runner, a triathlete, a world-class open-water swimmer and three semi-professional ultimate frisbee players. Lukasz didn't know frisbee was played at a professional level and calling it ultimate was a little much for him. But he wasn't really into sports, so what did he know?

The combination of people and their stories seemed surreal. Where he was from, software engineers were nerds with thick glasses, herded together in windowless rooms, well hidden from any customers. They were like him. Here, they seemed to be rock stars.

Ten more people until his turn. He stayed calm and created a game plan for his introduction. Competing with their adventures was impossible, and what was the point of bothering a bunch of strangers with his life story anyway? If only he could find something funny to say, an innocent detail that would make people chuckle but not laugh at him. He came up blank.

He knew this would happen. *Come on, you can do this.*

Five people to go, five stories, a maximum of twenty minutes. His heartbeat accelerated, a soft, rhythmic thumping inside his temple.

Nobody will judge you. This is just small talk. Make something up.

Lukasz hated small talk. He didn't see the objective or how it advanced the conversation. No informational value.

Three to go. A little more than ten minutes. I wonder what would happen if I went to the bathroom?

The anticipation was killing him. He didn't even listen to their tales anymore. He'd already forgotten the story he'd made up five minutes ago.

Two more. Six minutes, maybe eight.

Sweat broke out in his palms and armpits. It crept up his neck. When he was a kid, they'd called him weird. He'd felt it, too, a fuzzy background feeling that became more pronounced around groups of strangers and always seemed to be in his way. When he asked his parents about it, they'd said it was OK to be a bit weird. But he was a creature of science and 'a bit weird' wasn't good enough for him. He did some research and consulted a psychologist— the most uncomfortable hour of his life. Social anxiety was the name of his condition.

One more to go. Three or four minutes tops. Is this worth it? I could go home now and come back tomorrow. They wouldn't fire me for that, would they?

He shifted in his chair, moving his weight from one side to the other and back again. He'd studied the symptoms, and today, he had them all: the heat in his forehead, the cold in his feet. His brain knew the only way to get past it was to expose himself to uncomfortable situations. His stomach didn't agree.

The person to his left had finished. It was his turn. Now. Time to man up.

He froze. Twenty-five people in the room stared at him, their faces suddenly hostile. Raised eyebrows over evil eyes zeroed in on him, narrowing in on his very soul. The only warm and friendly person was the girl in black.

'Hello? It's your turn. Are you alright?' Shawn asked.

'Yeah ... yes, it's muh-my turn. My nuh-name is Lukasz. Uhm ... I'm from Belarus. I'm a ... duh-data scientist.'

'And?' said Shawn.

Lukasz's mind flat-lined. 'I ... I was happy when I guh-got hired.'

'Please! We don't care about your whole boring life story.' The girl in black heaved a sigh. 'Can we move on?'

The person on Lukasz's left side got the cue, chuckled and started talking. A handful of people shook their heads, but everybody moved on quickly enough. Ada gave him a wink, and he nodded back gratefully. She seemed nice.

Situation under control. Was this really so bad? he asked himself as he was supposed to every time his anxiety came back.

After completing the full circle of introductions, Shawn methodically covered all of Swoop's products and offerings. Device by device, app by app, feature by feature. Of course, Lukasz knew all of this already. His goal was to become one of the best data scientists in the world and join Swoop's renowned research team, an accomplishment that'd set his family up for life. The only way in was a recommendation by an employee far up the reporting chain, and to pull this off, he had to listen, prepare and work harder than anybody else.

Three hours and exactly zero additional knowledge later, the group followed Shawn to one of the many cafes for lunch.

The break came as a relief. Although Lukasz spent his day mostly listening, being in crowds drained him. Finally, a bit of silence. He carried his tray to an empty table far away from the others and enjoyed two full minutes of solitude before —

'Society's a bitch, isn't she?' The girl in black took the seat next to him.

Clutching his cutlery like a toddler, Lukasz had no idea how to respond. He couldn't appear rude on his first day, and he fought the urge to send her away; besides, even if she talked way too much, he kind of liked her.

She continued. 'I mean we already have to spend the whole day with all these morons, and now we're expected to have lunch with them. No thank you.' She shoved a spoonful into her mouth. 'And don't feel like you have to answer that sales jerk if you don't want to. He's a sales dude who's not in your reporting chain. Who the hell cares?'

Fixated on his food, Lukasz still didn't have anything smart to say. People didn't usually come and talk to him. All his previous relationships had evolved purely by circumstance: family, neighbours, working groups at school or common interests. Ada didn't seem to care about social norms. Or any norms for that matter.

A minute of silence passed, and Lukasz's chair became increasingly uncomfortable. He'd better come up with some words, and fast.

'What happened? I mean when you were hired,' he finally asked. 'People usually write blogs to get noticed by big companies. You must've been happy enough.'

Ada smiled. 'I'm not fucking people. Read my blog and you'll see. Truth be told, I was sort of forced into this.

Not that Swoop isn't a good company. Technically speaking, most of their infrastructure's actually pretty solid. But I'd have preferred to stay on my own rather than to give in to corporate capitalism.'

That didn't compute. Where Lukasz was from, everybody wanted to work for a successful tech company and get rich along the way. 'How does one get forced into a job?'

'Slavery, I guess. It still exists. Seriously, ask any of those poor kids working in the textile industry in fucking Bangladesh.'

'Yes, I've heard of globalisation. How were *you* forced into this job?'

'So you do understand sarcasm,' she said with a wide grin. 'Now that's something I can work with.'

Trying to keep his cool, Lukasz couldn't avoid a few eye twitches. He hated when people didn't provide clear answers to straightforward questions.

She rolled her eyes and checked her surroundings. There was a perimeter of emptiness around them that would've made others question their smell. 'I'm not supposed to talk about it. I can get into deep shit if I do. Do you understand?'

'No problem.' He didn't, actually, but he also didn't want to push her out of her comfort zone. 'No need to get into it. I was curious, since – '

'But I'm dying to tell somebody. I'm a blogger for shit's sake, I have to talk about stuff.' She took a deep breath. 'You seem like an honourable person. I just have this feeling. So I'll tell you, but you have to swear this stays between us. You know, with great power comes great responsibility and all that shit.'

His index finger tingled. Did he really want to know? Maybe it was a trap, and there'd be laughter all around him in a second. Exactly what he needed on his first day. *Calm down, Lukasz.* Trust had to start somewhere. 'OK,' he said with a shrug.

'So … When I said I was a blogger, it was only part of the truth. That was my official, uhm, day job. I was also … I guess you'd call it a hacker. Not in a life-threatening way, of course. I mostly broke into government systems to find the truth about politicians.

'I was looking into this right-wing douchebag who was supposed to become a federal judge. The guy was a real shit show, and we can't have one of those in power. So I broke into his mailbox at the Department of Justice — which was super easy by the way, thanks to those idiot admins working for the government. Anyway, nothing to see there. But I found out he was using an anonymous Swoop email to do his dirty work.

'I broke into their servers next, which was much harder. I found a bit of dirt, not even much … I mean, for an asshole like that. But worse, Swoop found me. I'm still not sure how they did it, but the next day, I had a home visit from a fucking FBI squad.'

Lukasz' knife scraped on his plate. Did she say FBI? 'Not good.'

'You bet your ass not good. They interrogated me and showed me the whole goddamn file they had on me. I couldn't deny any of it. They had me cornered real bad. But apparently, I'd found a weakness in their system they didn't know about, so they gave me a choice. I could go to jail until the end of time or join Swoop and help improve their security.

'As I said, I hate big corporations, they're demons of capitalism, but I didn't have a choice, did I? So now I have to play by their stupid rules for five years before they drop my charges. Five whole years. That's like … seven per cent of my life, assuming I live to, say, eighty. Totally sucks.'

A criminal. Lukasz had managed to befriend an outlaw on his first day. A risk he wasn't supposed to take. What next? This new place was full of surprises. He'd better get used to it.

'Thank you for sharing,' he said. 'Your secret's safe with me.'

Chapter Three

After lunch, Shawn led them to the security office to receive their official Swoop badges. On their way over, Clark, the chatty golf enthusiast, followed close behind Lukasz and Ada.

Waiting in line, he turned to them and said, 'So you're the famous Ada Fisher. Man, what are you doing here at Swoop? Shouldn't you be in a deep dark dungeon with your pals from Anonymous, trying to bring down some third-world government?'

'I already have all the secrets worth stealing. No fun anymore,' she said. 'Who the hell are you again?'

'I'm Clark,' he said as the queue shuffled forward. 'I like what you do, at least the articles about technology. I don't care too much for the social commentary bits, but I guess everybody needs a hobby.'

'Do you want an autograph or what?'

He laughed and snapped his heels together. 'No thanks, your highness, I'm good. Just wanted to say hi, is all.'

'Why don't you say hi to the other morons in the group?' asked Ada.

He tilted his head. 'Isn't it obvious? I'm an idiot, not a moron. Completely different species. I have to stick with you guys, the other idiots.'

'Hey, I'm not an idiot,' Lukasz protested.

'Sorry, that's how it is. I don't make the rules.'

It was Lukasz's turn. He approached the photographer, who stifled a yawn as he moved Lukasz into position before taking a quick snap from his corporate phone — the newest Swoop model. A few seconds later, a complex machine spat out Lukasz's very own badge. Even though the picture looked dull, he couldn't help but smile. The nerdy kid from Belarus had come a long way.

He crossed paths with Ada as he came back.

'I think Clark's alright,' she whispered. 'We can probably let him hang out with us a bit — only on probation, you know. One wrong move and I'll shoo him away quicker than he can say quicksort. Okay?'

Lukasz had mixed feelings. Two people entering his space in a single day? Using a breathing technique he'd learned in therapy, he tried to suppress his anxiety. A long breath in, through the abdomen, and out for six seconds. Another one in, and out again. He had to learn to become more social, and now was as good a time to start as any. 'Alright, but we keep an eye on him.'

He continued towards Clark and fell in line with him.

'Sorry, dude, I didn't catch your name,' Clark said. 'I had to establish trust with the alpha female first.'

'Lukasz, Lukasz Jankovic.'

'Yankovic? For real? Like Weird Al?'

'I'm sorry, I don't know what that is. Jankovic is a common name around Minsk.'

'Never mind. Hey, I've heard of Belarus. Dude, is it true they still have the KGB? Must've been tough growing up there.'

The pressure inside Lukasz's skull dropped a few pascals. Belarus was a small, isolated country. Few Europeans knew where it was; most others didn't even know it existed. The fact this guy had some knowledge gave Lukasz a bit of comfort. Maybe Clark wasn't so bad.

'Yes, that's right. Although it translates to KDB in Belarusian. They're not as bad as they used to be, but they still kidnap people occasionally.'

'Wow, Luke, this is sick. How'd you end up here then?'

'It's Lukasz.' He enunciated the *sz* as best as he could, but instantly knew it was wasted energy.

They chatted about his background until Ada returned and presented her badge. She'd pulled an absurd grimace in her photo and was barely recognisable.

Clark chortled. 'How'd you get away with this?'

Ada's giggle made the Noop next in line shake his head. 'He told me I was being inappropriate, but I kept doing it. He challenged me three times and finally gave up. Perseverance, baby! That's the key.'

'Luke was telling me how he kept running away from the KGB as he grew up in Belarus,' Clark said.

'It's Lukasz. And I—'

'They've got quite a hacker scene going on there,' Ada said. 'A guy from Minsk hacked into the network of the European Central Bank to steal information about the next interest rate or something. Right?'

Lukasz fidgeted with his badge. 'I don't know. I'm not associated with any spies or hackers.'

'This isn't about hacking. It's about fucking society,' Ada said. 'Whenever people are in control, they're trying to hide the truth. They assume the public doesn't have the balls to handle it. But trust me, people understand, and they find out eventually.'

'Power to the people, stick it to the man. Sound familiar?' Clark said.

'You're a real smart-ass. I'm not saying communism is the solution,' Ada said. 'But I'm pretty sure there's something better than what we have now. But why listen to me? I'm not in charge, I'm just opinionated.'

Once everybody had their badge, Shawn showed them the rest of the office: kitchenettes, game rooms with pool and ping pong tables, a woodworking area and a climbing wall. It was a gigantic playground for adults.

Clark and Ada argued throughout the whole tour and consequently ignored Lukasz's attempts to correct the pronunciation of his name. He forced his mouth to signal something of a smile. *I guess I'm Luke now.*

At last, the moment Luke had been looking forward to arrived: their team allocation. He could end up anywhere but hoped for a project focused on behavioural prediction, fraud detection or experimental network traffic forecasting. Whatever they threw at him, he'd embrace it.

Fifteen Swoop managers entered the room. Dressed casually, they weren't much older than their new fosterlings. One stood out—with his grey beard and big glasses, he looked like he'd engineered the internet all by himself.

In a ceremonial fashion, they called out names, one by one. Each manager explained what their team did and why their work was so important.

The old guy with the beard stepped forward first. 'Ada, as discussed earlier, you're in my team. Network security is what we do, and we do it better than anybody else in the world. Our top priority is to make sure our data, our most valued resource, stays secure. Given your … uhm, qualifications, I'm sure we can learn from each other, make our systems more secure and stay ahead of the curve.'

Impressed, Luke made a mental note to read Ada's blog when he got home.

Three more engineers got their assignments. Translation, web search, site reliability. Respectable roles for beginners, but nothing too crazy either.

Then it was Clark's turn. His team was creating a new, supposedly revolutionary chat app. For Luke, chat apps were about as boring as it gets in the world of software engineering. But they planned to integrate a few machine learning features to predict what kind of information the user wanted at any given time. If a famous actor was mentioned, the app would automatically pull up their Wikipedia page. At least this part seemed interesting.

Luke was last. With a thick beard and round face, his new manager looked like a cross between a human and an Ewok. His grey T-shirt, three-quarter pants and sandals had seen better days.

'My name's Nathan. I'm the tech lead for the settings team. You know, when you hit the settings button on your phone? That's us! Our job is to enable users to personalise their phone to make it more efficient in doing the things that matter to them. This mostly means a lot of buttons and checkboxes. But with the company's focus on machine learning and all that, we've decided to try out something new. Smart settings, we call it.

'One of those settings is the brightness of the screen. We obviously want people to see what's on their phone, but we also don't want to make it any brighter than necessary — saving battery and all that. We'd like to automatically adjust the brightness using machine learning. If we do this right, we can save two to five per cent battery on average, half an hour more power, every single day! All that will be your responsibility. You'll make a huge impact.'

Luke narrowed his eyes, trying to wrap his head around what he'd just heard. Ada and Clark could barely conceal their grins. Luke had landed the most boring job in the entire company.

Chapter Four

The restaurant was a regular employee hangout, a tacky affair. A bright shade of green that bordered on atomic radiated from the walls, only to be absorbed by the dark red tiles and brown ceiling. Diverse religious figures embellished the decor—a blue Ganesh, an orange Vishnu and a purple Shiva. Two large flat screens on opposite sides of the room showed the latest news from the tech scene while a cheap hi-fi system played the soundtrack of Bollywood's finest movies.

'The others in our group are all idiots,' said Ada with her usual charm. 'Seriously, did you see that guy's solution for the webserver code lab? Absolutely laughable. And on top of everything, they're lucky idiots. Did you see the projects they were assigned to? Behavioural prediction, user profiling, all the fancy stuff. Who the hell did they sleep with to land those gigs? Don't get me wrong, I'm not complaining. Security's my thing. But look at poor Luke here, stuck with screen on and off.'

Luke tried to stay positive. He could change the world later. 'Everyone complains about battery time these days and our project really can save energy. We can improve this dramatically using machine learning, better than humans ever could. It's exciting.'

Ada folded her hands in prayer. 'All hail the robot overlords.'

Clark grinned from ear to ear. 'Dude, but seriously, AI has made a quantum leap over the last couple of years. With all this power, we can make amazing things happen. Like turning things on and off. You know, the display … on and off. Oh, Luke, wait, there's another invention you should probably look into: it's called the light switch.'

'Funny,' Luke said. 'AI has so much potential, we could use it for just about anything. Don't you realize?'

'Dude, you already sound like one of those sales guys. But enough of your boring life. Ada, how's working with Methuselah?'

'He's great. Has to pee every fucking twenty minutes, but otherwise, he's a nice guy. Too bad all his protocols are flawed and easy to break.' She sighed theatrically. 'But I guess that's what I'm here for. Ada Fisher, working for the man.'

Tech Hour came on the TV, a popular show about the latest industry products and rumours. An employee had lost a prototype of the upcoming Swoop phone in a bar where it'd been found by a reporter, who now showed off his trophy with a smug smile.

'Vultures,' said Clark. 'Look at them. They feed on what we leave behind.'

Ada frowned. 'True, this guy's a real jerk. But, hell, you have to get your information somewhere when you're a reporter. Or a blogger. It's fiercely competitive.'

'I've got news for you. You're not one of them anymore. You're part of the machine now. Get used to it,' said Clark.

Ada gave her best annoyed expression as the program switched to an interview with Walter Hamilton about the latest and hottest startups. Everybody knew Hamilton — self-made billionaire and president of his own venture capital fund. One of the biggest fish in the small pond called Silicon Valley, a real tech icon. Not quite Bill Gates or Steve Jobs, but almost.

'That'll be us in a couple of years. Filthy rich, but without a damn backbone. That's what the corporate world does to you — makes you evil through and through,' said Ada.

'Probably not you and me,' Luke said. 'But maybe the future Clark here, age sixty-five. They even look alike.'

Clark fiddled with his cutlery. 'Not cool, man. Just because I'm black. That's plain old racism.'

While waiting for dessert, Clark and Ada toyed around with their new phones. Still not used to people pulling out their devices at every opportunity, Luke stared at his empty plate. He, too, wanted to play with his new gadget but thought it was rude at the dinner table.

'What a shitty way to go,' Ada said suddenly. 'Thirty years and then bam … brain cancer.'

An inkling of a shiver ran down Luke's forearm. 'Who are you talking about?'

'This guy, Chris.' She held out her phone. 'He died last night. I just saw his obituary on the intranet.'

The picture showed Chris at dinner with his team, smiling, with a truckload of food and empty beer glasses in front of him.

'That's his official employee photo?' Luke asked.

Clark stiffened as he stared at the picture. 'Guys, I know him … He's a product manager from one of my sister teams. My boss introduced us yesterday. I was supposed to work with him on a cross-functional project. The thing is, he looked very much alive and healthy in the morning.' He typed on his phone and showed them an email he'd received from Chris a day earlier. 'See. It's the same username.'

Their desserts arrived, and they ate in silence. Clark kept shaking his head. Ada seemed to be deep in thought. Luke attempted to overcome his discomfort by processing the facts in a clinical way. Brain cancer was a rare disease, but Swoop was a sizable company; all sorts of random things happened if enough people were involved. His statistics professor used to state *Once the population is large enough, any circumstance, no matter how unlikely, becomes a possibility*—a mathematical way of saying anything is possible. But the abrupt decline in Chris' condition—

'Something doesn't add up here,' said Ada. 'I searched for late-stage brain cancer symptoms, and several sources confirm he'd have had a severe fucking headache throughout his last two weeks. Like the damn mother of headaches where you want to curl up and die already. Plus, frequent seizures, incontinence and random neurological deficits, whatever the hell that is. No way anybody could work in that state. Clark, are you sure we're talking about the same guy?'

He showed her his phone again. 'Yeah, man. Check yourself. One hundred per cent: same email, same first name, same last name, same face. It's him.'

'Holy shit,' said Ada.

Luke's doubts grew into a mental itch. 'Maybe he was poisoned. It says here this can happen quickly if you're exposed to high levels of radiation.'

'He didn't work in a nuclear plant, dude. He sat behind a desk in an office, in front of a computer screen. Like we all do. Radiation's not very likely,' said Clark.

'Maybe he was a spy and they killed him. You know, like that Russian guy,' Ada said.

That brought a chuckle from Clark. 'Said like a true conspiracy theorist. Let me ask the waiter for some tinfoil, so we can build you a nice big hat.'

'Funny. Look at me, the crazy cat lady with her weird hair, suspecting mysterious schemes behind every corner. But seriously, don't you guys think something's off here?'

Luke's cramping stomach conceded. 'We should go home. We have another long day ahead of us tomorrow.'

Clark took out his credit card and gestured to the waiter. 'I got it, guys.'

Ada glimpsed the card, stared at Clark, then the TV, again the card, then back to Clark, her eyes wide open. She typed something on her phone and her jaw dropped. 'Clark Hamilton ... You're Clark *Hamilton*. As in Walter fucking Hamilton's son ... Damn ... You're filthy rich!'

Clark blushed and cursed his carelessness. 'Please ... guys,' he said. 'Please don't tell anybody, OK?'

Chapter Five

'Come on, move along, we've got a full house today,' said the security guard.

Luke had been looking forward to his first company-wide all-hands meeting, one of Swoop's traditions. Every week, Umesh and his inner circle shared internal updates, announced new projects and addressed the big and hairy questions. Juicy stuff.

As they walked further into the auditorium, they caught their first glimpse of Umesh Patel, Swoop's legendary CEO. Everybody knew his story. Indian-born, his family settled in San Francisco when he was six years old. A maths genius, he got into programming and created a computer game at age fourteen. The first one put him on the map; the next two made him a millionaire by the age of sixteen and got him into Berkeley. Halfway through his degree, he invented a ground-breaking new operating system for mobile phones, back when every vendor still did their own thing. He dropped out, founded Swoop and had been revolutionising the world ever since.

'Check out the big guy,' said Ada as they shuffled into their seats. 'Why's his arm in a sling? If he's sick, Swoop's stock price is gonna drop to the bottom of the ocean. Our shares are gonna be worth jack shit. And what's this announcement everybody's so fucking crazy about?'

'What announcement?' asked Luke.

'Well, that's the damn point, Captain Obvious. Nobody knows. But people seem to think he's about to reveal something huge.'

Clark shook his head. 'One week into the job and you already know "people"' — he made air quotes — 'I haven't even made it through the tutorials yet.'

Luke was genuinely puzzled. 'You should take this more seriously. Have you seen the infrastructure code lab? They make the algorithm scale to a million nodes.'

'You too?' said Clark. 'I thought Ada was the only one smart-assing around all the time. Jesus, you guys really make an effort to make me feel dumb.'

Ada shushed them. 'The general's about to address the troops.'

'Hi, folks,' Umesh started. 'I hope you're all pumped because we have quite a bit to cover. This week is Swoop's fifteenth anniversary! Yay! Can I have a big round of applause please?'

People tentatively clapped their hands. Luke had already received more than ten emails about upcoming birthday parties, marketing efforts and Easter eggs to be released on Swoop phones. No surprise there.

'Don't worry, I won't make you sing "Happy Birthday" or anything like that,' Umesh continued. 'But I do have a little gift for every one of you to thank you all for your hard work. You won't get it before the end of this presentation, which is my way of making sure everybody stays until we're done.'

A few people chuckled, but there were no surprised faces. The majority seemed to have expected a giveaway.

'But first, let's greet those who haven't actually done anything to deserve this yet. Don't worry, you'll get one all the same. A warm welcome to all the Noops!'

The screen showed the names of all recent new hires. The list spread over several slides. Luke spotted his name and couldn't help but smile. Clark and even Ada, the undisputed queen of sarcasm, did, too.

After Umesh's introduction, a handful of VPs came on stage and covered the latest and greatest product launches in their area. A man in a black suit hovered in a dark corner at the far side of the stage. He barely moved and seemed completely untouched by the unfolding events. A shudder ran from Luke's neck all the way down to his feet. Something about this man made him uneasy. His eyes, perhaps? Luke forced himself to ignore him and concentrated on the presenters.

After the round of VPs, Umesh came back on stage. 'So ... fifteen years of Swoop. Crazy, right?' The screens showed pictures of the early days when Swoop was only a handful of employees working from a tiny basement room with no windows.

'Fifteen years working with the brightest minds on the planet, fifteen years in which we brought a whole new level of data into the hands of humanity. A whole new way of thinking about information. Facts about our world, advice from experts and amateurs alike, tools to control our health — we brought all this to the fingertips of our users. It's something to be proud of, folks.'

The smiles in the audience grew wider and wider. Everybody likes a compliment and, in this regard, the tech elite in the auditorium was no different to a five-year-old. Maybe this was true for many things.

'But we didn't stop there. We always pushed further, beyond what others thought to be possible. We brought the internet to users who didn't know they needed it. Today, more than seventy-five per cent of the global population has access to it; that's almost two billion more than five years ago. Think about this magnitude for a minute ... six billion people, all using one gigantic, interconnected network. And our company played a major role in this milestone.'

The crowd cheered, sending a swell of warmth through Luke's body.

'And I have another number for you. One I'm especially proud of. Only four years ago, we had an idea. An idea of a unified, cloud-based operating system that could run on any device. Laptops, servers, mobile phones, smart speakers, fridges, cameras, vacuum cleaners, all running on the same system, making interactions incredibly easy for both users and developers. That was the vision of CoreOS. Today, we achieved what Microsoft wasn't able to pull off with Windows, what Google couldn't accomplish with Android, what Apple failed to reach with iOS. Today, our CoreOS runs on over ten billion devices.' A low *uhhh* went through the audience. 'That's more devices than people on the planet. That's a one with ten zeros. And we — you — made this possible.'

There were high fives all around. A guy three rows ahead punched the air. Nobody had expected the numbers to be so high. Luke had definitely joined the best company in the world.

'We made communication simpler. We made interfaces more intuitive. We empowered users, making their daily tasks more efficient. It's this constant questioning of the status quo, the relentless push beyond feasibility, the healthy disregard for limits that makes Swoop so special. This is what we do like no other company, and it's what we should be most proud of. I want to thank every single one of you for your contributions. Great job, folks!'

Everybody jumped off their chairs in a standing ovation. Luke soaked in the hype. It took a while until the room was quiet enough for Umesh to continue.

'And because we never stop … because we always keep pushing, we're ready to head in a new direction. Machine learning's made a quantum leap over the last couple of months, and here at Swoop, we have some of the best researchers in the field. Brain-computer interfaces have evolved beyond the research lab towards production readiness, and with our acquisition of Whitefeed, we've made sure we have this covered as well.

'Now we're ready to announce we've brought these technologies together. We'll use machine learning to filter the flood of information; to show users exactly the things they want to see when they want to see them. We'll use it to make decisions for them, faster and more accurately than any human could ever do. We'll know what our users want before they know it themselves. We'll create devices acting as individual assistants in people's lives, freeing them from their daily chores and leaving them more time for more interesting things.

'And most importantly...' He paused theatrically. 'Our users won't need any keyboards or mice to control all of this. They'll be able to control it directly with their minds. Think it, and it will be done. That's our new mission. Think it, and it will be done!'

Thousands of pupils around Luke doubled in size. He couldn't help but join the cheering. He hadn't been this excited since he'd predicted the weather with his own machine-learning model a few years ago. Their equity packages weren't going to be worth jack shit; they'd be worth millions.

A La Ola wave rushed through the crowd. It was a little ridiculous, a room full of adults behaving like toddlers on Christmas Day, but Luke was swept up in it too. He couldn't quite describe it but sensed he was part of something grand, something that would change the future, right then and there.

'About those gifts I mentioned earlier...' Umesh gave a wide smile. 'We already took the first steps in this new direction. Three months ago, I created a team with the goal of bringing Swoop's leading artificial intelligence together with Whitefeed's innovative interfaces. This team is led by the fabulous Dr Wu.' A slender woman emerged on the side of the stage, waved nervously into the crowd, and vanished as quickly as she appeared.

'Dr Wu is as smart as she is shy, and we convinced her to take a sabbatical at Tsinghua University in Beijing to lead this project. The team has been working around the clock to present to you … this!'

He held up a mobile phone in front of him, barely visible from Luke's seat. A camera projected it onto the big screen. Sleek and modern, it was similar to the other Swoop phones but not exactly like any existing model. A bit larger maybe.

'This is our newest flagship phone, which we'll announce at our SwoopX conference in two weeks. It has all the latest hardware, a great camera and runs the newest version of CoreOS.'

People cheered again, but this time, Umesh held his hands up and calmed them down.

'Wait, wait, wait, folks, wait! We always announce a new phone at SwoopX, that can't be the big news, right? No, I have something better. What I wanted to show you is … this!'

The room went dead quiet. Luke expected him to open a new app or show a new feature. Instead, he stood there and did nothing.

A few seconds later, a warm female voice spoke cheerfully through the PA system. 'Of course, I can show you the weather forecast for tomorrow. It will be sunny, seventy-five degrees, zero chance of precipitation.' Simultaneously, the phone screen showed additional details about humidity, an hourly temperature breakdown, and so on.

It took Luke a couple of seconds to realise the voice originated from the phone. But what triggered it?

Umesh flashed a wide grin. 'I guess you're wondering where that came from. Well, I can tell you. It wasn't a technical glitch. It was me asking the device for the weather forecast ... with my mind!'

Thousands of jaws dropped to the floor. An avalanche of achievement and belonging swept over Luke. The woman in front of him asked her neighbour, 'Is this for real?'

'Now, I'm pretty sure we have a few sceptics in the room who think this is all fake and staged. Well, I told you I have a gift for you. On your way out, you'll all receive one of these, so you can check it out yourself. Consider yourself a beta tester.'

A collective *wooooow* rose from the room, followed by a wave of applause and countless *woohoos*. People yelled at each other, wondering if they'd witnessed the start of a new era. Luke's initial scepticism was swept away by a rush of euphoria. If, later on, anybody asked him for the definition of 'going nuts', he'd recall this scene. It felt like they were making history.

Chapter Six

From the outside, the venue didn't look like much – a plain grey building, probably an old warehouse, in a deserted alley somewhere in the outskirts of San Francisco. A single red door led inside, offering a glimpse into the lavish interior every time it swung open. The muffled beat inside formed a pattern that morphed into a cover of Michael Jackson's *Billy Jean*. Rock meets techno, driving home some extra hipster points.

The long line moved slowly. A Swoop employee dressed as Leia Skywalker checked the guests' badges and handed out vouchers for complimentary drinks. Her outfit was spot on and made Luke, wearing a retro Darth Vader shirt, feel underdressed. To her right stood the mysterious guy Luke had noticed during Umesh's speech, a soldier in a suit with a deadpan expression.

'I did a bit of digging on that guy,' whispered Ada. 'Xavier Sanchez. His official title is Head of Site Security.' She took another step towards the entrance.

'What does that even mean?' Clark asked. 'Standing in the background all day like a scarecrow?'

'He's doing his job extremely well then,' said Ada.

When it was their turn, Leia smiled and handed them special vouchers for unlimited drinks. 'Usually, there's only one drink on us. But this is our starting gift for Noops. Enjoy and welcome to the family!'

Black and purple velvet everywhere, the inside mixed extravagant with down-to-earth elements like wooden bars and stools that could've been from a Wild West movie. Waitresses carried trays of cocktails, shots and long drinks, glowing in bright colours. Empty beer cans were strewn everywhere, and drinks were spilled on the floor. It was nearly nine o'clock, and it seemed most employees had come right after work. Work hard, play hard.

The place reeked of tequila and lime mixed with sweat and hairspray. This week's *Star Wars* theme had been embraced by all guests, and apparently, wannabe alien creatures needed plenty of hairstyling. During a song Luke didn't recognise, a dozen Wookiees waved their arms in a symphony of uncontrolled ecstasy. Nerd heaven.

Ada grinned. 'Look who's making a fool of himself on the dance floor.'

Clark facepalmed. 'Oh man, it's Shawn the sales dude bouncing around like a ping pong ball.'

'Guys, let's move before that nitwit sees us. Time's ticking. We better make use of those unlimited drinking vouchers.'

When they reached the bar, they found one of the other new hires from their group. Luke didn't remember his name but recalled he was Australian and had sailed around the entire continent before joining the company. His glossy eyes suggested he'd been drinking for a while, sipping on one fancy single malt while waiting for the next.

'I know you, mate,' he said. 'You're the shy guy from Europe.'

'I ... uhm, yeah I guess that's me,' Luke didn't know whether to be offended or happy to be recognized.

'Good on you!' He pointed towards their conglomeration of upcoming drinks. 'Dig into those as long as you can. Who knows if you're still around tomorrow?'

Luke was about to ignore him and move on, but his stern demeanour gave him pause. 'What do you mean, still around? Swoop doesn't fire people unless you leak secrets or something, right?'

The guy guffawed. 'No, no, no ... Mate, I mean walking and breathing, being amongst the living. Maybe tomorrow you'll spontaneously have brain cancer and die, like all the others.'

Luke remembered his uneasiness about the obituary on the intranet. 'You mean what happened to Chris? A tragedy.'

'Right-o. Except it wasn't a random tragedy. He was murdered, mate. I tell you. And he wasn't the only one. There were at least five of them.'

'Five Swoop employees?'

'No, as far as I know, just him at Swoop. Four more in other tech companies, all over the last few weeks. Same thing, mate. No previous symptoms, then melanoma in the brain and dead within a day. A buddy who's been at Swoop a while told me all about it. Bloody insane, mate.' He turned back to his whiskey.

Before Luke could process this information, they received their drinks: a beer and three shots each.

'To decadence,' Clark said and raised his glass. 'To our new corporate life, which conveniently comes with a truckload of corporate booze.'

'I hate nothing more than religion, but Amen to that,' cheered Ada as another shot went down.

Worry made the tip of Luke's toes tingle as he stared into the untroubled crowd. Shouldn't he be studying? 'Guys, you know the area pretty well, right? My Airbnb runs out soon and I'm looking for an affordable suburb.' His beginner's salary had seemed plenty at first, but then he realised how high rents were in the Bay Area.

'Try the middle of the fucking desert,' snorted Ada.

Clark's eyebrows gnarled. 'Dude, go anywhere cheap and the commute becomes terrible … You know what? Why don't you move in with me? I have a spare bedroom, and my apartment's close to work. Why don't we team up?'

Luke stepped backwards. So much trust from somebody he'd only met a few days ago? 'That's very kind, but I couldn't afford it.'

'Bullshit, man. I don't want your money. I'm paying for the place whether you're there or not.' He sighed and added, 'Come on, you already know my dad's loaded. The rent barely makes a dent in my allowance. I seriously don't mind.'

'Maybe just for a couple of days? To give me a bit more time to find my own place. I don't want to be a burden.'

'Done deal,' Clark yelled. 'Now let's go and enjoy this party.'

Ada rolled her eyes and chuckled. 'That's exactly what the world needs, you two broing up.'

As they strolled away from the bar, Luke glanced back to the Aussie sitting on his stool. He mouthed, 'Watch out,' and stared back into his glass.

A queasy sensation lingered in Luke's stomach throughout the night. And it wasn't from the tequila.

Chapter Seven

Luke had dinner alone in yet another Swoop cafe. Their main campus in Santa Clara featured seventeen restaurants, each offering a different cuisine. This place was desperately trying to look Italian. Large olive oil tins, boxes of pasta and giant pepper mills lined the shelves on the walls between black and white posters of almost forgotten Italian movie stars: Sofia Loren, Marcello Mastroianni, Laura Antonelli, Sergio Leone. On the menu, nothing but pizza.

He was halfway through his first slice when Ada showed up and sat next to him. How did she always find him?

She examined him a little longer than necessary and gave him an unexpected hug. 'You know, I realized it must be hard living so far away from your family.'

Luke froze in his chair. Was this Ada's non-evil twin sister?

'I mean having no friends except for Clark and me must be really fucking annoying.'

No, it was still her.

'Anyway, remember that Australian guy from the party the other day?' she said. 'Crocodile Dundee on a boat? I've been thinking about what he said, you know, about those people dying.'

Luke's fingers twitched. 'Maybe it was the alcohol speaking.'

'Yeah, but what if not? What if there's funny business?' Ada asked.

'What do you mean?'

'Come on, first Chris, now these other people? All suddenly dying from brain cancer? It smells iffy. Seriously, we should check it out.'

Luke focussed on the portrait of an actress he didn't recognize on the far end of the room. 'Maybe it's a coincidence.'

'Coincidence my ass. Let's at least double-check what the Australian told us, OK?'

Luke nodded. 'Sure ... But for the record, we're not planning to do anything illegal here. We're just curious, right?'

'Potayto, potahto. Take out your laptop. We'll have a look.'

They brought up the web page of the Santa Clara Police Department. Like any government website, it was dull but functional. It offered a database for crime statistics and a register for sexual offenders, but nothing about recent deaths. They moved on to Google and found an online directory of obituaries. They filtered the last six weeks and found twenty-eight entries in and around Santa Clara. Christian Turner came halfway through the list.

Christian was born on September 4, 1994, and passed away on May 17, 2021. Christian was a resident of Santa Clara, California, at the time of passing.

The blurb was automatically generated; it gave no condolences or emotion.

'At least we know this list's accurate. Shame it doesn't show the cause of death,' said Ada.

They checked the other twenty-seven entries. Only six were aged thirty-five or younger, which they assumed was the upper end of the spectrum for tech employees. If the Australian's story were true, then at least four of them had to be victims of some variation of brain cancer.

They narrowed their search to these six cases. One of them died in a car crash; they ruled it out right away. The others didn't reveal the cause of death, but they found online condolences for four of them. Two had entries created on behalf of their company, which indeed turned out to be in the tech business.

One confirmed, Chris Turner. Two potential matches, tech employees with unexplained causes of death. Three unknowns. One eliminated.

Luke leaned forward. 'Let's start with the potential matches.'

Ada pulled up the Facebook profiles of the two tech employees. Apparently, people had no sense of decency and left all sorts of public messages for the deceased on their profile page. In both cases, they found comments about their unforeseen departure. On one, two friends discussed a possible family history of melanoma in the brain.

Two confirmed. Luke fidgeted with his pen. Were they onto something?

LinkedIn and Twitter validated two of the three unknowns worked for tech companies. The third was unemployed a.k.a. working for Uber and Airtasker.

Two eliminated.

They searched for the remaining names on Google and found a local newspaper article from three weeks ago lamenting the death of a rising star—a huge open-source contributor in the field of cryptography. Cause of death: brain cancer.

Three confirmed. Luke's entire arm twitched.

'Let me try something,' said Ada. 'One of the obituaries mentioned a last-ditch effort to save her life, right? At the Stanford Cancer Institute. As it happens, I worked with the infrastructure department at Stanford back when I was a student. They had a system for real-time medical data, a complete mess in terms of security. I bet they never changed the master password.'

Any system is only as good as its administrators, and indeed, they turned out to be a lazy bunch. Ada logged in and soon found a page showing the cancer institute's internal statistics.

'Looks like they're finally anonymizing the data, something I told these dimwits years ago. Look, here are the medical profiles, but the names are redacted. Bummer ... but wait, there's one other thing we can check, maybe we'll get lucky.'

The institute maintained aggregate statistics about their patients; part of this was a daily updated dataset with the number of successful and unsuccessful treatments — the latter being a euphemism for people dying while in the hospital's care. She adjusted the date ranges and checked the stats for the day before and the day of the victim's death.

Luke finally understood. 'So we know she died that day, while in the care of the institute. And on the same day, they had exactly one death, caused by a malignant brain tumour. Hence she died because of brain cancer.'

Four confirmed. Two eliminated. One question mark. Luke's stomach turned sour. What if somebody traced their steps on the web?

The last case turned out to be a dead end; they couldn't find any information online.

'We'll have to go old school with this one,' Ada said.

Via Facebook, she found the name of the victim's mother and in the phone book, she found her number.

Ada dialled, waited a couple of seconds and put on her most generic call-centre voice. 'Hello, my name is Varga, I'm with the Department of Health and Statistics. It seems there was a system error regarding the death of your son. I'm terribly sorry, but I need to confirm the cause of death with you real quick.'

She waited for a couple of seconds and nodded. 'Thank you so much for helping us out here. And ... I'm sorry for your loss.'

All five confirmed.

Luke had lost his appetite. His gut was on fire. They were onto something. He didn't know the how, the what or the why, but they'd started descending into a deep dark abyss, and he needed to know what was on the bottom.

'Fucking look at that.' Ada slammed her phone down on Luke's desk.

He jumped; he'd been so deep into coding he hadn't noticed her arriving. 'It's nice to see you, too,' he said, looking up from his keyboard.

Her hair was a mess, multi-coloured strands stood out in every direction. 'Just read it, ok?'

The phone showed an article titled *Promising Startup Eradicated*. He skimmed it and read the last paragraph aloud.

...and ultimately, their visionary research became their own demise. Tragically, everybody involved in the experiment died, the entire company of three leading neurological researchers and two software engineers. The loss of life is unfortunate, but the fact that their research may now be buried forever is a real setback for humanity.

Death. There it was again, a shark circling the island of his new life. 'This sounds awful. Did you know them?'

'What? No, I didn't. Luke, use your stupid brain. Didn't you read what they were looking into? Effects of electromagnetic waves on the nervous system.'

'I guess they set up their experiment the wrong way and obliterated their brains. Horrible.' His trembling hands almost dropped Ada's phone. What a way to die.

'Don't be an idiot. That's not what they were doing—
I know, I wrote a few articles about them. They only
measured our exposure to ambient electro smog—they
didn't create their own. This is all related, brain cancer for
shit's shake. Another five dead.'

Luke tried to stay rational—somebody had to—
reiterating probabilities and correlations, reminding
himself Ada was the queen of conspiracy theories. But his
stomach fought its own battle, sending deep primeval
signals that something was wrong. Why did he move to this
strange country?

'Maybe we should find the Australian guy from the
party, see if there's a connection,' he said.

'Hell yeah. I already spoke to Shawn the sales dude,
the most annoying five minutes of my life. Seriously. Guess
what? He asked me if I wanted him to be my mentor. Fuck
no. Anyway, he said the Australian's name is Brett Lynton.
His desk isn't far from here.'

Lynton's workspace was deserted. One seat further
along, sat a slightly older and distinctly grumpy person
they identified as his manager.

'Sorry, we're looking for Brett, Brett Lynton,' Ada
said.

The manager looked up from his monitor and rolled
his eyes. 'If you want anyone in my team to help you out,
we got an official queue. If it's urgent, you talk to me, not
to them.'

'This isn't for work. We're friends.'

Brett's manager narrowed his eyes and gave them a
good look over. Then he shrugged. 'Brett didn't come in
today. In fact, he hasn't been here the entire week. Haven't
heard from him at all. Maybe he got cold feet. Happens
sometimes to the new guys when they find out what

they've gotten themselves into. All the new contracts have a special clause, anybody can back out during the first month without a reason. If you ask me, it's the most annoying thing ever. All this effort spent on interviews and hiring, and now I have to start all over.'

Luke stared at Ada in disbelief, craving to run away but unable to move. Cold feet? Hopefully, this was just a poor choice of words. Or did the deadly shark just swim dangerously close to his shore?

Chapter Eight

'Dude, you're staying with me. End of story.' Clark sipped his sake and flung another eager look at the three bowls of ramen and the dwindling shaft of steam emerging from them. The enticing smells and authentic décor transported Luke and his friend right into a quiet Kyoto back alley. They'd ordered for Ada as well, but she was late as usual.

'I don't want to be a burden,' said Luke.

'Bullshit. You've got money issues, right? Don't give me that "everything's fine" again, I know something's going on. I don't care what it is, I got your back.'

Luke took a long breath of spice-laden air. 'It's my parents. We never had much, but we used to be ok. Now my mum got sick and … well, they're struggling. They won't admit it, but a friend told me they basically live on stale ends of bread. And I'm not even there to help. I'm sending them money, as much as I can spare.'

'Sorry, man. Don't feel bad about it … Money isn't everything, you know. My family has so much of it, we can't even spend it. If I could, I'd trade it all for a little less pressure. But I'm the son of the great Walter Hamilton, stuck with this mountain of expectations but unable to get anything off the ground. I've been launching startups since I'm sixteen and I've butchered every single one of them. Why haven't I figured it out yet?'

'I don't understand. You'll probably inherit it all one day and won't have to think about work ever. You don't need to figure it out.'

'But it's not *mine*. Every schmuck in the Valley has their own company, but me … nothing! That's why I joined Swoop, to learn a thing or two.'

They swallowed at the same time, and Luke realized how this shiny cradle of technology embodied the best and the worst of capitalism. But it was good to have a friend, a friend who —

'Product managers are a bunch of idiots,' Ada stomped into their booth and immediately dove into her food. 'Just because the problem's simple doesn't mean the solution's simple, too. They always assume coding's easy, it doesn't occur to them there's actual work involved. These MBA douchebags don't know what real work is, all they ever do is fucking PowerPoint presentations.'

Luke exchanged a smile with Clark and said, 'Amen.' Back to ordinaries.

'Dude, I'd like to join the complaining, but you still haven't told us what you're working on.' Ada had told Clark a heavily censored version of how she ended up at Swoop a few days earlier, and he hadn't stopped asking questions ever since. 'More hacking?'

'No more hacking for this girl. My job is to fix the bug I discovered, remember?'

'But what exactly is that vulnerability?' said Luke.

Clark fumbled with his chopsticks. 'Yeah, man. How does the whole hacking thing work anyway?'

Ada sighed. 'For shit's sake, why do people always make such a fuss about this stuff? Everybody seems to think some weirdo in a basement hammers around on his keyboard and the entire world explodes.'

'I'll explain this to you in simple terms. Say you want to read data on a server without being authorised, then you have to figure out a way to get access. Often, you can come up with the right password by trying a bunch of them. I mean a proper shitload. Or you find an open port and you tamper with whatever's running there. There are lots and lots of different ways, depending on where you can find an entry point.'

'Sure, but what's the hole you found?' asked Clark as he poured himself another sake.

'I'll tell you, but you have to promise to keep it to yourselves,' said Ada, checking over her shoulder and lowering her voice. 'I mean it. This one's pretty hot shit, OK? This can bring down governments.'

'You're such a drama queen,' Clark said.

'Swear it.'

'Fine,' they both agreed.

'I found a way to exploit a memory overflow, which is a bit of a last resort for hackers. Honestly, I got lucky. I tried lots of ways to crack CoreOS, but it's actually designed pretty well. Anyway, you know how code gets compiled into machine language, the famous zeros and ones everybody talks about?'

They nodded. Computer Science 101.

'The thing is, any bunch of zeros and ones can be interpreted as two different things. Either a command, like a calculation or whatever. Or data, like the word "Hello". For a memory overflow hack, you put some data into the memory of a program that doubles as executable code. Then you point the processor there to run it, and voilà, the program executes your code, which can do anything you want, like giving you admin access or crazy shit like launching nuclear rockets.'

'Two problems,' said Luke. 'First, how do you get your data into the program's memory? And second, how do you make the program run it? Programs only execute what they're coded to do, you can't make them do something else.'

'Ha … but if you're really clever, you can,' Ada said with a smug smile.

'You lost me at zeros and ones.' Clark shook his head and left for the bathroom.

'Alright, let's start with getting the data into the system's memory. First, write the machine code you want to run and use a tool to convert it to the corresponding text. Then you enter it. Most programs allow users to enter text, right? And the computer loads it into memory. Like when you log in somewhere, you enter your username. That's text. The moment you hit enter, it goes into memory, where it's available to do silly things like checking whether this user actually exists.

'That's exactly how I got my data in. I knew CoreOS saved the last twenty passwords in memory, probably to do some smart security detection thing I don't care about. So I wrote a bunch of code to give me full system access, converted it into completely gibberish text, broke it into twenty parts and entered those parts one by one into the password field of the login screen.'

Luke nodded. 'So now you had your code sitting there, ready to be run. How'd you make CoreOS execute it?'

'That's where the luck comes in. And the oldest bug in the world. Say you want your user to input eight digits, but they give you nine. Users always do this shit, right? If you store this to memory unchecked, what happens? The ninth digit overrides whatever comes next in your memory. And if that's executable code, then you got your way in. You simply make the ninth a number that translates to the command "jump to the badass code I smuggled in during the first step", and at some point, the program will go there and run it. Boom, you're in.'

Luke scratched his chin. 'I think I got it. You look for code that's physically after data from user input. You make the data longer than it should be, and it overrides the code. Then your override gets executed. Pretty clever.'

Ada's eyes glowed.

Clark arrived with a tray full of ice cream and sponge cake. 'The dessert looked awesome, I thought I'd bring you guys some.'

They dug into their food, but Luke was still thinking about Ada's hack. 'This all sounds a bit unlikely. How'd you find this bug? I mean CoreOS must be millions of lines of code. Where is it?'

'That's the lucky part. I made educated guesses by trying out every possible user input. I experimented with various lengths and entered something just over the limit to see what happened. Not manually, obviously, that'd take ages. I wrote a program years ago that probes for that kind of stuff. And in CoreOS, I found my way in via the captcha. You know, the image that shows six hard-to-read digits in a picture, and you have to enter them to prove you're human? Well, enter seven and you're in.' Ada grinned so widely, she looked like the Grinch.

Luke's eyeballs almost popped out.

Even Clark understood the consequences, his mouth hung open. 'Dude' — he looked around and continued in a hushed voice — 'are you telling us there's a critical bug in the operating system used by more than ten billion devices? And the way to exploit it is to type seven instead of six digits? That's it?'

'They need to be the right digits. And don't forget you need to smuggle in the code beforehand. But yeah, fucking crazy right?'

'And you haven't fixed it yet?' Luke's discomfort materialized in a crack in his voice.

Ada shook her head. 'Nope, it's still there.'

Clark's piece of cake fell off his fork, he didn't even notice. 'Is this really so hard to fix? Check the input. Coding 101. Or move the input data somewhere else where it can't mess with anything?'

'Now you sound exactly like my douchebag PM. It's not that easy. Yes, this particular hole would be fixed but reorganizing the machine code would place the data somewhere else, making another part of CoreOS vulnerable. And without lengthy analysis, we wouldn't know which part. So we keep it where we can see it until we fix it for real. So far, nobody else has found it, I know that for damn sure. It's why they were so eager to make me keep my mouth shut.' Ada radiated pride.

Shaking his head, Luke tried to slow down the frequency of his shallow breaths. Given the stakes, he thought Ada should work day and night instead of wasting time with them, but she just seemed pleased she'd found a critical issue in that oh-so-perfect operating system everybody in the world seemed to trust.

'Relax,' she continued. 'Don't throw away all your Swoop shares just yet. I'm working on a systematic way to avoid this stuff altogether. Basically, I'm adding a step in the compiler that makes sure user data and executable code are never allocated next to each other, requiring changes in the memory layout, which is obviously one of the crazy parts of the whole operating system. You have to use static analysis to...'

Ada kept going for a couple more minutes, but now she'd lost Luke and Clark entirely. They were still processing the fact that half of all devices on the planet were vulnerable, and the mad genius who discovered it was sitting next to them.

Dead people and hackers. For a brief moment, a recollection of home crossed Luke's mind, where people had their own issues, but life seemed to be simpler. Too late, he was deep in the rabbit hole now.

On his way home, Luke checked his emails. A fresh one from Ada dropped into his personal inbox.

Luke, I'm feeling a bit nostalgic. I promised this would never see the light of day, but now I have to share it with someone. I don't know why I trust you so much, but I do. I wrote an app that combines all the steps we talked about and gives you instant access to you know what — at least until the fix is in. It's super convenient, and it runs on your phone. Who knows what this could be good for? It's encrypted, but that big brain of yours should be able to figure out the password :)

Luke had been handed the mother of all hacks. The damage that could be done. Indeed, this could bring down governments.

The right thing was to instantly delete the message. He didn't want to jeopardise his job at Swoop or his life as an upright citizen. His thumb hovered over the delete button.

He closed the email. The temptation was too great. Besides, he had no idea what the password was.

Chapter Nine

Luke watched Clark, who sat at the kitchen table and stared at the fridge. A bowl of cereal waited in front of him, its contents squishy, almost entirely dissolved. Luke hated seeing his friend like this. Over the last three months, they'd shared everything and went through the highs and lows of their new jobs together. But during the last two weeks, Clark had become quiet and withdrawn. Retracted from life, he'd spent a lot of time at his dad's and hadn't spoken much. Was he struggling at work?

'How're you?' Luke asked.

Clark turned towards him, his empty eyes slowly focussing. 'What?'

'How are you?'

'I'm good, man, I'm good,' Clark said. 'Did you install the latest update? When you think of somebody's name now, it automatically shows you stuff about them. You know, last calls, emails, calendar. And if you don't know them, whatever's on the web. Pretty cool, don't you think? This way, you always know who you're dealing with.'

Luke had been equally enthusiastic about his new phone and its machine-brain interface at first, but he'd quickly lost interest. In the end, it was no more than a toy for a bit of extra convenience. He'd gone back to the good old touchscreen weeks ago. 'Seems like a nice feature. But I can't concentrate on anything else when I'm using this thing. Besides, typing's much quicker.'

Clark added more cereal to his bowl, giving the soft contents a crunchy top. He still made no effort to eat it. 'Yeah, it's hard, man. I guess over time we'll get used to it, and our brains will rewire. It'll be super normal in a couple of years, you'll see.'

Luke hated to repeat himself. He took a deep breath. 'Clark ... how are you?'

'Dude, I told you I'm fine. For real.' His gaze went back to the fridge.

Luke didn't know what to say. He sat in silence for a good five minutes, staring at the same point, waiting for it to tell him how to end his friend's misery.

Clark finally said, 'Do you know why the Roman Empire fell?'

Luke wasn't sure whether this was a real question. 'I think it became too big, too hard to maintain. So they split it up into smaller and smaller pieces until it finally vanished. Like divide and conquer, only backwards.'

Clark frowned. 'Dude, no, that's not it. I'll tell you what it was. It was decadence.' He said the word with such vehemence he spit into his bowl. 'They became rich and lazy until they spent most of their time either eating, vomiting and screwing around with little boys.'

'I believe the Greeks were the ones with the little boys.'

Clark rolled his eyes. 'Whatever, bro. My point is, the real Romans, I mean the people originally from Rome, they fought hard to conquer their empire. They were brave and fierce, and nothing stood in their way. Once they were at the top, they celebrated their brains out. And fair enough, they'd earned it.

'But man, they became comfortable with what they had. They let others do the fighting and only cared about the finer things in life. Then they had children who had all this stuff from the get-go. No fighting, no starving, just wealth and games and orgies. They had everything, and that's exactly when progress stopped, and the empire fell apart.'

'Orgies seem fine to me.'

'I'm serious, Luke.'

Luke rubbed his thumb against his sweaty palm. 'Then what are you saying? Why are we talking about Romans?'

Clark exhaled sharply and looked him straight in the eyes. 'Jesus, I told you I'm doing great. Do I need to send you an email, so you can analyse it in detail? I'm just wondering about the Romans and their connection to our … situation.'

Anger turned Luke's hands into fists, but he relaxed them again; he needed to be a better friend than that. 'Whatever's going on, you can tell me, right?'

'Man, you're not getting the message. Leave me alone, dude. Seriously.' Clark's chair crashed to the floor as he stood and went to his room.

Luke let out a deep breath. Dealing with his own emotions was enough of a struggle, others' dramas even more so. He desperately wanted to help. But how could he if Clark didn't tell him anything?

A minute later, Clark came back with a large duffel bag over his shoulder. 'Sorry, man. Look, I need to be alone for a bit, OK. No big deal. We're cool, right?' He didn't wait for an answer. 'I'm gonna spend a couple more nights at my dad's and probably take a few days off work. But I'll be back Wednesday. Let's have lunch then, alright? Wednesday?'

Luke sighed. 'Sure, Wednesday.'

Later, Luke often looked back at this moment and asked himself what would have happened if he'd pressed on.

A few days later, Luke sat at his desk and checked his watch—11:57 am. Time to grab lunch and meet Clark.

Something was off with his friend, and today he wouldn't take no for an answer.

When he arrived, the cafeteria was deserted. He checked the time again — exactly noon. He didn't see his friend anywhere, which was no surprise. Clark was routinely late, Luke was used to it and didn't mind; it gave him a bit of alone time.

12:03 pm. Luke browsed the news on his phone. There were all sorts of scandals about politicians, ranging from rudeness to embezzlement to sexual assault. Other politicians harshly condemned each person in question, only to make similar headlines a few weeks later. Luke shook his head.

12:13 pm. He finished skimming the list of articles. It was also an unwritten law that Clark would never let Luke wait more than ten minutes. Did they miss each other? No. Luke had kept an eye on the door the entire time.

Clark, are you coming? We're still having lunch, right? Luke texted him.

He went back to the news while his food grew cold. The cafe filled up, and several people asked him whether the spot next to him was already taken. He scanned the room like a searchlight as despair took over.

12:22 pm. No answer to his message. No Clark.

He looked up the number and hit the dial button. A few rings and that was it. Not even a mailbox. Why couldn't his friend walk through the door, smile and tell him life was great again?

He sent another message. *Are you ok? Talk to me. I'll eat now, then you can find me at my desk. Come!*

12:39 pm. Luke finished his meal and returned to his workspace. On a regular day, he was deep into the zone by then. But he didn't usually wait for twenty minutes to get started.

He unlocked his computer and tried to focus on his code. Something was wrong. He didn't believe in gut feeling, but today, even the most rational part of his brain couldn't deny the plunging sensation in his stomach.

12:51 pm. Informing his manager on the way, he left the building through a back door and paced to their apartment. It usually took ten minutes door to door. He made it in less than five.

Why was he rushing home like that? Clark hadn't been there in days. Luke was guided by a sensation that didn't make sense. Would he need the Post-it note on their fridge with Walter's emergency number on it?

12:57 pm. Cold dark silence struck Luke as he opened the door to their place. It smelled intense, stale.

He tried to control his jitters. *You're driving yourself crazy. He's at his dad's place and doesn't want to talk.*

Stealing through the living room, he reached Clark's door. It stood half-open. A shudder ran down his spine. He was positive it was closed when he left this morning.

Luke peeked inside.

And then it hit him. It hit him so hard he couldn't breathe, couldn't think, couldn't blink. He could only stare.

Clark's lifeless body sat crumpled against the wall, his shirt open, a big hole in the middle of his chest. His face reduced to pale purple agony. Next to him, a gun.

Horror shredded Luke's temporal lobe.

The pool of blood around his friend seemed surreal, but the smell assured Luke this was reality, terrible and raw.

He gagged.

Luke stumbled out of the room, ran out of the apartment, onto the street and down the road. Clark's foggy grey eyes were too much to bear. He needed to be as far away from the corpse as possible.

After a few blocks, dizziness and nausea took over and he slowed to a stop, his heartbeat heavy and desperate.

He had to face it.

His friend was dead.

Chapter 10

June 1990

Another cable car rumbled steadily towards the next stop. Exactly on time, young Umesh noted. Twenty-seven carriages he'd seen today, and each one passed within five minutes of its schedule. He'd grown up in India, where trains were always late—an hour's delay was still considered on time. The clockwork and precision with which the cable cars operated in this new place astounded him. They shook and rattled as much as the trains back home, but they showed up reliably, always per plan.

People outside sweated as they walked along the streets in the shimmering air. It was even hotter in Umesh's small apartment, but he didn't mind. India was a place of ever-present heat; this was nothing to him. Three months in California didn't make him forget home, where things were less convenient and more chaotic. Right now, he was quite comfortable sitting by the kitchen table, looking out the window.

Umesh spent a lot of time looking through this particular window. He'd started school two months ago but hadn't made any friends yet. Shy, short and skinny, the other kids constantly made fun of his accent. Did he have one? English was just English to him—and he spoke the language well enough. Rather than playing with friends he didn't have, he sat and observed.

All the kids in America cared about were comic books, superheroes, toys and TV. He'd seen these things before or had at least heard of them, but here they were ever-present. Every kid in his school had more toys than fingers on their hands, and they spent many hours watching TV, every single day. He didn't know why they were so obsessed with these things. He had his window, and he was happy with it.

The adults were even stranger. Mobile phones had emerged on the mass market, and in San Francisco, a city of early adopters, they really caught on. People walked around with these brick-sized devices, talking to their friends or wives about meaningless stuff. As if it couldn't wait ten minutes longer until they were home.

To Umesh, these things were of little importance. But maybe he didn't understand them yet; after all, this was a new world for him. So he sat by his window, watched and learned.

Chapter Eleven

Santa Clara Police Station was located on El Camino Real, a 600-mile-long road connecting twenty-odd Spanish missions on its way from San Diego to San Francisco. As one of the main traffic arteries winding through Silicon Valley — congested most of the day — it linked tech companies small and large.

The building featured a plain limestone facade and a black roof, not completely flat but not exactly pointy either. Its E-shape resembled a thousand other office buildings in the state of California. Fifty shades of beige. It had palm trees in the front yard, which Luke thought was a nice touch. All in all, a rather calm-looking affair.

Inside was a different story. Detectives rushed around, carrying brown folders and ignoring the constantly ringing phones. If the police station were a body, the detention cells were the bowels, the interrogation rooms the heart, and the detectives' bullpen, where Luke sat, was the brain. The open space office had twelve desks arranged in six pairs, in two rows, each equipped with a standard-issue office chair and a standard-issue detective. Eight of them were in, most of them working on reports or speaking to witnesses. The air hummed with activity. Everybody seemed to be involved in Clark's case, and they all wanted to make a good impression. It wasn't every day that the son of a famous billionaire died.

As Luke waited — in a chair more basic than the detectives' ones — nausea crept up his throat. He didn't know whether it came from his encounter with a corpse, the blood, so much blood, or the fact that his best friend had been murdered. He couldn't comprehend the brutality of it.

'Sorry for the wait. We're dealing with a lot of paperwork right now,' said the detective. In his early forties, with a thick moustache, he looked like a Mexican Burt Reynolds. 'My name is Lopez. I'm the lead detective on the case.'

Not any case, *the* case.

'As you can imagine, a lot of people are working on this. But since you're a key witness, I'll deal directly with you. Makes things easier, doesn't it? Anyway, sorry for your loss. Probably quite a shock. You want coffee?'

Luke's whole body was numbed with exhaustion. The adrenaline was finally wearing off, and his last coffee had been many hours earlier. He weighed the risk of vomiting with the possibility of falling asleep and decided falling asleep was worse.

'Thanks, that'd be great.' His hands trembled. He told himself there was no reason to be nervous but didn't believe his own words.

Lopez gestured to one of his junior detectives, a petite woman with a pixie cut. She looked drained, exactly like somebody who'd been doing the legwork for a major case all day long. She nodded and disappeared.

Lopez opened one of the folders on his desk and produced a set of glossy photographs. They must've been taken and developed within the last hour. Luke wondered if every murder received such prompt treatment.

'So, you found Mr Hamilton exactly as in these pictures?' Lopez asked.

Luke forced his gaze on the photographs for a single second. 'Cuh-correct. I … it took me a while to process. I called 911 from outside.'

'I see. How come you went home in the first place?'

Luke shook his head, unable to explain. 'I had a feeling.'

'A feeling? Let me get this straight. This was just past noon, correct? In the middle of your workday, you had nothing better to do than to go home and check on your housemate?'

'Yes, I did...' Luke finally understood. 'Am I a suspect?'

'Please answer the question, Mr Jankovic.'

'OK ... OK,' Luke said, too tired to argue. 'I was worried. I hadn't seen Clark since last Friday. He seemed confused and distracted, but he didn't want to talk about it. He promised he'd explain everything today. We were meant to have lunch, but he didn't show up, so I went home to check on him.'

Detective Lopez typed diligently on his computer. 'Do you have any idea what he was so upset about?'

Where was this going? Luke just wanted it to be over. 'No. I wondered, but I didn't find an answer. Maybe he was struggling at work. We both joined Swoop three months ago, on the same day. He was still excited, but I suppose he didn't perform very well. I don't know why anybody would kill him, though.'

Luke needed to breathe. He'd been focussing on delivering his report clearly and concisely. After all, this was the police. This was the law. It was more important than his fears and abilities. He figured he was managing the situation well, but it stripped all his energy.

Lopez raised an eyebrow. 'What makes you think somebody killed him?'

'What? I ... There was blood ... What else do you think happened? An accident? I thought ... isn't this why I'm here? To help find his murderer.'

'Mr Jankovic.' Lopez got Luke's last name perfectly right, a little patch of comfort in the rocky sea of terror. 'First of all, no, you're not a suspect. I just had to verify your statement. Mr Hamilton was wearing a fitness armband at the time of his death. One of the fancy ones that measure your pulse. His heart stopped beating at exactly 11:26 am. You used your badge at 8:32 am to swipe into work and then at 12:53 pm to get out. It wasn't you.'

Within a couple of hours, California PD had searched their apartment, taken pictures and conducted quite a bit of background research. Swoop would've handed over the information they needed quickly enough, but no doubt a ton of paperwork was required to make that enquiry. Lopez and his team were on top of their game.

'Also, it was suicide,' he added.

Shock radiated from Luke's hypothalamus all the way to his stomach. The little comfort detective Lopez had given him faded, replaced by the picture of Clark's body chiselled into an inner retina. Luke could still make out every detail: the blood-stained shirt, the derelict colour of his skin, the blank look in his eyes. And the hole in the middle of his chest.

'I don't understand. Wasn't he...? I thought he was shot.'

'I know this probably looks like homicide to you,' Lopez said. 'But to the trained eye, a couple of signs tell us it was suicide. First, his shirt was unbuttoned. People getting shot don't do that, because they don't see it coming. But suicide victims rarely shoot through clothing. It's an odd thing, but a strong signal.'

'Second, the shot was angled slightly upward. From the bloodstains, we know he was sitting there when it happened. Pretty hard to shoot somebody sitting on the ground from below. But if you have a gun in your own hands and aim it at your chest, that's what it looks like. Also, the wound was star-like, which means close proximity.'

'Third, there's no evidence of a struggle. People rarely go down without a fight.

'Fourth, the gun next to your friend and the gunpowder on his hands. Why would he have that if someone else shot him? I'm sorry. But he pulled the trigger himself.'

Luke's gut churned. Trying to hold it together, his mind resorted to what it was best at — evaluating the facts. No matter how he looked at it, what he'd just heard didn't compute. True, Clark had seemed a bit unsettled, but in no way badly enough to end his own life. And if he did, why would he shoot himself in the chest and not the head? It didn't sound right. Yet, Lopez seemed like a trustworthy, competent detective and his reasoning made perfect sense. A fine piece of police work.

Had Luke missed the signs? Was he so ignorant of others' feelings that he hadn't seen how desperate his friend was?

'I know it's a tough pill to swallow,' Lopez broke the silence. 'But you can't look into peoples' heads. No way of knowing what's going on in there. All we can do is verify the evidence, which is pretty clear in this case. I'm sorry.'

Luke shifted uneasily in his chair. He wanted to believe the officer's words, the assessment of a professional, but he couldn't. He needed sleep. Tomorrow, things would make more sense.

'Thank you, Detective Lopez. You and your team did a great job. And so quickly. I guess not everybody gets this treatment.'

Lopez tilted his head and narrowed his eyes. Then he relaxed. 'OK, look. Between you and me? Yes, your friend had a bit of a VIP procedure here. We were going to process it fairly quickly anyway, given who he was. Then your friend's father stomped in here as soon as we notified him. Made quite a scene. I guess that's understandable given the circumstances. He insisted we drop everything for this case, chased us around like a maniac and asked us to wrap it up as soon as possible. At first, we ignored him, but as you probably know, the man's a bit of a figure around here. Within five minutes, he had the mayor on the line, ordering me to do whatever he required. Money really opens doors.

'He's still here, doing his psychological debriefing downstairs to make sure we can discharge him. Mandatory for family and close friends. I'd like you to do one as well.'

Once the last details, paperwork and signatures were taken care of, Lopez asked the detective with the short hair to show Luke to the psychology department. On the way, she grabbed him another coffee.

Battling fatigue, his brain finally ramped back up. The sight of a psychologist's office brought back painful memories of Luke's anxiety therapy a few years earlier. If only brains could be programmed like computers. As he sat down on the uncomfortable hallway chair to wait for his turn, he noticed the door was open a crack, an oversight that allowed Luke to peek inside.

Behind a dark wooden desk sat the psychologist, a woman in her sixties, her grey hair in a librarian bun. She looked like she'd seen it all, and the array of degree certificates behind her bolstered his assessment.

In the opposite chair was Walter Hamilton. Luke had watched enough interviews with him on TV to recognize him without seeing his face. Inventor, self-made billionaire, president of his own charity fund, as close as it gets to a rock star in the world of technology. And now childless. His slumped posture emitted apathy and defeat.

Luke ignored his prickle of discomfort at invading their privacy and tuned in.

'...oftentimes thinking back to a recent conversation with your son will create a permanent memory you can cherish, even though he's now gone,' the therapist said.

Even from his limited point of view, Luke could sense Walter's misery.

'I told your detectives already, I don't remember when I last talked to Clark. It must've been weeks ago, and I don't have the slightest idea what we spoke about. I'm a busy man, I always have ... things on my mind ... but I can't believe I don't even remember our last words.' He sounded angry, angry with himself, the police and the whole world.

What was that? Walter hadn't seen Clark in weeks?

Before Luke could process what he'd heard, the psychologist continued. 'It'll come back to you, almost certainly. Now go home and rest. No work and lots of sleep, that's my professional advice.'

Walter took a deep breath and got up without another word. On his way out, he noticed Luke and raised both eyebrows. Luke desperately tried to look inconspicuous. Was his eavesdropping obvious? After a second of awkward silence, Walter nodded and moved on.

Then it was Luke's turn. A hint of sickness passed through his stomach as he faced the doctor. He expected inkblot cards and multiple-choice personality tests, but none of that happened. Instead, they talked for an hour, an endless string of questions about Luke's mental state, his relationship with Clark, and the extent of guilt he felt.

It wasn't as uncomfortable as he thought it would be, but only half his mind was present. The other half pondered where Clark had been before his death. *I'm gonna spend a couple more nights at my dad's*, he'd said. Luke remembered it vividly, he had an excellent memory for these things. Could it be possible that Walter's statement was inaccurate? Straight-out dishonest? No, his pain seemed real. Besides, this was still the police.

There was only one conclusion. Clark had lied about his whereabouts.

Chapter Twelve

By the time Luke was cleared to go home, it was way past midnight. Swoop's HR department mandated he take the next day off, so after a quick exchange of text messages with Ada, he shut down his phone and his alarm clock, fell into his bed and had a long and dreamless sleep.

When he opened his eyes, it was still dark outside. He looked around, his thoughts dizzy and nebulous, and realised he'd been sweating. His clothes were drenched and so was his blanket. He checked his watch — 6:13 am — groaned and turned around, determined to go back to sleep. He rolled from side to side but soon realised it was hopeless.

He got up and went to the bathroom. As he passed Clark's room, a chill swept from deep inside his bones to the outer layers of his skin. A distant rustling and a soft whine he couldn't identify came from inside, maybe a bird or a rat, or his imagination. He didn't feel ready to go in there and check.

He took a long shower and rinsed the sweat off his body, weighed down by overwhelming sadness and shock over his friend's death. After twenty minutes under the hot water, the world felt slightly less horrible.

A splash of red appeared on his hands. He didn't know whether it came from the water or his body, but he could swear it hadn't been there a minute ago. It stuck to his palms and then disappeared as quickly as it had shown up under the steady stream of water.

Blood? Dirt? Rust? His imagination toyed with him. Maybe he was losing his mind.

A couple of seconds later, an ocean of red surrounded him. Instead of comforting, clean, transparent water, blood came out of the shower rose. This time, he had no doubt.

No rust, no dirt. It was blood, thick and red and disgusting. It covered the floor, the walls, the glass door. Litres and litres of it. He tasted it in his mouth, his eyes filled up with it, his vision blurred. Choking, he grasped for the handle to turn it off.

Abruptly, it stopped and the shower spat out clear water again. It took a minute for the last of the blood to wash out of his hair and off his body until the last speck of red disappeared down the drain. Once he was clean, he cut the water.

No trace remained, not a tiny bit of proof.

Reality seemed to be slipping away. What had happened didn't even seem special. His friend was dead, there was blood in the shower, no big deal. Nothing to see here. And somehow, perhaps most worrying of all, he was okay with that.

He dried every centimetre of his body. When he left the bathroom, the same noise emanated from Clark's room again, louder than before, like breathing, low and deep, combined with the high-pitched whistle of air moving through a narrow pipe.

He stood in front of the door and swore he wouldn't go inside. He'd find the imprint of bloodstains on the carpet and the smell of death, but otherwise nothing except dust and Clark's stuff. He wanted to see none of those things. But his legs worked by themselves, stepping closer to the door as if driven by some outside force. He observed himself putting his fingers on the handle.

What am I doing?

His hand pushed down and opened the door.

And there he was, sitting in exactly the same position in which he'd died. With the same hole in his chest. Clark.

Or what was left of him. He was breathing heavily and struggled for air, since most of what he was trying to suck into his lungs escaped through broken capillaries in the deep crater in his rib cage.

An overwhelming urge to flee rushed through Luke's every cell. Alas, he wasn't in control of his actions. He was caged in his own body.

At first, Clark didn't seem to notice Luke, busy with the simple task of breathing. Every muscle in Luke's body wanted to close that door, lock it and throw away the key. But he couldn't.

The thing that was once Clark turned around and eye-balled him. The zombie's gaze pierced right through him. It tried to speak, but only hisses and whistles came out of his mouth.

Luke didn't need to hear it to know what he wanted to say. He could read it from his lips. One word, repeated over and over: *Why?*

Luke realised he'd been walking steadily towards Clark, the undead, and was already halfway across the room. He tried to turn around, but his legs didn't respond.

A second later, the thing stood and walked towards him, quickly closing the distance.

Normality reframed. Suddenly, the blood in the shower and the zombie in the apartment took on the face of terror.

Luke jerked his upper body around in one final act of self-control. He didn't get far. He stumbled, slipped and dropped to the ground.

The fall lasted longer than it should have. Luke plummeted for ages, watching the ceiling, the thing that once was Clark and the whole room fade away. It all disappeared into nothingness until pure black surrounded him. He was in space, falling towards Earth. The planet came closer and closer, until he could make out more and more details. First continents, then mountain ranges and countries, finally cities. He was closing in on Belarus, on his hometown outside the ancient city of Minsk, on his old house. He was rushing towards the ground like a meteor, only fractions of a second before hitting the roof.

Then he woke, his heart racing. It was already noon; he'd slept for almost twelve hours. The apartment was as silent as a graveyard.

Chapter Thirteen

April 1992

Umesh took another bite of his Samosa. He'd been at school for almost a year, but he still ate alone. Everybody else bought their snacks from the school kiosk, but he had homemade food every day. Not that his parents didn't have money to provide for him — in fact, they were doing quite well in the new world — but they believed the love they put into their food, made with their own hands, translated into happiness and health for their child.

And Umesh was satisfied with what he had. Small and skinny for his age, he considered himself healthier than his chubby classmates. Plus, he didn't have to queue for food and got to eat outside in the schoolyard under his favourite tree. These were his little breaks from boredom in a world where he had no friends.

'Can I sit next to you?' asked a voice from behind. Umesh picked up an accent, a pretty thick one. He didn't know where it was from, but it didn't belong to a native English speaker.

'I'm taking a break,' he said.

'Me, too. It's my first day here. Look, I also have my own food. I don't like it, but it's mine. Can I sit next to you?'

Umesh turned around. The other kid was as short as he was, and, judging from his clothes and ancient-looking lunchbox, up for a tough time with his classmates. Umesh pictured himself on his first day.

'OK,' he said, awkwardly shuffling to the right.

'I'm Xavier, with X,' the other kid said. 'I'm from Spain. My name used to be Javier, with J. But my parents swapped the J with an X when we came here. I think it looks cool.'

'I'm Umesh,' he answered. 'Do you want to try one of my Samosas?'

Chapter Fourteen

'How're you holding up?' Ada said over the phone. 'It's all over the news. These bastards don't even care about Clark. Seriously, all the fuss is about Walter Hamilton's great empire and what's gonna happen to it now that he's lost his heir.'

'I guess they write what people want to hear.' Luke wasn't interested in the media, didn't really care about anything at the moment. All he wanted was to stay home and feel miserable.

Ada sighed. 'You're too nice, you know that? Screw this! Our friend died, the whole world is going to shit, and you're still being diplomatic. You need to let it out, Luke. Insult somebody, fucking anybody. Come on, it's just you and me on the line.'

Luke wanted all these things. He longed to slam a door, punch a wall and vent all these wretched feelings, but his rationality wouldn't let him get out of his own self. 'I don't see why I'd do that. It doesn't change anything. I'd rather be alone.'

'I'm just saying. It might actually help you to show some anger … you know, to deal with things.'

'I'm perfectly alright,' Luke lied. Ada's ability to read him so effortlessly bothered him.

'No, you're —'

'Hang on, I've got a second call.' Luke checked his display. 'Shawn Work. Introduction Shawn?'

'The sales simpleton? What does he want from you?'

'I don't know, but work is still work. I need to take this.'

'Fine,' said Ada and hung up.

He stared at his screen for a few seconds and turned off his phone.

Luke didn't do much of anything during the following days. He stayed home, thought about Clark, his dream and the mysterious string of brain cancer victims. Death seemed to haunt him. Isolated from the world, he harboured dark thoughts and even darker feelings. Had he failed his friend?

His phone rang occasionally, a few calls from Ada, and some from Shawn — the last person on earth he wanted to talk to. He answered none of them. He didn't want to hear about mentorship or condolences or whatever it was they wanted.

A professional team of crime scene cleaners came and sanitised Clark's room. They scraped off the blood and wiped away fingerprints and all other physical remnants of Clark's life. Then, the whole place fell silent, the kind of silence that oozed through the walls and floors. Luke developed a grudge against the apartment; he avoided going into Clark's room.

Whatever he tried to distract himself, two questions kept coming back to him.

Did Clark really kill himself?

Luke was terrible at reading people — he was painfully aware of that, now more than ever — but even he'd sensed Clark's distraction and detachment. Clark had been unsettled before he died, that was a fact. But all this had only been going on for a week or two, no signs of depression beforehand. Could anybody decide to take their own life without a significant trigger within a matter of days? Probably not, he decided after a whole afternoon of research. Clark's behaviour didn't fit what any of the textbooks said, none of the common symptoms matched. But Luke was no psychologist, and, as the detective had said, it was impossible to understand what was going on in someone else's head. Still, something deep inside him questioned the police's assessment. His head wanted to trust the detective, believable as he was, but his heart didn't buy it.

Where had Clark been last week?

That part made even less sense. Clark had said he was going to spend a couple of nights at his dad's place, but Walter had told the police he hadn't seen his son in weeks. Certainly, he would've remembered an overnight stay the day before, even in his huge mansion. And why would he lie? The only logical conclusion was that Clark had been hiding somewhere else during the last days of his life. The big question was where? And why?

After seven days of solitude, Luke was looking forward to going back to work. Finally, he'd get out of the apartment, meet other people and do something productive to take his mind off this mess. A new start. When he arrived, his boss sent him straight to Swoop's corporate psychologist. So much for distraction.

Looking like the hallway in a primary school for severely depressed kids, the corridor in front of the shrink's office was plastered with depression awareness posters. *I'm OK, you're OK ... Got the blues? ... Don't do it.* If he were remotely considering suicide, these posters would've pushed him over the edge.

A set of chairs next to the office door formed the waiting area. Ada sat in one of them, staring at her feet. When she saw Luke, she smiled. 'I guess we're both officially declared psychos.'

'Sorry for not answering your calls.' Luke fixed his eyes on the ground. This was his first conversation in more than a week. 'I ... I needed alone time.'

'I figured, no big deal. You can tell me, you know. People deal with things in their own ways, and that's OK. Tell me next time, huh? I was ... worried. You good?'

He smiled at the thought of Ada speaking more than two sentences without a profanity. 'Yes, I'm alright. We only knew Clark for a couple of months, right?'

'Glad to hear your friends don't rank very high on your list of fucking life priorities.' She grinned. Swearing was back, and the world became a little more normal. They looked at each other and burst into laughter. It felt good, for the first time in an eternity.

'You know what I mean,' Luke said. 'I don't need another psych exam to confirm my mental health.'

Ada's eyes narrowed to slits barely wider than matchsticks. 'But?'

'But what?'

'Come on, Luke. For shit's sake, something is nagging you. You don't believe in your own sanity right now, do you?'

That caught Luke by surprise. Ada had, yet again, seen right through him.

He looked around and continued in a hushed voice. 'It doesn't make sense. Why would he kill himself? He was OK, really OK. What if it has something to do with those brain cancer deaths? I bet Clark was still looking into it without telling us.'

The door opened and the psychologist gestured Luke inside.

Ada whispered, 'Don't tell the psycho guy, or they'll throw you right into the fucking nuthouse ... See you tomorrow at the funeral.'

The doctor was a male version of the psychologist from the police station: grey hair, glasses, turtleneck. The session went as the previous one, even the room looked surprisingly similar — the same set of diplomas, books, comfortable chairs and soothing colours. Except this one was more modern and expensive. The corporate touch.

Luke elaborated on his friendship with Clark and how he was coping. Everything he said was met with a calculated 'And how does that make you feel?' The session was one hundred per cent out of the textbook. It ended with a long string of 'On a scale from one to five' questions, obviously calibrated to evaluate his own suicidal tendencies. Luke felt nothing as he answered them. He hadn't been particularly fond of psychologists before, but now he started to hate them.

'One last thing,' the doctor said. 'Based on what I heard from you today, you need closure. Don't try to interpret Clark's death or second-guess the police work. Closure will only come with peace ... peace with the status quo. Digging deeper will lead you down a path of unhappiness and uncertainty, just as it happened with those cancer cases. That didn't give you either closure or happiness. If you want my professional opinion, let it be.'

The words hit Luke like a sharp slap. When did he mention their cancer research? Their conversation replayed in his mind as he got up and hurried out of the room. No, he was sure he never brought it up.

As he closed the door, still dazed, he saw Xavier Sanchez at the other end of the hallway. Not bothering to pretend to do something else, he just stood there, observing silently, eyes on the action at all times. Luke was well aware this was no coincidence. Xavier wanted him to know he was being watched.

Chapter Fifteen

Luke hated funerals. Nobody was fond of a confrontation with death, but the finality of it twisted his bowels like an evil meat grinder. On the way over, he'd bought a pack of Xanax. He swallowed three of them. They numbed his gut and took away the pain, but not the overwhelming sense of powerlessness.

Worst of all were the people, dealing with grief in their own ways. Luke's aversion to crowds and inability to handle emotions fuelled his social anxiety to a higher order. Not to mention his own grief, a constant gnawing misery.

And the crowd came in large numbers. The ambivalent look on their faces gave away that most of them had never even met Clark. The bulk of them were probably Walter's business associates, no doubt showing up to prove their professional loyalty. The younger group was slightly more involved, golf buddies and former colleagues from Clark's many attempts to create a successful startup. True mourners seemed to be a minority, easily identified by their sobs or suppressed tears. Family. He spotted Walter in the front row, next to his ex-wife, who Luke had only seen once in a picture.

The service was nothing like any funeral Luke had attended before. Since the Valley was firmly atheistic, it wasn't held in a traditional funeral home and there were no religious references. Instead, he sat on a huge, fenced lawn in Palo Alto, between a thousand strangers, facing Clark's urn on a podium. A whole life reduced to a few grams of carbon. Rumour had it Walter was planning on sending his remains to space with the next SpaceX rocket.

Ada was his only comfort, sitting next to him and listening politely for once. Each speech was brief and followed a common theme: life was too short, nobody could predict when and how it ended, so everybody better use their time and make the world a better place. Generic, besides the point, and condensed into a ten-minute format. Like a TED talk.

Once the official part ended, the chairs were taken away and replaced by bistro tables for finger food and drinks. People socialised and settled into business as usual. Luke was sure deals were made, perhaps even by Walter himself, which relaxed him in a way. It made the world more orderly.

'That shady guy Sanchez is here,' Ada said. 'I saw him earlier.'

Luke didn't know what exactly it was, but the guy creeped him out. 'He was talking to Shawn a few minutes ago. Pretty sure he was watching us at work yesterday as well. Something's up with him.'

'Agreed. That's why I did some research. He and Umesh go way fucking back. I found an old article about Sanchez losing his wife in a terror attack in Egypt. After that, radio silence for a couple of years. Then, ten years ago, he came back to life and joined Swoop as head of security. I found a few hints that he was with some sort of special ops team during those quiet years, which means next to him, Rambo looks like a little girl scout selling cookies. He's a complete maniac.'

There it was: a fanatic, capable of anything. And he had his eyes on them. 'How do you get this information? Did you hack into something again?'

'Me?' She chuckled nervously. 'No way, remember I'm clean now. But you know, I used to be a tech blogger, which is as much about people as it's about computers. I still have my sources.'

'What sources?'

'Friends.'

'What friends?'

'Hacker friends,' she whispered.

A waiter offered them a round of drinks. The thought of alcohol made Luke gag. He continued in a hushed voice. 'You don't think he has something to do with Clark's death? If he was special ops, he probably knows how to make it look like a suicide.'

'Anything's possible with such a freak.'

Luke nodded, staring at the urn in the distance. His friend. 'What if he also pressured the shrink at work into telling me to let things slide?'

'Wait ... he told you, too?' Ada asked. 'I thought it was an odd thing to say, psychologically speaking ... Drop it my ass!'

'And he knew about the brain cancer stuff. I didn't tell him that. Did you?'

Ada shook her head, her eyes wide open and alert. 'OK, so here's a theory. It's all Xavier. He's behind all those deaths. I'm not sure how, and I know it's a stretch, but bear with me. Assume Clark kept investigating secretly, maybe he wanted to impress us. Let's be honest, he wasn't doing great at work, so this was his chance to earn some street cred. Anyway, I think he solved it. Not sure how, but Xavier was probably watching and took him out when he got too close. Everything's fucking connected.'

Perfect. A conspiracy theory, exactly what he needed right now. Pain rippled through his stomach. Did those pills wear off already? 'Sounds like an action movie. This stuff doesn't happen in real life.'

'Where do you think writers get their damn ideas from?'

Luke closed his eyes. The image from his dream of Clark the undead haunted his inner eye, still mouthing a single word. *Why?*

'A few days before he died, I spoke to Clark. He didn't make much sense ... but he mentioned the Roman Empire.' He swallowed hard. 'Maybe he wanted to tell me something. OK, what do we do? We didn't get super far last time we tried to play Sherlock Holmes.'

'Here's the thing. If my theory's right, Clark got somewhere. And if he found something, then hell, so can we. Maybe we need another angle.'

'Not another angle. We need help.'

'The cops? No way, Luke. They're set on suicide, and who knows if that's a cover-up. I'm just saying, it's possible. No, we need somebody else, someone we can trust. Xavier has resources, and if he's best buddies with Umesh, then there's a shitload more where that came from.'

'How could we ever match that? We'd need a powerful ally.'

Ada smiled. 'Who has a vested interest in Clark, is well connected, filthy rich, and has basically unlimited resources?'

They waited another hour until the crowd thinned out, keeping to themselves, always with an eye on Xavier. After a group of young women had said their goodbyes, they made their move.

'We're sorry for your loss,' Luke said.

Walter nodded as he gave them a look over. 'You're the Fishers' kid, aren't you? I knew your parents. They were pioneers back in the good old days when we all worked out of our garages.'

Ada didn't beat around the bush. 'How well do you know Xavier Sanchez?'

Walter lifted his eyebrows, his lips stiffened. Maybe the name triggered an old memory, consciously or subconsciously, maybe he was offended by Ada's manners, or maybe it was a random movement caused by a misfired synapse. But it was there.

'Never heard of him. Why?'

'We think he has something to do with ... I mean with Clark's ... his—' Luke didn't manage to get the words out, fighting off the urge to vomit. Walter's expression of pity and aggression said it all. Luke had seen that look over and over as people watched him struggling with his anxiety.

'—with your son's death,' Ada finished his sentence.

Walter turned his head back to her. 'And how would that be?'

They explained how they found out about the brain cancer cases and how their Australian colleague disappeared, about their investigations and Ada's newly formed theory.

'...and Sanchez was around every single time,' she said. 'We think Clark came close, maybe too close. So Sanchez killed him.'

The more they spoke, the more Walter's face reddened. His right eye twitched as he struggled to contain himself. 'Are you experts in forensics?' he shouted. 'Experts who know better than the police, the psychologists and me? Clark was my son ... my son! I knew him better than anyone else. If something was going on, I'd have known. But, oh yeah, right. The two of you have known him for about five seconds. So, of course, you're way more qualified and you know everything. Right? Right!' He stared at Ada, then deep into Luke's eyes, into his very soul.

Luke wanted to curl up and die, right then and there.

But Ada stayed cool. 'Don't you see? There are too many coincidences. And I'm pretty sure a man like you doesn't believe in chance.'

Walter took a deep breath, letting the air out slowly. 'Look, I know you're upset. I'm upset. But not everything is a conspiracy. My son took his life. It's a sad thing for all of us. But unfortunately, it's true. I saw the police reports, and they're pretty clear. My son was in distress, there's no point denying it. We all have to accept the facts and trust the professionals. Just because you two don't like it doesn't mean it didn't happen. Besides, nothing will bring him back.' His eyes locked on Ada's. 'So I'm asking you nicely. Let it go. Don't cast a slur on my son's memory. Clark isn't here anymore, and I need to accept that. I need to move on. And so do you.'

He walked away but stopped after two steps. 'And believe me. If I have to repeat myself, I won't be this nice.'

He got into a black SUV and the driver took off.

Luke was glad he was still standing. He'd come close to fainting under Walter's intimidating stare. 'That went well.'

Ada shook her head. 'I don't believe a single word he said.'

Chapter Sixteen

After the funeral, they went straight to Luke's apartment, the dreadful place that once had been a symbol of his friendship with Clark. He needed to move somewhere else. But at least Ada was with him now.

They made coffee and warmed their hands on the hot mugs. Once Luke's stress had worn off, his energy levels had dropped; a quadruple shot of caffeine brought him back. He looked at the ground, the table, the fridge, the door to Clark's room. A week ago, grief had been a somewhat abstract concept. Now the funeral was over, and the dust had settled, it became real. Clark was gone. All that was left of him was that door.

'Do you actually believe in this theory of yours?' he asked. 'I mean really? Xavier killing Clark? Maybe we're … you know, overreacting?'

'I don't know.' Ada clung to her mug. 'Looks like we're the only ones who give a shit. But that doesn't mean it can't be true.'

'Anything can be true. But maybe we're just making up explanations for something we don't comprehend.'

'Honestly, no idea. Maybe I'm wrong, maybe I'm not. But something isn't right here. I know it. I can feel it. And I need to know what it is.'

Luke closed his eyes and nodded to a fleeting image of Clark. 'OK.'

He got up, walked to Clark's room and tore down the police tape. The act was symbolic rather than rebellious; Santa Clara PD had officially released the crime scene a few days earlier. Somehow, he felt lighter already. 'Let's see then. The detectives didn't find anything in here, but maybe they missed something.'

Clark's room looked roughly as it had before, except for two things. First, all the drawers and doors were open. Most contents were still in their place — not like in the movies, where the whole place was turned upside-down and everything was on the floor — but obviously, the room had been searched. Second, there was a shadow of blood on the wall where he'd discovered Clark's body a week earlier. The cleaners had done their best, but Luke could still see the exact shape. He willed his focus away from it.

Swallowing hard, Ada crossed the doorstep and went straight to Clark's desk. 'I'll start here. You go for his wardrobe, since, you know, you're a guy. Check everywhere. Lots of people actually do hide secrets in their fucking socks.'

Clark's clothes had been shuffled around, but the general order was still intact. His wardrobe was expensive but not excessive. Polo shirts from Lacoste and Marco Polo, jeans from Tommy Hilfiger and Hugo Boss, shoes from Nike and Adidas, and two suits, both tailor-made from outfits Luke didn't recognise.

Luke examined the pants first, hoping to find a scrap of paper in their pockets. Nothing. He moved on to Clark's shirts, checked their pockets and found them all empty as well. He continued with the socks, looking inside every single one, then moved on to shoes and underwear. No note, no money, no hint whatsoever.

Ada still seemed busy searching stacks of paperwork in Clark's desk drawers, so Luke moved on to check the shelves. He'd never paid attention to Clark's collection of books before — multiple volumes on programming languages, algorithms and databases; a whole section with biographies of the greats of computer science, from Steve Jobs, Steve Wozniak and Bill Gates all the way back to Grace Hopper and Ada Lovelace; a full shelf dedicated to management strategies and technical leadership. Not a single work of fiction. A literary reflection of Clark the hard worker, the startup founder who never had any measurable success, the son who always tried to live up to his billionaire father's expectations, but never did — and never would. Luke wanted to burn them all.

He continued with Clark's golf bag, which contained, apart from the obvious equipment, a stack of business cards. Apparently, deals really were made on golf courses. He shuffled through them and tried to find a pattern, but they seemed like a random set of names and companies. Reporters, venture funds, Google, Apple, Facebook and a few startups. He turned the bag upside down and a bunch of golf balls rolled out of a side pocket. He chased them around the room.

'Done with the desk,' said Ada. 'A bunch of bills and everyday paperwork. No scribbles or messages on anything. But look at this.' She held a torn-out page from a notebook, densely covered in green handwriting. 'It's a break-up letter from his ex-girlfriend, Vanessa. Writing love letters on paper is already weird, but a break-up letter? Seriously, wow. Anyway, it's dated four months ago. Did he ever mention her?'

Luke hit his head on the shelf under which he'd found one of the golf balls. A girlfriend? His thoughts spiralled with doubt; he thought he knew his friend. 'No, never. Do you think he was still sad?'

Luke was no expert on break-ups. In fact, he didn't have much experience in romantic relationships at all. Years ago, he had a girlfriend, Theresa. He'd liked her, truly and honestly, and they had a good time as long as it lasted. But then it was over, and that was that. No emotional rollercoaster, no tears and no wars of roses. Maybe they hadn't been in love.

'I don't know,' Ada said. 'He didn't seem very stirred up when we met him, did he? But then, you can't look into people's heads. Suicides are tricky. Being dumped is probably high up the hit list.'

'Taking your life for a woman? It seems ... exaggerated.'

Ada pulled her phone out and typed for a minute. 'Not even for her?'

Vanessa was in her early twenties, tall, blond and stunningly beautiful. Even Luke could see that. 'I don't think appearance matters,' he said.

'You don't, because you're naive and a fucking robot. But in the real world, it matters. Especially when your name is Clark Hamilton, and you're interested in something other than numbers and data.'

Luke had to bite his lip. He didn't mind the bit about robots or numbers. Machines were efficient, objective and logical. But naive? Luke wasn't going to be anybody's puppet. He hated her for saying that. But Ada was his friend, and he understood her point.

'Alright, assume he suffered from the break-up. How was he hiding all this from everybody? I lived with him for three and a half months! But let's say it's true. This means the detective was right. Suicide. End of story.'

'Not so fast, Schumacher. Maybe there's more to it,' Ada said. 'We should talk to her.'

It wasn't much of a lead, but they got one step closer towards the closure they craved so desperately. On his way out, as he switched off the light, Luke's gaze wandered across the floor in a last attempt to find something they'd missed. He spotted one of the golf balls below Clark's desk. When he bent over to pick it up, he saw a small bright triangle sticking out from behind the back panel of the table.

A few millimetres of yellow paper cut into his conscience, a Post-it note which must have fallen behind the desk. Something the police had missed. He pulled it out and held it up to the light.

Clark's handwriting. Finally, a clue.

Luke's heart hammered inside his chest; his voice broke. 'Ada, look at this.'

Back at the kitchen table, Luke stared at the cryptic piece of paper in front of him. It didn't contain a lot of information, and the little it had didn't mean anything to him.

Two lines, eight characters each. Could this be the answer to it all?

The first line was 'Scaevola'. Latin or maybe Greek? Possibly a name. Or something entirely made up, like a codename or a pseudonym.

The second line contained six digits and two slashes. 09/22/21. A date. American formatting, four weeks in the future.

What was the connection between these two bits of information? And how did it relate to Clark? Maybe a username and a password. People used dates as passwords all the time, particularly the birthdays of their beloved ones.

Ada already had her laptop out. 'Found it,' she said. 'Scaevola is either an Australian flower or a Roman guy called Gaius Mucius Scaevola, who lived around 500 BC. The flower's only claim to fame is that it spread beyond the Australian continent and populated the rest of the Pacific, which is apparently a rare thing. The Roman dude was an assassin, famous for his bravery. Looks like he held his right arm into a fire pit until it was completely burned up, just to make a fucking point. Scaevola actually means "the left-handed" in Latin.'

Luke's thoughts scattered. 'Rule out the plant. It's too generic, only relevant if it meant something super personal to Clark, like the first flower he gave to his first girlfriend. We'll never know, so what's the point thinking about it?'

'Obviously,' said Ada. 'And didn't you mention Clark rambled about Romans?'

He did. For the thousandth time, Luke cursed his inability to read people. Had the answer always been there, in plain sight? Why didn't he pick up on it?

'Yes ... Scaevola the Roman hero sounds like a perfect alias, so maybe this is a login and password for a website or ... a game.' He paused. Were they overthinking again? 'What if Clark spent his nights foraging a fantasy world as an orc named Scaevola? A simple guilty pleasure.'

'That's what I thought at first, too,' Ada said. 'People write down their passwords all the time. They're not supposed to, but most are idiots and do it anyway. The easiest way to steal somebody's PIN is to break into their place and look for Post-it notes with four to six digits. The world is full of morons.

'But this date's not a password. People use birthdays or wedding dates, that sort of thing. This one is in the future, which doesn't make sense. You want to use something you remember, and you can't remember stuff that hasn't happened yet.'

Ada had a point. Any non-random password was essentially a mnemonic, an aid for the brain. The future was uncertain, and uncertainty was no help at all.

'Could be a codename for a project, maybe at Swoop. You know how we always have cool internal names, and then the idiots from marketing change them to something lame and mass friendly. And the date could be a deadline, a release date or a milestone.' Ada typed on her keyboard as she spoke, the familiar page of Swoop's intranet on her screen.

A realization shook Luke's gut. 'Wait! Isn't this traceable?'

Ada flashed a tired smile. 'Yep, for a mere mortal like you. But Swoop doesn't want anyone to know what their security engineers do all day. We have special accounts.'

Luke instinctively looked away from the screen. Ada was back in the world of hackers, a place he'd rather avoid. 'If you say so.'

'I can't find any project or team called Scaevola. Nothing containing that word across all our internal sites … But hang on, maybe it's not that obvious.' She opened several other tabs in her browser and expanded her search.

A few minutes later, just as Luke was about to give up, she said, 'Here it is, in the archive of our internal mailing lists. Sent by a pretty high-up manager to another one about three weeks ago … They're talking about product launches and timelines, and the last line says, "We need to coordinate this with the Scaevola launch". That's it, the only reference.'

Luke's stomach plummeted. It wasn't a game. A group of people shared a secret, and they were hiding it carefully. 'It's a project. Looks like this was supposed to be a private email between those two people. One of them added this mailing list in CC and then the other one hit "reply to all" accidentally.'

'Why can't we find it anywhere then?' said Ada. 'All Swoop projects are visible to all employees. Except…'

'… except if somebody has special access like you do?'

'Holy shit,' said Ada. 'What does Clark have to do with all this?'

Luke cursed himself. Why did he find that note? They'd opened Pandora's box, and there was no going back.

Chapter Seventeen

August 1993

History wasn't Umesh's favourite subject, far from it. He was a creature of science and excelled at maths, physics and chemistry. In these courses, his grades were straight As, and he didn't care much about anything else. Especially history, which in his opinion was merely the recounting of things that had already happened, like playing a pre-recorded tape.

Lately, however, he'd become a little more interested in this subject due to the current topic: The Roman Empire. Umesh didn't know much about it, but the teacher's introduction caught his attention. A single city rising to immense power, conquering the country around it and then most of the known world. An empire that lasted more than a thousand years. Clearly, the Romans must've done something right.

'...and the people of Rome were pretty desperate during that siege,' the teacher said. 'Imagine a city, fully surrounded, no way to get food in or out, no way to communicate with the rest of the world. It wasn't like they could pick up the phone and call for help.' The teacher chuckled but didn't get much of a response from his crowd.

'So they made a plan, a pretty sneaky one. They recruited three hundred youths, teenagers not much older than you guys, to assassinate the Etruscan king Porsena. Gaius Mucius made the first attempt. He got into the camp of the enemy and killed their leader. Or at least that's what he thought. You see, it was payday, another thing that was more complicated back then. They didn't have bank accounts or anything like that, so every soldier was paid in cash each week. On paydays, the king's scribe managed all the business, so Gaius Mucius accidentally identified him as the true leader of the Etruscans. He'd killed the wrong person.'

'He was of course arrested and questioned. He famously declared, "I am Gaius Mucius, a citizen of Rome. I came here as an enemy to kill my enemy, and I'm as ready to die as I am to kill. We Romans act bravely, and when adversity strikes, we suffer bravely."'

'And what do you think he did to prove his bravery? He put his right arm into a fire pit and held it there until it was completely burned off. I'm not talking blisters here, I'm saying he burned his arm down to a stump without even flinching. It took an enormous, unthinkable amount of willpower to do that.'

Umesh was mesmerised. He wasn't sitting in his classroom anymore; he was right there, thousands of years ago, witnessing the astonishing feat of an ancient hero. He could almost smell the burned flesh.

'It's just plain dumb,' said the kid sitting next to him, a class clown who didn't rank very highly on Umesh's ladder of respect. 'Look how smart I am, I burned my hand.' The entire class laughed, except for the teacher and Umesh. 'And it's probably not that hard. I bet anybody can do it … I mean it's holding out your hand, how hard can it be?'

'Are you volunteering to prove your point?' the teacher said. 'I have a lighter with me, right here. I'll buy you the biggest portion of ice cream you've ever seen if you hold your hand over the flame long enough to get a blister. Think about it, ice cream and the admiration of the whole class, all for a little bit of red skin that will be gone by next week.'

The kid's parents were wealthy, and he was spoiled; he could get all the ice cream he wanted. But the second part hit a nerve. Umesh knew he was desperate for attention and approval from his classmates.

'Deal,' the kid shouted as he jumped up from his chair.

The teacher ceremonially shook his hand and lit a tiny flame. The kid cocked his head, looked at it for a couple of seconds and stretched out his hand. He couldn't keep it there for a single second.

'What's wrong? Is it … hot?' the teacher asked with a smile.

'No, it isn't,' the kid protested. 'It was a reflex.'

'Aha,' the teacher said. 'That's the whole point. You have to muster enough willpower to suppress your reflexes, which have been hard-wired into our brains for millions of years. Not an easy feat, and that's exactly why-'

'I want to try again,' the kid interrupted him. 'Now I know how to do it.'

The teacher shrugged, 'Sure, be my guest.'

This time, he kept his hand still for a couple of seconds, before letting out a muffled scream. He looked at his hand. No damage. He tried it twice more but couldn't provoke as much as a heat rash. He walked back to his chair without another word, keeping his head low and his shoulders lower.

Umesh couldn't resist a spiteful chuckle.

'Don't feel bad about it,' the teacher said. 'That's why this guy is in the history books and we still talk about him two and a half thousand years later.

'This incredible feat of willpower earned him the respect of the Etruscan king. He was released, made an envoy and sent back to Rome to start peace negotiations. The two rival kings settled their dispute, and the Romans were free again. As a reward, Gaius Mucius received a generous portion of farming land and the nickname "the left-handed". Or "Scaevola", as they say in Latin.'

Umesh gaped, deeply moved. The story was probably just an old tale, but the idea of the mind triumphing over the body through sheer willpower intoxicated him. He was well aware his physical appearance didn't impress anybody, but he could work on his self-discipline and determination, his courage and his fortitude, and use these to shape his path in this world.

Scaevola. He'd always remember that name.

Chapter Eighteen

'This is Jacky O'Connor, live from the 101 between Redwood City and Palo Alto.' The reporter's voice came out crisp and clear through the car speakers. The Uber driver had a full entertainment system built into his hatchback, allowing his passengers to watch TV, play games or browse the internet.

Luke didn't particularly feel the need to be entertained during the half-hour ride to Palo Alto, but the previous guest had left the news channel on, and he couldn't figure out how to turn it off.

'Last Thursday, a brand-new Tesla Model 3 lost control at about sixty miles per hour, right here where I'm standing. The young man operating the vehicle crashed through the divider into the traffic on the opposite side, where he hit three cars in rapid succession and lost his life. None of the other drivers got hurt beyond bruises and scratches.'

'Over the last few days, investigators have been speculating about an error in the car's software system, an accusation Tesla vehemently denies. About a month ago, the company rolled out a new version of their self-drive module, allowing drivers to completely disengage and watch TV while their car takes full control. The carmaker created an expert task force to investigate the circumstances of the crash. This team has now released their preliminary report, in which they reach the conclusion that the assistive systems were not in fact activated at the time, and the vehicle was fully controlled by the driver.'

'Meanwhile, doctors conducting the autopsy discovered that the deceased suffered from a fatal brain aneurysm. The twenty-eight-year-old, who worked as a product manager in a life sciences startup, had a stroke affecting one of the main arteries in the brain and passed out while driving at full speed. According to the medical team, this type of stroke is extremely rare and affects less than one in a million people.'

'Officials now agree nothing could've been done to prevent this tragic death. Despite all our efforts to develop smart technology, there are unfortunately still aspects of our lives we can't control.'

Luke reached for the pack of Xanax in his pocket. A brain stroke, in the news. Was there a connection? Metaphorical billboards screamed death all around him, yet he couldn't understand their message.

Luke left the car wondering about the connection between project Scaevola and the mysterious string of deaths. The pills eased his stomach but didn't calm his thoughts. Why couldn't he shut up his brain? He had to focus on the task at hand: speaking to a stranger, and a stunning one at that.

The house, located in a quiet alley close to the centre of Palo Alto, reminded him of an old English castle. Thanks to Ada's research, he knew the father of Clark's ex-girlfriend was a VP at Google and shamelessly rich. But it was one thing to know they had money and another to stand in front of their intimidating mansion. A realtor's dream. Luke's nightmare.

Once again, he rehearsed the sentences he'd prepared. His therapist once told him to read his notes aloud whenever he was particularly nervous, but Luke was worried somebody would hear him. If only Ada could be with him now.

But she had other work to do. The police were about to release Clark's personal possessions, and Ada hoped to get her hands on his phone. By law, only close relatives were allowed to collect those belongings, which meant sooner or later, Walter would stop by and pick up the whole lot. The chances of obtaining Clark's phone after that were close to zero, so Ada decided to rush to the station and take it before that could happen. Luke had no idea how she planned to pull it off, but something told him the less he knew the better.

He waited in front of the enormous wooden door, the intimidating eyes of its lion-head knocker reminding him of his comfort zone boundaries. Trying to convince a rich and gorgeous stranger to share details of her relationship with a dead person seemed like an impossibility.

He was about to turn away when a maid opened the door. Her stern expression left no doubt that Luke better state his business quickly or get the door slammed in his face.

'May ... muh-may I...' He closed his eyes and focused on the words he'd prepared. 'May I speak to Vanessa ... please?'

The maid raised an eyebrow and examined him from head to toe. Evidently, she decided he posed no threat, because, in a voice that could summon the most defiant toddler within a radius of a kilometre, she yelled, 'Vaneeeeeessaaaaaa!'

Luke attempted an awkward smile and shifted his weight from one leg to the other. If only the maid would take her eyes off him.

Behind her, a man in his fifties came down the stairs, presumably Vanessa's father, mobile phone in his hands and headphones in his ears. He seemed to be on a conference call and lowered his voice when he saw the stranger at their door. He turned and disappeared towards the back of the house.

A second later, Vanessa came out of one of the many doors on the ground floor. She was even prettier than in her picture, wearing hot pants made of denim and a pink top with a unicorn on it. Luke began to sweat.

'Do I know you?' she asked.

'You … don't. I'm a friend … a friend of Clark, I mean. Could I … Do you mind if I ask you a few questions?'

'I … I'm sorry,' she said, checking the direction where her father had gone before. 'I heard about the funeral and wanted to go. But my dad told me it was a bad idea, he said it wouldn't be appropriate. Looking back, I think it was a mistake.'

A few awkward seconds passed. Luke didn't know what to do or say. His prepared sentences were gone. What now?

'But you better come in,' she broke the silence. 'Do you want tea or coffee?'

Luke's clenched jaw eased. 'Coffee … yes, that would be great.'

The maid, who'd remained beside them the whole time, nodded and disappeared. Vanessa led Luke through the living area into a sunroom alcove that was bigger than most inner-city apartments. Large windows overlooked their backyard, which boasted the greenest grass he'd ever seen and white marble statues of Greek philosophers shining under the California sun.

Vanessa's father sat on the living room couch and typed on his laptop; Luke could hear the faint clattering of the keyboard from his spot. Surely, there had to be a more private place in this mansion. Luke channelled his discontent into a questioning stare, but Vanessa didn't budge.

'How did you know Clark?' she asked.

'Roommates ... I mean we were roommates for the last few months. At Swoop ... we started working at the same time. He asked ... invited me to live with him.' Luke was already exhausted, his inner battery drained by the tension. If only he could do these things online.

'He was always generous,' she said. 'I can't recall him mentioning a roommate, but that must've happened after we broke up, right before he joined Swoop.' She looked at him and tilted her head. 'So, how can I...?'

Time for the big question. Luke fumbled for it in the depths of his short-term memory. 'May I ask ... Why did you break up with him?'

Her eyes narrowed. 'What makes you think it was me who broke up?'

Luke closed his eyes and visualised his childhood bedroom. The sight of his old bed always comforted him. 'Your break-up letter. I saw it, a fine gesture. Writing a letter, I mean. Shows you care.'

Vanessa's cheeks blushed to a delicate shade of red that made her even prettier. The maid came back with the beverages and put them carefully on the table.

Vanessa waited until they were alone again and took a deep breath. 'Now I'm embarrassed. I wrote that letter after Clark had already ditched me.' She sighed. 'Nobody had ever broken up with me before, and I guess my ego couldn't take it. Part of me pretended it never happened, so I decided to break up with him ... again. Or instead, I don't really know. It was utterly meaningless, but it helped me, devastated as I was. It took me a couple of months to get back on track. My therapist helped me work things out. And then he died. Just like that. I don't know what to think anymore.'

What she said didn't make sense. Why would she break up after it was already over? Facts were facts. Reality was reality. But then, people did all sorts of weird things when they were emotional. Was it inappropriate to continue?

Then she gave him the answer he was looking for. 'What killed me back then was Clark was perfectly fine, you know. He told me it wasn't working out for him anymore, and he didn't have any feelings left for me. And that was it for him. And I ... I thought we'd grow old together.' A tear rolled down her cheek. 'I felt like a book read out and put back into the shelf, done and dusted. Not a nice feeling. And seeing him just fine made it much worse...'

She sobbed, and Luke felt more helpless with every passing second. Why weren't there any tissues in the room? Calling the maid was out of the question.

Just when he couldn't stand the silence anymore, Vanessa finally said, 'Anyway, didn't you want to ask me something?'

Luke already had what he'd come for. Not what he'd expected, but the truth, he was sure of that. He thought for a second and then tried a shot in the dark. 'Did he ... uhm, did he ever mention a confidential project to you? Project Scaevola?'

In the corner of his eye, he saw Vanessa's dad look up from his laptop, his eyes emitting surprise and bewilderment. Luke's brain automatically logged lurking danger. A fraction of a second later, her father's stare was back at his screen.

Before Luke could process her father's reaction, Vanessa said, 'Sorry, this name doesn't mean anything to me.' Her face hidden behind her hands; she was properly crying now.

Luke's phone vibrated, a text message from Ada. Time to go. But how could he leave her in this state?

Her father intervened. 'That's enough now,' he said, leaving not a trace of doubt. Luke immediately understood why he was a VP.

As Luke hurried away, he sensed Vanessa's father's piercing eyes burning a target on his back.

Chapter Nineteen

Luke held Clark's phone like it was radioactive. 'How did you trick the police into giving you this?'

'Trade secret,' said Ada with a wink.

'Come on!'

'Let's just say they agreed to hand it to Walter's assistant.'

'His ... what, you?'

Ada smiled. 'All you need is a forged power of attorney and –'

'Unbelievable.'

'Told you, you don't want to know.'

Luke shook his head. 'So what now? I don't know his password.'

'Coffee, that's the fucking secret. With enough coffee comes energy, and with energy comes perseverance, and that's exactly what we need. Make the biggest damn pot the world has ever seen. We have a long night ahead of us.'

Luke had been afraid she'd say that. He tried to rub the tiredness out of his face. 'So you're finally showing me your CoreOS hack in action.'

'Ha, I wish. But unfortunately, our corporate phones have a modified version of CoreOS, you know with all that annoying employee tracking stuff. It's an entirely different build, which means my hack wouldn't do the trick. I'm afraid we'll have to work for it.'

Luke clutched his mug. He was about to cross the threshold into the den of hackers, an underworld of shady characters and illegal activity. He'd do it for Clark. 'OK. How can I help?'

Her laptop showed a perfect copy of Clark's phone screen, displaying the login window. Next to it, Luke saw a text editor with a long list of words, one in each line. Ada added new ones as she spoke.

'I'm preparing a list of phrases we can use as passwords. This little script tries each one of them, which is obviously way faster than typing the damn things. By doing that, we also avoid the limit of three retries before the phone locks itself. These morons built this stuff directly into the user interface, so it's easy to get around by directly talking to the backend. Now we have to find the right password.'

Luke raised an eyebrow. Maybe he was going to be fine after all. 'This is what you call hacking? Trying lots of different passwords?'

'No, this is not hacking,' Ada said. 'Despite what you might have seen in those dumbed-down movies, the easiest way to break into a system is to guess the password. I'm only trying to be efficient. Why make it harder for yourself and not try the easy stuff first? This leaves absolutely no trace and is completely legal. In fact, it's impossible to tell the difference between knowing a password in the first place and guessing it, right? Means I'm not breaking this stupid agreement with the FBI and can keep my job.'

Luke gave an absent nod. A judge would probably disagree.

'What I need from you are ideas. Any combination of letters and numbers that would've meant something to Clark.'

Ada was already up to several pages and had covered the most obvious terms. With their combined brainpower and a little help from the internet, they found almost a thousand candidates. They had birthdays of his close family, graduation dates, names of relatives and their pets, pseudonyms, their favourite musicians and so on. The amount of information they were able to gather using social media shocked Luke.

Ada hit a button and the list increased rapidly. On the simulated screen, one candidate after another was entered automatically into the password field.

'It's a shame he didn't use a four-digit pin like most people,' said Ada. 'That'd be much faster, only ten thousand possibilities, right? But it's OK, that's why I created this script. It extrapolates the data we entered by using everything forward and backward, replacing certain characters with letters, and doing a couple of other semi-smart things. See how our measly list grew to ten times its original size? It's the kind of stuff you do when you're a good hacker, not like all those amateurs. We should be through in about fifteen minutes. Or faster, if we have a match.'

It was already past midnight, and Luke was starving. All that coffee helped his concentration but made him hungry. 'I'll order pizza. Margherita for you?'

'Sure. Something tells me we're not done here anytime soon.'

He placed the order, drained his mug and thought about what Clark's ex-girlfriend had said. Human behaviour still amazed him. Her father's reaction was suspicious. How could a Google executive be involved in all this? Did this run deeper than they imagined? What if they couldn't handle what they discovered?

An outburst of Ada's swearing drew his attention. 'Fuck. Screw this shit. No match ... Ugh, this is frustrating. I guess that means I actually have to work for it. Damn, I don't have all my proper stuff on my laptop anymore.'

Oh no. It was going to happen after all. He'd be a criminal. 'Are you sure you want to do this? We could both end up in jail.'

She exhaled loudly and paused. As silence polluted the air between them, Luke imagined himself behind bars, in a tiny cell with murderers and rapists. His gut cramped. He wasn't made for this.

'Not if you don't tell anybody,' Ada finally said. 'The only traces I'll leave will be on this phone, which nobody even knows we have. And to be sure, we can completely wipe it afterwards, just in case ... We owe this to Clark.'

Luke closed his eyes. 'OK.'

Ada nodded and hacked away. Now it looked like the real deal. She typed frantically, switching between several terminal windows, her eyes never leaving the screen. She barely blinked. For about half an hour, Luke roughly followed her actions, but then he lost track and gave up. He sat beside her and made sure her coffee and food supply didn't run out.

Two hours later, he finally caught up again. 'Let me get this straight. You're sending text messages to the phone, and each message contains special characters that are actually code. And with this code, you try to give yourself access to everything. Correct?'

Ada didn't look up. 'More or less, yes. But those exploits become public pretty quickly and get fixed even quicker, so there's only a limited number of things I can do with those shitty little texts. Think single-line commands. Plus, it's protected by this extra son-of-a-bitch corporate Swoop app that prevents pretty much anything that doesn't look like Clark's doing it. I don't know how this exactly works, so all I can do is trial and error. It's like trying to shoot flies with a fucking bazooka in a dark room. And I was never into this phone hacking stuff, so all this is taking me a bit longer.'

Unable to help, Luke decided to broaden his search for brain-related deaths in the Valley. After an hour spent turning over every stone, his back was stiff and his neck corded, and he didn't find anything new. Frustrated, he created a spreadsheet where he entered all known cases, with names, dates and other information he could use for future tracking.

Thirteen rows of data were in front of him. Eleven definitive cases, five mentioned by the Australian, five related to the electro smog startup, and the Tesla driver. And two maybes, Brett Lynton and Clark. Every single row a life not lived to its full potential.

No matter how he sliced and diced the data, he couldn't find any meaningful connection. All victims worked in the tech industry, but everybody within a radius of maybe a hundred kilometres did. Being young and mostly male wasn't a distinguishing factor either.

An ancient part of his brain wanted to throw his dreaded laptop out the window, hoping his worries would disappear with it. He wanted to slam his fist on the table until it was bloody. What happened to his analytical mind? How could he, the best data science student of his country, not find any clues in thirteen measly rows of data?

Luke was asleep when Ada's elbow woke him. 'Luke, I'm in. I cracked the fucker.'

It was 3 am and Luke's brain needed a few minutes to get up to speed. At least now he was able to contribute. Knowing the exact time of death, it should be easy to reconstruct Clark's last couple of hours.

The browser history didn't reveal anything out of the ordinary. Clark hadn't searched for psychological help or ways to end his life—a common pattern with suicide victims. His history was all about news, technology, life hacks and golf.

They checked his Facebook account and found nothing obvious: no signs of ex-girlfriend obsessions, no unusual private messages. In fact, he'd contacted a series of obviously single women, fishing for a date. It all confirmed what his ex-girlfriend had told Luke earlier – Clark hadn't suffered from post-breakup depression.

Luke's arm hair stood up as they opened Clark's location history and literally retraced his last steps. They were following a ghost through the last moments of his worldly existence.

Clark had been at home for the last few hours of his life. No surprises there.

But as they scrolled back further, Luke spotted something he didn't expect. This time, the analytical part of his brain caught up and sent a flare of alarm throughout his entire nervous system. 'Wait … go back a couple of days. There.'

Ada scrolled back and forth on the location timeline. Then it hit her, too. 'Shit! We had it all wrong. It wasn't Clark who lied, it was Walter. Clark was at his dad's place for three fucking days.'

Luke's eyes flickered. He couldn't believe it; not because he'd been wrong, but because the possibility hadn't occurred to him that Walter, in the midst of his grief, had lied to them. Alarm turned into anger. 'That's why he was so weird at the funeral. But why? Why lie about it?' Luke's lungs scrambled for air.

'Not a damn clue. Honestly, I don't want to think about the implications, that's a question for tomorrow. I can't think straight anymore. We need to go to bed.'

But Luke was wide awake. How could she think about sleep now? 'Shouldn't we check the most obvious thing first?'

Ada yawned, not bothering to cover her mouth. 'What do you mean? Did I miss something?'

'I can't believe I'm ahead of you for once. Think old-fashioned. The call logs.'

Ada sighed. 'How many times do I have to tell you, people don't make phone calls anymore. And by people, I mean everybody but you.'

She pulled it up, nevertheless. When Luke saw the last call, he plummeted into a dark chasm of simple but horrific truth. Clark had received a phone call right before his death.

'Fuck,' Ada said. 'Holy fuck. He spoke to his dad seven minutes before he died.'

Chapter Twenty

'…and now this guy follows me on Twitter. I mean what an honour. Maybe I'll become a famous influencer, you know, telling people what to do and all that.' Nathan laughed so hard he almost choked on his food.

The words passed through Luke's head without registering. He hadn't slept much over the last couple of days. The food in front of him didn't look appealing, and he was even less interested in his boss's stories. But he couldn't just get up and leave.

'And remember I'm listening to this freaky podcast on my way home?' Nathan said. 'Weird Deaths?'

Luke didn't but nodded anyway.

'Usually, they talk about bizarre accidents and stuff like that. And there's been crazy shit on the show, I can tell you. I mean, I know it's weird to listen to death and all that, but I'm really enjoying it, even if it makes me feel like some sort of freak. Or maybe that's the whole point. Who knows? You should definitely check it out.

'This week's episode wasn't about circumstances, but probabilities. They found this couple dead together in the bathtub. Apparently, their brain stopped working somehow, right when they were taking a bath. From what I got, they kinda drowned. By itself, that's not really weird, at least by the standards of the show. But the chance of that happening to any single person is about one in a hundred million. Super-duper rare.

'What blows my mind is it happened to both of them. Together, at the same time, in the bathtub! And there's more, they had the same job, both software testers. Can you believe it? The guys from the podcast calculated the probability, accounting for the fact they were a couple and their ages and all that. Guess what? It's about one in ten to the power of twenty-four! A ten with twenty-four zeros. You know what it's called? A Yotta! I actually had to look it up. You know Mega, Giga, Tera, and so on. If you follow that all the way to the end of the scale, that's where you find Yotta. It's literally the highest number with a name.' Nathan made a gesture as if his head was exploding.

A wave of adrenaline pulled Luke's consciousness out of limbo. Why did they die? Did he say software engineers? How unlikely was this? Now he was all ears.

'Their brain stopped working?' he asked.

'Yeah, some kind of freak brain stroke,' Nathan said. 'But that's not the point here. You have to think about the probabilities, Luke. It's not just rare, it's never ever in the lifetime of this universe will this ever happen again rare...'

Nathan kept talking, but Luke turned inwards again. Two more deaths, both related and insanely rare. Two more rows for his spreadsheet. He understood probabilities and their implications well enough. None of this was a coincidence, not anymore. A train of death was steaming through the Valley, and he was running behind. He needed to figure out what powered it.

Luke and Ada had spent the best part of an hour in the sushi joint. Disappointed and disillusioned, they played a game they used to enjoy when Clark was still alive – they guessed what people on the other side of the conveyor belt wanted to eat and snatched it up before it could make its way around. It was fun and mean in equal parts, they used to love it. Today, they did it out of boredom.

Luke wasn't even hungry, his mouth tasted sour. Over the last two weeks, they'd searched and validated, turned around every stone and examined every file on Clark's phone. Without the slightest bit of success.

'Let's face it,' he said. 'We spent so much time on this, looked everywhere, and barely worked. It's a miracle we're still employed. And what did we find? Nothing.'

'We know only three things for sure. One, there's a mysterious project. Two, Clark was involved somehow. Three, Walter lied about Clark's whereabouts and the phone call. These are facts.'

'Then there are the theories. The police were probably wrong about Clark's death, to say the least. Or' — he cleared a lump in his throat — 'or they're actively covering up a murder, and Walter or maybe Xavier is involved. Whoever's behind all this, they're hiding it well. This is all very vague.'

'If you say it like that,' said Ada, 'then yeah, it sounds pretty fucking thin. But I mean, come on, you know as well as I do something stinks here.'

Luke moved too slowly to catch a plate of sashimi; the sushi train carried on without disturbance. He couldn't care less. 'Agreed. But we can't find anything. Two weeks, Ada. And we've been on it every single night. I don't know where else to look.'

The plate Ada took didn't upset anybody. She wasn't disappointed either. 'Hell, this is frustrating.'

'What are our options? Confront Walter again? I don't think that'll lead anywhere. Same with the police, it's a closed case.'

Ada didn't reply.

Luke's mind was a deflated windbag, helplessly dangling in the air. He missed his friend, and the least they could do was to find out why he passed away. But do the dead even care? What was the point of all this? Nothing could bring him back. He hated the world for that.

Back at his desk, Luke didn't know what to do. He typed the same sentence over and over into an empty text document, a Belarussian rhyme he'd learned as a kid. Never in his life had he gotten this stuck. When he had a problem, he'd always worked as hard as he possibly could and found a solution somewhere along the way. But not this time. No matter what he tried, he couldn't figure it out. What killed him was he knew the answer was out there; he knew it deep inside his every cell.

So he typed irrelevant Belarussian nursery rhymes and sulked. His once tidy inbox was a mess of unread emails.

After wasting a few hours this way, he grew bored and moved on. In an act of both defiance and frustration, he randomly browsed Swoop's behavioural database, which contained everything about their users from their phone calls to the applications they installed. Thanks to his work on machine learning, he had virtually unlimited access to this data. Everything except email addresses, names and phone numbers, which were replaced by hash IDs — long and meaningless combinations of numbers and letters designed to obfuscate people's real identities.

He studied the behaviour of a handful of arbitrary users and followed their virtual footsteps. Who they called, what model their phone was, their screen brightness at any time of the day, and so on. If only he'd known Clark's account ID, Ada could've saved her efforts breaking into his phone. But that was the point of the whole anonymization procedure. Don't spy on your friends.

The one exception was Umesh Patel. To set an example for transparency and trust, their charismatic CEO had made his ID public on Swoop's intranet. People suspected Umesh had several phones and used the one with that ID only for irrelevant things. True or not, it allowed a tiny glimpse into the life of their famous founder, which most employees found profoundly fascinating. There was an internal website called 'UmeshTracker' where a dedicated community attempted to de-anonymise the mesh of IDs around their CEO, a bit like a computerised, planet-scale version of Memory.

Luke's clearance gave him access to a richer set of data than those folks running the website, allowing him to pull up Umesh's daily activities. The UmeshTracker people would probably give their right arm for a screenshot of what he had in front of him.

Skimming the data, Luke found Umesh's behavioural patterns weren't so different from most other people. He slept a bit less than the average person, worked more, and exercised frequently. But otherwise, his habits seemed pretty average. Billionaires were humans after all.

He zeroed in on Umesh's location history, which turned out to be relatively boring. His movements were mostly between Swoop's main campus and a residential address in Palo Alto, which Luke quickly memorised as his home address, and the occasional event downtown.

As he opened the call logs, Luke found himself looking over his shoulder. Not that he was doing anything illegal; he had legitimate access to this data. But his moral compass made him pause as he thought back to his home country with its bloody history marked by endless conflicts. Belarus was called 'Europe's last dictatorship' for a good reason: its authoritarian government, which routinely and violently suppressed the opposition. Freedom was an aspiration rather than a reality. Growing up, fear of the secret police was ever-present, so personal freedom meant a great deal to him.

But then, Umesh consciously made this data available to his employees. Luke proceeded.

Most calls in and out were to a single ID, regularly during business hours, and occasionally stretching late into the night and weekends. The pattern matched the relationship between a hard-working CEO and his even harder-working assistant. A second ID showed up a little less often, but steadily around night-time.

Luke shrugged. Maybe a secret lover — everybody had needs.

He was about to close those files when, in a flash of inspiration, he checked the day Clark died. He didn't suspect any involvement of his CEO per se, but the more data the better.

Umesh's morning followed the regular pattern. But one call caught Luke's attention, about ten minutes before Clark's death. The cryptic caller ID sparked a faint vibration in the depths of Luke's memory. He'd seen this ID before. Where was that?

He opened UmeshTracker to check if they had a guess who it belonged to. They sure did. A shiver went down his back. All sounds faded, and he was alone in the universe in front of his screen with his discovery. He closed his eyes and checked again.

And again.

He confirmed it three more times, his muscles stiffening further with every affirmation. Where was his Xanax?

The combination of letters and digits of both IDs matched perfectly, one by one. He rubbed his eyes and stared at his screen.

'Luke ... Luke, you don't want to come with us for lunch?' he heard one of his colleagues ask.

Jerking his focus back into reality, he quickly closed the file before his boss could see what was on his screen.

'You ... you go ahead,' he said. 'I'll join later.'

Once they were out of sight, he pulled it up again.

It was still there. He hadn't been dreaming.

According to UmeshTracker, Umesh had spoken to Walter Hamilton ten minutes before Clark's death. On any other day, this wouldn't seem like a big surprise — two Silicon Valley giants having a casual chat. But not this day. This couldn't be a coincidence.

Luke's mind raced. He had Hamilton's ID now, so he was able to pull up Walter's phone calls and confirm a terrible hunch. Twenty seconds after hanging up with Umesh, Walter had called another ID. From that timestamp, Luke already knew who it belonged to. Clark.

Cold punched his gut. Did he really leave his pills at home?

Maybe he'd made a mistake. It couldn't be true. Maybe he'd mixed up some numbers.

He cross-referenced the location history for Clark's ID with their home address. It matched. And all activity related to this account ceased precisely with Clark's time of death.

No mistake. This was his friend.

Now the timeline was established without doubt. Umesh called Walter, then Walter called Clark and then Clark died.

Luke held his breath. There was one more thing.

He opened Walter's account and narrowed the location history down to the time of Clark's death. His heart turned into a rock, cold and solid and unable to beat.

Walter was with Clark when he died.

Chapter Twenty-One

Luke almost fell through the door when Ada opened it. He marched to her couch, sat down and tried not to have a panic attack. Her living room was messy, as usual. Clothes, coffee mugs and dirty dishes lay everywhere. Her apartment had always felt tiny, but today it seemed barely enough to encompass him.

'What the hell are you doing here?' Ada asked.

'I discovered something.' He told her about the connection between Clark, Walter and Umesh, irrefutable digital footprints painting a frightening picture.

'This is fucking huge!' The veins in Ada's neck stood out like knotted rope. 'You don't think Walter…'

Luke had wondered about it before. It couldn't be. 'I don't think anybody's capable of doing that. Clark's his son! But he's obviously hiding something. And what about—'

'Damn it, you're living in his apartment! Walter's still paying for it, right?'

Luke noticed the clock on Ada's wall was out of battery. The hand still twitched but didn't have the power to turn. 'Yes.'

'Well, you're staying with me now, at least until we know what's going on. End of discussion.'

Luke's heartbeat accelerated. 'Maybe you're right.'

'You bet your ass—' Ada's eyes widened to the size of golf balls. 'Shit, are those files traceable? Tell me they don't know you sniffed around in there.'

'I checked, they're not audited. Part of the whole transparency thing.'

Ada closed her eyes and nodded. 'OK, so what do we do? I bet everything I own the police are in on this.'

'I don't know…'

Luke's phone buzzed. A web alert he'd set up on cancer-related news articles.

Engineer dead from rare brain disease.

No. Not another one. With trembling fingers, he opened the page.

A senior software engineer working at Microsoft was found dead in his apartment in Menlo Park earlier today. The thirty-three-year-old didn't show any previous conditions or symptoms and appeared to be in good health at the time of his passing. His body was discovered by his housemate Dr James Alperstein after he hadn't shown up for lunch or replied to any calls.

Dr Alperstein, a world-renowned neural researcher, volunteered to perform the autopsy and discovered his rare condition. The cause of death initially seemed to be a deadly brain aneurysm, but it was later revealed that his medulla, the part of the brain responsible for breathing, simply failed. As a consequence, the victim suffocated while otherwise being alive and well, a particularly tragic form of death.

Dr Alperstein ensured us this syndrome is extremely rare and, while the death of his friend was immensely unfortunate, his condition is not contagious or likely to affect others.

Luke was suddenly surrounded by a wall of catatonic silence. Ada was talking and gesticulating wildly on the other side, but no sound made it through.

This was his fault. People were dying because he couldn't figure it out. Real people. Eradicated because of his inability. He needed to be better than this.

Chapter Twenty-Two

'They'll find out,' Luke said as he badged into the rear entry of Swoop's building number one, home of the executive team. 'We shouldn't be here.'

'So what?' said Ada. 'Two employees doing a bit of late-night work. What's so fucking suspicious about that? I'd say it's rather commendable.'

He cursed her carelessness. 'Not once they realize we broke into our CEO's office to steal his personal files.' Everybody knew Umesh recorded all his phone calls, so he could hold people to their promises. If Luke and Ada got their hands on those tapes, they'd have proof.

'Relax, nobody will find out, least of all the nitwits from security. Remember what they told us during the introduction? No guards or security cameras in any of the work areas in this building. Too many ultra-confidential things happening in here, they can't afford to have this on camera. And if we're right, we'll be … you know, protected. We're solving a murder here, Luke.'

'So let's break into his system and steal it from the comfort of our home. I thought you were a hacker.'

Ada rolled her eyes. 'Of course. But even the great Umesh Patel, who thinks everything should be accessible anywhere, doesn't trust the cloud with these recordings. He stores them on old-fashioned DVDs in his office. He had his assistant buy ten identical DVD drives to make sure he can still read them in the distant future, in case the format becomes obsolete.'

'How do you know all this?' said Luke.

Ada shrugged. 'People want to know what's going on in the life of a billionaire CEO, every fucking aspect of it. Gets you tons of clicks. And bloggers are pretty badass about getting this type of information.'

They made their way through the rows of empty desks. Occasional cones of light fell on seats where people worked late-night shifts. All of them wore big headphones and were completely in the zone. Nobody paid them any attention.

Ada's ability to enter the main lobby with a sense of belonging baffled Luke, who awkwardly tried to mimic her movements.

They needed to reach the second floor above the fake jungle canopy where Luke had started his journey of technology and death several months ago. Their employee badges didn't grant them access; it was one of the few restricted places on campus.

By day, it was rumoured to be easy enough to sneak in by tailgating an authorised employee – not legal in the world of Swoop's internal security and a thorn in the eye of the executive team who worked there, but not exactly the end of the world either. In fact, a common dare for the most audacious new employees was to snap a quick selfie with Umesh's office door and get the hell back out. If this strategy was good enough for selfies, then it'd work for them, too, Ada had told Luke earlier that night.

The problem was, nobody went in or out, not at this time. Luke's neck stiffened as they waited for more than an hour behind a thick layer of enormous plastic ferns, ready to run and slip through the door.

But nobody came.

'I was hoping we could avoid plan B,' Ada finally said. 'But I guess it's the only way.'

Luke rubbed his eyes. 'Plan B?'

Ada led him to the opposite corner of the lobby, where a metal spiral tube came out of the ceiling, its lower opening concealed by a monstrous tropical flower. A steep, shiny polished chrome slide.

'This comes right down from the exec floor.' Ada pointed upwards. 'It was one of the first perks they had installed after moving into these offices. Guess that's what CEOs do for fun. We have to crawl up.'

'Impossible. Way too steep and way too slippery.'

'We have to try, it's our only chance. Only one of us has to make it up. The door opens from the inside.'

After a quiet, heated discussion, they agreed Luke had to be on top. Ada was taller than him and didn't have the strength to pull herself up, which made her better suited for support. He crawled as far up the tube as he could by pressing his hands and legs against the inner walls, shuffling up bit by bit. He didn't get far.

'I'm stuck, it's too steep,' he said. Droplets of sweat ran down his forehead.

Ada planted her feet firmly on the ground, squatted down, grabbed his ankles, and pushed him up as far as she could. Luke felt the lift and scrambled towards the top. Then Ada reached her limit, and he got stuck again. In the darkness, he couldn't even see how far he'd made it.

'Higher,' he whispered. 'I think I'm pretty close.'

Ada let out a muffled grunt and stiffened, arching and stretching. Luke reached upwards, inching his fingers further, bit by bit. But still, he couldn't reach the top.

Hanging there, unable to climb any further, he ran a quick calculation in his head. Together, they accounted for about three and a half metres of body length. Due to the angle of the slide, he figured the reality was closer to three. He estimated the ceiling of the lobby at about four metres.

Not enough. Not even close.

A wave of paranoia swept over him. What if somebody discovered them? They wouldn't be able to run away.

Trying to reach higher, his feet slipped, and he lost control. He clutched at the walls, but his sweaty fingers couldn't find a grip. Slowly at first, then faster and faster, he slid down until he crashed into Ada. They tumbled outside the tube and landed hard on the floor.

Pain shot through his limbs. He tasted blood from a bitten lip. But he felt alive. They were foolish and weak, and their attempt to break into the office of one of the most powerful people on the planet was probably doomed, but at least they were doing something.

He checked the time — well past midnight.

'Shit,' said Ada after catching her breath. 'I'm gonna have bruises all over.'

'You OK? Nothing broken?' said Luke.

'Yeah … All intact, except my pride.'

They sat in front of the slide and stared at the point where it came out of the ceiling.

'I need to reach higher, so we have to get you further up as well,' said Luke. 'You need to stand inside the tube, not in front of it.'

'You're insane. I'm already shaky enough with my feet on the ground. Now you want me to stand on this slippery piece of scrap metal?'

'We can build something. Look.' He pointed at the fake plants.

They improvised a step on the slide's mouth by tying a bundle of fake vines around the tube and strengthening their construction with branches.

Ada looked at their work and sighed. 'More fucking bruises, right there.'

She stepped onto their makeshift platform and tested it under her weight. It stretched and twisted but didn't give in. Happy with this result, they repeated the climbing procedure. This time was more difficult for both of them since Ada had less stability.

Once Luke's feet were above Ada's shoulders, he saw a dim glimmer of light from the top. Not much, but hope. 'Push … push … push with everything you have.'

Ada tightened her grip around his feet and thrust him up. He spotted the edge of the platform, but he still couldn't quite reach it.

'A little bit more … a little bit…'

Both were on their toes, fully extended, when Ada mustered a final push. Luke grasped the edge with his fingertips. He took hold just as Ada collapsed underneath him.

But he still had to lift himself all the way up. His grip was only a few centimetres wide; he needed all his strength to flex his muscles and inch closer to the top. A cramp formed in his left arm, shooting pain along his torso.

With his last bit of energy, he pulled himself over the ledge. He wasn't made for this, but he'd done it. Lying on the ground next to the slide entry, he let out a deep sigh.

Once his heart slowed down, he opened the upper door and kept it ajar with one of his shoes, descended the staircase, and opened the lower door where he found Ada waiting impatiently.

The mix of adrenaline and awe made Ada's eyes sparkle as she entered the deserted floor. They were in the legendary heart of their company, where decisions were made affecting billions of users and trillions of dollars.

'It's down there.' Ada pointed towards the far end of the floor where a massive animal skeleton resembling the shape of a fully grown elephant towered over them. Luke swallowed. The beast's eyeless sockets seemed to follow his movements.

'It's a mammoth, an actual fucking mammoth,' Ada said. 'I'd heard we had one but never believed it. It's meant to symbolise how a sweeping change can transform the earth, like when dinosaurs were replaced by mammals like this one. Then humans swept away the mammoths. The circle of life — or death is more damn like it. This is apparently one of the best-preserved in the world, it must've cost a fortune. They call it Edgar.'

Luke shook his head. He didn't understand symbolism, never cared for its ambiguity or interpretation. Clear and precise statements were his world. The facts and only the facts, simple and true.

They stole through empty desks arranged in small clusters rather than long rows like on the regular floors. Nobody worked here in the middle of the night. As they approached Umesh's office, the beast from the ice age loomed above them, creepy and mysterious, giving off the aura of a deserted amusement park.

Umesh's office door was closed but unlocked. The inner sanctum. Luke glanced over his shoulder before stepping inside. 'I can't believe he doesn't lock his office.'

The room was spacious but not ostentatious. A big round glass table in the centre surrounded by eight white chairs was flanked by two huge, overstuffed couches. On the far side, a large futuristic desk had been pieced together from spaceship parts made of metals and other materials Luke couldn't identify. Behind it, shelves were filled with random pieces of art — granite depictions of indigenous people, abstract wire sculptures, blown glass and a tiki head made of stone, which Luke thought was tacky and way too big.

Ada opened a file cabinet, then paused and turned to Luke. 'We're doing this, right?'

So far, they hadn't done anything wrong, at least nothing that couldn't be explained by a few white lies. Rummaging around in their CEO's office crossed a line.

Luke swallowed hard and nodded. 'For Clark.'

He got to work on Umesh's desk. In one drawer, he found a stash of employment contracts waiting for signature — proof the billionaire still personally signed every new hire. Another one was full of mobile phones of different makes and models, which their CEO, known to be meticulous about user experience, probably used to verify all Swoop apps ran smoothly on every device. But there were no DVDs, CDs or other forms of data storage.

'The recordings aren't here,' said Luke. 'Did you find anything?'

Ada, busy sifting through shelves of company paperwork and stationery, shook her head. 'But I'm sure they exist. I talked to someone who's seen them, and I totally trust this guy. He said they were in a black DVD rack with a lockable plastic door.'

Luke scanned the room for anything that came close to this description. 'Maybe he moved them somewhere else.'

The lights turned on at the other end of the floor. Luke's stomach clenched. Someone was up there with them.

They rushed towards the office door when another set of lights came to life, closer this time. Whoever was up there was coming towards them, and quickly.

They'd stayed way too long. His gut roiled.

A third cluster of lights turned on as they reached the door. The whole floor was illuminated now, showing the mammoth in its full might. Only Umesh's office remained dark.

'Too late,' hushed Ada. 'They'll fucking see us. We have to hide.'

Luke mustered all his courage to backtrack. He gestured to the couch—bulky, good cover.

They rushed behind it. Not enough space to duck down.

'Push,' Ada whispered.

They inched it forward. Squatted down. Luke's head ended up on the floor, giving him a view across the room.

They made it just as a silhouette entered Umesh's office. A man dressed in black. A ghost in the darkness.

Luke recognized him before he saw his face. Xavier Sanchez.

He held his breath. The urge to take a stomach pill hit him. He had to resist; the sound would betray them.

Xavier stopped in front of the glass table, scanning the room like a radar, his head moving left and right. He zeroed in on the couch. His eyes narrowed.

Luke's heartbeat pounded inside his temples. They were well hidden, but if anybody possessed superhuman senses, it'd be Xavier.

After a few long seconds, Xavier checked over his shoulder and strode to the tiki head behind Umesh's desk. He touched behind its oversized ears. *Click.* The face popped open to reveal a safe with a keypad and a fingerprint reader.

Luke forced his concentration away from his stomach onto Xavier's fingers as he entered the six-digit combination. The pattern looked like a tiny spaceship flying from left to right. He recognized it as a stylised version of the AUM, an ancient Indian symbol representing the state of absolute consciousness, pretty much the opposite of their modern technology-driven way of life.

Xavier pressed his thumb against the fingerprint reader, and a tiny LED turned from red to green. The safe opened.

The safe contained stacks of paper and three identical devices that looked like oversized mobile phones. Xavier took one of them, put it in his pocket and closed the safe. Once more, he looked around. Then he left as quickly as he'd appeared.

Luke peeked out of his hiding place and saw Xavier disappear between the clusters of desks and chairs. He wiped the sweat from his face but didn't dare to move. After ten minutes, the lights turned off automatically, and he relaxed.

Ada went straight to the tiki head safe and found the little button behind its ears. The front opened.

Luke felt a sense of achievement as he watched her examine the keypad. 'I saw the combination. It's a little spaceship, 1-2-5-6-7-8. But that won't help us without the fingerprint. Anyway, I saw inside. No DVDs.'

Ada smiled. 'Not bad, Mr Jankovic ... Not fucking bad at all, spying on Mr Creep himself. Are you sure there were no DVDs?'

'One hundred per cent.'

'OK, let's leave that thing alone then. If it logs every transaction, they could use this to nail us.'

They left Umesh's office, passed Edgar the mammoth, crossed the floor, went down the stairs and entered the lobby. The tension in Luke's body began to ebb away.

They were about to exit the building when Luke heard a voice from behind. 'You two, stop!'

Xavier. Within a second, Luke's heartbeat escalated. Where did he come from? It had been absolutely silent for the last few minutes. But there he was.

Ada found her balance first, and in her most innocent voice, said, 'Hey there, what's up?'

Xavier's face was stern as a rock. 'What are you doing here?'

Luke had seen him lurking around many times before, but he'd never heard him speak. His Spanish accent had influences from all over the world and a military tone. Luke had an ear for these things.

'Working,' said Ada. 'You know, computers, programming, all that stuff. Can't you see our badges?'

Xavier examined their badges and double-checked their identity on his phone. He ignored Ada's expression of annoyance. 'What I meant was, what are you doing here in the lobby? Now, at this time of the day?'

Luke saw Ada's scrambling for an answer and jumped in. 'We're picking up something we forgot this morning.'

Xavier looked up. 'You don't work in this building, either of you.'

Ada pulled her phone out of her pocket. 'I left my phone on a colleague's desk. We're still allowed to talk to our colleagues, aren't we? He works over there, to the front and right. His name is Dex.'

Luke had no idea who Ada was talking about.

Xavier's gaze tightened. 'So why are both of you here?'

'Does it matter?' asked Ada. 'Since when can't Swoop employees enter a company building? I have half a mind to file a complaint against you for harassment.'

Xavier's expression changed — not to fear or anger, but a faint smile. 'You may try. Go ahead, first thing tomorrow morning, you'll see where this gets you. But first, I asked you a question. Why are you both here?'

Luke fought off another cramp in his gut. 'Because we're a couple, OK? Ada's my girlfriend.'

Xavier raised an eyebrow and checked his phone. 'We don't have any record of this. You're aware that every relationship between employees has to be declared? This is a serious breach of our code of conduct. Contact HR first thing tomorrow.'

Xavier's phone rang. Without another word, he left the building and answered the call.

Luke's legs trembled.

'That was close, damn close,' said Ada. 'Let's get the hell out of here, boyfriend.'

Chapter Twenty-Three

February 1994

When Umesh realized how late it was, he stopped typing. Didn't he just come home from school? The sun was about to set, and the shadows of the many stacks of books in his room grew larger. If he hurried, he could still fix that annoying bug before dinner.

A sparkle appeared in his eyes, the same he had every time he thought back to the day when his father gave him this computer, a simple machine, nothing crazy even by the standards of the time. But it had the new Windows 95 pre-installed and a full suite of software development tools. His parents had noticed his knack for maths, so they'd saved money and bought him something that utilised his brain to its full capacity. They knew he didn't care much about games or entertainment, so instead, they bought him a book about C++, which according to their neighbour, who worked for AT&T, was the latest and best programming language.

Fascinated by the inner workings of software, Umesh read the book overnight and wrote his first program the very next day. A couple of weeks later, he created an application to help his dad manage his shop's finances. But that wasn't enough for Umesh; he needed to truly immerse himself in a project. That's when he became interested in games.

His parents were right; he didn't care about playing, except for professional curiosity. He wanted to create his own adventure, to share a glimpse of the world as he saw it without actually having to talk to anybody. Filled with riddles and labyrinths, with mystical creatures and strange characters, this game would be almost impossible to win.

Over the next couple of weeks, he'd spent every night in front of his screen and most of his weekends, except when his parents forced him to take a break to go to the park. Obsessed, both with an impeccable coding style as well as the perfect storyline, he'd typed until his brain hurt.

'I don't know how you do it,' a voice said from behind.

Umesh turned abruptly. Lost in his world of coding, he'd forgotten Xavier had come home with him. 'Do what?' he asked, rubbing his eyes.

'Coding without proper tools. Seems like you're making it harder just for the sake of it.'

Umesh frowned. He used a normal text editor for coding, plain and simple. More sophisticated tools called IDEs — Integrated Development Environments — made software engineers' lives easier by highlighting the code's syntax and other nice things. But Umesh thought they dumbed down programmers by doing the thinking for them. He liked to do things the basic way, the old-fashioned way, to use his full mental capacity. 'It helps me stay on top of my game. If I let this thing write my code for me, I'll forget how things work.'

Xavier laughed. 'I highly doubt it, given the time you're spending on this thing. It's coming along nicely. Honestly, I admire you.'

Xavier moved his chair forward a little, his thigh touching the outside of Umesh's leg. Umesh felt a warmth he couldn't explain. Maybe he was tired. He turned around just as Xavier jerked his head back to the code.

'What does this line do?' Xavier pointed at the display.

'Which one? There's a lot of code on my screen.'

Xavier gently touched Umesh's hand and moved the mouse over a random snippet of code. 'That one.'

'Seriously? That's a simple loop, counting to a hundred. What happens inside, now that's way more interesting ... See how it prints a tree on the screen? It starts at the bottom and then paints smaller and smaller branches as it goes up. This whole thing here produces a little forest with a hundred trees.' Umesh wasn't entirely sure Xavier processed his words.

He swivelled around in his chair, forcing Xavier to back away. 'You know what? I totally forgot ... I got what you came for! Here's the latest version for testing, we're up to 0.6.10 now.' He took a floppy disk from one of his desk drawers and waved it in Xavier's face. 'One more round of bug fixes and we can call it 0.7. Thanks again for all this, it helps me make the game as stable as possible.'

A tired smile passed Xavier's lips as he put the disk in his pocket.

Chapter Twenty-Four

They'd expected a shabby backroom infused with the smell of coffee and cigarettes, a desk full of paperwork, and a fat guy with a thick moustache behind it. Instead, they found a lean, tall man with no hair from his neck upwards. His desk was clean and minimalistic, and so was his office. He had two large Macintosh screens in front of him, one mounted on a flexible bar so it could be turned towards visitors. A metallic nameplate, placed precisely in the centre of the desk, read 'John McLeary, PI'.

Ada had been chewing on her nails from the second they'd entered the lobby. Luke, the calmer of the two for once, was relieved they'd agreed to turn to a professional. The situation felt way beyond his control, and surely, a person accustomed to dealing with life's shady side would be better at this.

'We found your ad online,' Ada said. 'A friend of ours committed suicide, at least that's what the police said. But it's bullshit. We need to know what's really going on. His father's involved, an asshole billionaire, and probably a couple of other very fucking powerful people.'

The investigator didn't flinch, just nodded. He'd probably heard similar introductions before, working in a high-pressure world where the fabric of the social network was weak. Luke hoped this man, a professional who'd seen it all, would help them find the truth between their theories and suspicions.

'Understood,' McLeary said. 'I won't lie to you. You're probably chasing ghosts. I'm not saying you're wrong but searching for reason is a human way of dealing with grief, especially unexpected passing. Most of the time, there are completely normal, harmless explanations for what you're experiencing.'

Luke was immediately impressed by his professionalism. Ada, slamming her palm on the meticulously polished table, seemed to have a different opinion. 'I told you we're wasting our time. Let's get out of here.'

The investigator continued, undeterred. 'I can still help you. I have contacts in the police department, and I'm able to access information the two of you can't. I've been doing this for almost twenty years now, and trust me, if there's anything going on, I'll find it. Or confirm for sure the police report is correct. Why don't we start from the beginning? Tell me everything you know, everything that happened. Don't leave out any detail, no matter how irrelevant and unconnected it may seem.'

Ada shrugged. 'Fine.'

They shared their research about the string of brain cancer-related deaths and Australian Brett's disappearance. They told him about Clark and Walter's reaction at the funeral. About the phone calls, the location history and the connection between Walter, Umesh and Xavier.

The investigator's mouth twitched as he listened. 'OK,' he said finally. 'You did your homework, as much as you were able. And I agree, some of this smells weird. Now let the expert handle it from here.'

Luke nodded. Expert, that was the keyword. Nothing in the world made more sense than this man and his feng shui office. Luke turned towards Ada. 'What do you think?'

'I don't know...'

'We came here because we can't do this ourselves. We need help. Do you have a better idea?'

'Fine,' Ada said again, clearly not convinced.

'This won't be cheap,' McLeary said. 'If two of the most powerful people in the Valley are involved, both billionaires, they'll have access to tremendous resources.

And experience. You don't get to the top without a few corpses in the closet. Which means I need to be extra careful, and I need to be compensated accordingly. I can do it for ten thousand. Take it or leave it.'

Luke moved in his chair. It seemed a hefty amount, but what did he know about this stuff? 'I guess all good things have their price.' He glanced at Ada, who seemed to have given up all resistance. 'We can do that.'

'But only when the job's done,' Ada added. 'Not getting any results is something we can do by ourselves.'

The investigator smiled. 'I can do fifty-fifty. Half now and half when I'm finished. Standard for jobs like this, I have upfront expenses to cover. Take it or leave it.'

Luke turned to Ada and said, 'Sounds fair. I'm sure we can do fifty-fifty.'

'Fine,' said Ada yet again.

Three days later, McLeary called back. It was late, Luke and Ada were at her place, watching TV. Being around her helped him get through his days.

'I'm sorry to tell you, but your friend Brett is dead,' he said over the speaker of Luke's phone.

Ada cleared her throat. 'He's not our friend.'

'Ada!' Luke said. 'That's terrible. How did he...?'

'There's no official record, but I talked to his parents, and they declared him missing. So I called in a few favours and found an unidentified body in the morgue of Hutchinson, Kansas. The local cops have no clue what happened, but something was definitely wrong with his brain. It's him.'

Luke's throat urged to swallow but his mouth was dry. The more he tried, the more the itching sensation expanded from his thorax throughout his whole body. 'Kansas?'

'It's the middle of nowhere, not a place where you just hang out. Hard to tell, but he probably tried to hide. Looks like they found him … I think you're on to something with this whole story.'

Silence. For a long time, shallow breathing was the only sound on the line.

McLeary finally moved on. 'And I found some information about your friend Sanchez. You were right about him, he's as serious as they get. A lot of security personnel are ex-military, but this guy's the real deal. He came to the States from Spain as a kid and grew up in San Francisco. He opened a European restaurant, had a wife and a kid. They were on vacation in Egypt when they got caught up in a terror attack. The wife and kid both died, but Xavier survived.

'That's when he got into the French Legion and stayed there for seven years. People usually quit after three, their first contract, enough to erase their past. But Xavier kept going and fought all over the world, mostly in covert operations in Africa. Then he probably got too old for this stuff and returned to California. He's been at Swoop ever since. Any questions so far?'

'Fucking Rambo! I told you there's no messing with this guy … That's impressive research, Mr McLeary,' Ada admitted.

'Just covering my bases,' he said.

'Anything on Walter and Umesh?' Luke said.

'Not yet, but I'm on it. In fact, I'm in front of Umesh's house right now, monitoring comings and goings. Xavier got in about an hour ago, then a blond guy with a ponytail stomped out a bit later. He looked pretty angry.'

'Shawn? Sales dude Shawn?' said Ada. 'I thought he'd be too dumb for serious shit like this, to have a line to the top.'

Luke agreed, but what did he know about people? 'Any idea what he was upset about?'

'Not a clue. It's quiet now, but I want to keep an eye on it. I might have to stay here a little. Give me a couple of days and I'll let you know what I find.'

Chapter Twenty-Five

'The wait's killing me,' Ada said. 'We have to do something. He was supposed to call back yesterday. And now he's not picking up his phone.' She kept stirring her soup. They were having lunch in yet another one of Swoop's cafes. They continued visiting a new one each week, a tradition they'd started with Clark. They had three more to go, then his footprint on their life would shrink a little more.

Luke's stomach had gotten worse with every passing day. It was barely past noon, and he was on his third Xanax. He hadn't weighed himself in years but was sure he'd lost a few pounds. Stoically, he held onto the belief that this investigator would solve all their problems. 'We said we'd give him a week, a full week. He has two more days. He's probably busy, I doubt we're his only clients.'

Ada grunted.

'By the way, the paperwork came through. We're officially life partners … At least according to Swoop law.'

She almost choked. 'Partners in crime, that's all, you creep. In a couple of weeks, we file for divorce. I still don't know why you insisted on that.'

'You heard what McLeary said about Xavier, he's dangerous and smart. Our story needs to check out.'

Ada's face melted. She looked right through Luke.

'Come on,' he said. 'It's not that bad to be in a fake —

'No … fuck … the news. Shut up and look at the TV.'

Luke swivelled around to see the screen across the room. He caught the closed captions mid-sentence.

'…which makes six confirmed deaths of otherwise healthy individuals within less than a month, all caused by brain aneurysms or other brain-related forms of cancer. And these are only the official numbers. The real figures are probably higher.'

A sharp pinch travelled through his nervous system. He knew they were at least twice as high.

'A working group of statisticians at Stanford has commenced an investigation to find out if this is a temporary blip or if there's a more systematic cause. One researcher suggested our excessive use of mobile phones and other wireless technology has finally caught up with us, fuelling anxiety about the ongoing 5G rollout. The statement, however, remained short on how exactly this would lead to such fatal consequences.'

The pinch turned into a steady, miserable electrostatic hum. Mobile phones? Weren't these things tested thoroughly?

'All this, of course, is of little consolation for this ill-fated homeless person who tragically died today. Local police are trying to determine the identity of this John Doe. If you have any information whatsoever, please contact...'

Luke turned back to Ada. Her face was white as chalk. What was wrong with her? More death was terrible, especially as the numbers started to look like a pandemic, but that wasn't it. There was a whole other level of shock written on her forehead.

'Ada, what's the matter?'

'The picture ... Look at the picture.'

The screen showed a headshot of the victim a split second before the program moved on, just enough time to recognize the poor fellow. Now Luke got it. Lightning impaled him. No illusion, no misfired synapse. Real, physical pain.

They'd been looking at John McLeary, their investigator.

'Fuck. Complete clusterfuck. He died the night we spoke to him,' said Ada without looking up from her phone. 'Says here his body was found the next day in a parking lot at the other end of town. He was wearing shabby clothes and an old sleeping bag … that's why they think he's homeless.' The colour in her face was back, the paleness of shock replaced by the bright red of acute anger.

Luke popped another pill. His mind was whirling, and he needed to silence everything else. Assumptions and connections formed in his head, and slowly a picture emerged. Not a pretty one. 'We killed him.'

Ada looked up from her phone. 'What?'

Luke's face was stern. 'Look at the facts, a simple chain of causality. He told us he was going to run surveillance at Umesh's house the whole night, and we have no reason to believe he changed his mind. Right? This means Umesh or Xavier or somebody else in their circle did it. They must've noticed he was on their heels and got rid of him. We knew what these people are capable of and we sent him anyway. We killed him.'

'We don't know what happened. It could be something unrelated. Maybe he worked undercover as a hobo for another client.'

'That's not likely. Look at the report, brain damage. Again. This didn't just happen. Umesh and Xavier aren't only responsible for the death of McLeary, this links them to the other cases. Probably to Clark as well. It's all connected.' He hyperventilated as angst reached his lungs.

Ada didn't look convinced. 'I don't know…'

Luke grabbed an empty plastic bag and breathed into it. They'd entered the danger zone. Concentrating on his childhood bed, his happy place, it took him five minutes to calm down. His hands firmly on the table, he finally said, 'Look at the statistics. What are the chances all these things happened at random? Statistics?'

'I don't know … fifty-fifty?'

Luke shook his head. 'Come on, way lower. The probability of multiple linked events occurring randomly drops dramatically with the number of events. That's eighth-grade math. Say there's a ten per cent chance McLeary was on another client's job, does that sound reasonable?'

Ada nodded slowly.

'And assume there's a one per cent chance he had a brain-related precondition — it's probably too high, but let's go with it. Then the chance that he randomly died of brain cancer *while* being on another job is a tenth of a per cent. If we add probabilities for everything else into the mix, the overall chance drops to a very small number.'

Ada didn't seem convinced. 'How little?'

Part of Luke's brain was in its comfort zone now, distracting him with numbers and logic. The other part was busy ignoring the agony running through his veins. 'Scientists have a hard limit for discarding a theory when the chances are smaller than one in the number of atoms in the universe. In McLeary's case, it's somewhere around one in a few million. Roughly like being hit by lightning or winning the lottery. Not good enough for a science journal, but practically speaking still impossible. Flipped around, this means it's overwhelmingly likely that McLeary was killed by them. Or in turn, by us. Statistics.'

'I still don't know … But you're the numbers guy, so I guess you're right.'

'As I said, his death is on our hands.'

Ada seemed to have a sudden epiphany. 'Shit. We have to assume the worst then … They're onto us.'

'How? I doubt investigators give up their clients.'

'He didn't need to.'

Luke shook his head. Did he miss something? Was his logic off? 'What else?'

Ada got up. 'Come with me, I have a theory. I'll show you.'

The door to McLeary's office wasn't locked. They entered and found the whole place turned upside down. Filing cabinets sat open, their contents spread over the floor. His computer was gone, the drawers of his desk gaped wide and his office chair had been torn apart. Whoever had been in there didn't care about surgical precision. The place was properly trashed.

Luke stood in the middle of the room and tried to make sense of this mess. Cursing himself for missing a vital piece of the puzzle, his breathing accelerated. No, he wasn't going to lose it now. Willing the gasps to stop, the conscious choice to survive kept his focus in the here and now. He took a deep breath. 'So they know we sent him. Somewhere in this mess was a file, a receipt, or another paper with our names. Or on his computer, which they're probably examining right now.'

'No shit,' said Ada. 'We got lucky during our late-night encounter with Xavier, but now we have to assume he knows for sure. And we know what that son of a bitch is capable of … Luke, we're in danger … Like actual fucking danger.'

Individual beats of Luke's heart merged into an indistinguishable blur. The office walls shrank around him. Was there enough air for both of them? 'I can't do this anymore. We go to the police. Not the local cops but the FBI. Right now.'

Ada seemed as close to a nervous breakdown as Luke. 'How does that help? Apart from Walter's location history, we don't have any proof. And that's on your Swoop computer. Hell, we got this data illegally, Luke. The police didn't believe us when Clark died, and they won't listen to us now.'

Luke picked up a shattered picture frame from the ground. It showed McLeary with a man who had to be his father — he looked like an older version of him. They held up a piece of paper Luke recognised from their first visit to this office: McLeary's PI license. The photographer had captured their pride.

Ada grabbed him by the arm. 'Luke, going to the FBI will only make it worse. Look what these people did to a private investigator. The FBI will make them really fucking mad. And without proof, the feds won't help us.'

In Luke's battle of adrenaline versus sanity, a switch toggled into active mode. Flight became fight. He was tired of being sick and afraid. He had been for a long time. 'We get proof, proper proof. We need to find these recordings, whatever it takes. The call between Walter and Umesh. It must be related to Clark's death. That must be good enough for the FBI.'

Frustration was written all over Ada's face. 'The recordings weren't in Umesh's office.'

'They must be somewhere, right? And I don't believe they're completely offline.'

Ada swallowed, and for a few seconds, Luke saw fear in her eyes. Then the mask slammed back on. 'So, what? I have to hack one of the most powerful people in the world, who also happens to be a tech genius. They say people grow with their challenges. Well, let's find out. But first, we need to get the hell out of here. It won't help our case if the cops find us here.'

Luke's stomach eased a fraction. Maybe the last Xanax finally kicked in. Or maybe because any plan was better than no plan. 'Where do you want to set up camp?'

'We split up. If they come for us, at least one of us will survive to tell the story. I'll get cracking on Umesh's account, it'll probably take me all night and then some. I'll call in sick. And you ... you ...?'

Luke frowned. Shouldn't they stick together in times of crisis? But she had a point. 'I'll go to work, anything else looks suspicious. If one of us is missing, that's a coincidence. Both of us, not so much.'

'Luke, it's where Xavier—'

'Yes, and that's exactly why I need to show up. Because it's the last place where they expect me to go, knowing what happened here. Think about it from their point of view.'

Ada sighed. 'You and your logic. I guess you're right, it'll confuse the hell out of them. But for the record, I don't feel good letting you go into the lion's den all by yourself.'

Luke forced himself to smile. 'Get over it. I'll be fine.'

Chapter Twenty-Six

Luke's computer came to life with the familiar sound of spinning hard disks and humming coolers, showing the Swoop logo on his login screen. Once he provided his credentials, his presence would be logged in Swoop's central user database. In combination with the touch of his badge and his internet browsing behaviour—reading emails, checking the lunch menu on the intranet, and so on—it'd create a web of digital footprints, traceable to the last bit. Data mining algorithms and digital forensic experts would later classify this mesh of data as a normal day of work. A standard behavioural pattern, manifesting millions of times every day all around the globe.

But this was not an ordinary day for Luke. Outwardly, he maintained a picture of normality; inside he was a mess. He'd barely slept or eaten. All he could think of was Ada's attempt to compromise the security of one of the most influential people on the planet. The danger she was exposed to. Was it even possible to take enough precautions? Wasn't this exactly how they caught her the first time? And Xavier's crosshairs were already locked on them.

By 9 am, Luke was convinced it was a mistake—him being at work, and Ada's foolish endeavour. But it was too late for doubts. They'd agreed on absolute radio silence to minimise the digital footprint between them. Plausible deniability. So Luke had to spend the whole day at his desk, pretending to work while he wrangled with his own conscience over the consequences of their doing.

Ada. Would he lose another friend today? It crossed his mind that the depth of his feelings, the searing pain in his gut, could be more than those of one friend worrying about another.

He cut off those thoughts. It wasn't the time. Maybe when all this was over, whatever *this* was.

He went to grab a coffee. The thought of caffeine almost made him puke, but he always had plenty, and anything else would look suspicious. It was already 10:25 am, and he couldn't focus on work. He couldn't stare at his screen for eight hours straight, so he chose a kitchenette far away from his desk and wasted time there and back.

He ground a portion of coffee beans and carefully filled the portafilter with it. Over the last few weeks, he'd mastered the craft and knew density was key. He inserted the filter into the corresponding pouring slot, set the water pressure to exactly the right value, adjusted the timer to match the water pressure, and hit the start button. His work was immaculate. What a shame it would go to waste.

With the hot mug in his hands, he approached his work area. About thirty metres away, an anomaly caught his eye, a subtle difference in the normal picture of the office space around his empty desk.

Xavier.

Luke froze. Would it be the biggest mistake of his life to return to his seat?

The enemy stood right next to Luke's workspace, talking to his manager, scanning the room for his target. Him.

Luke's brain was in full stasis when a reflex kicked in. The motion came from the depths of his brain stem, overriding the more evolved parts of his self. He dropped to his knees, spilling his precious coffee all over his pants. Even through the fabric, it scalded his leg. He bit his lip to keep silent.

Right in time, he took cover behind an empty desk, shivering and hoping. Did anybody see him?

He willed away his misery and discomfort, and crawled to the desk's edge to risk a cautious look.

Xavier was still there, chatting to his manager, his head a Luke-seeking radar.

Luke took a deep breath and weighed his options. His first thought was to play dumb. He'd need an excuse for the spilled coffee, but otherwise, he could pretend everything was normal. Xavier would probably question him in a private office. Maybe there'd be violence. But if he denied everything, he might continue his life without any major consequences. After all, he hadn't done anything wrong, had he? But he had a hunch Xavier didn't care about trivialities like right or wrong.

A huge risk.

His other option was to run. If he got away, he'd avoid any short-term consequences but would have to deal with the long-term ones. He'd look suspicious, that was for sure. There was no point in ever coming back to work. His job, his visa, the dreams he'd nursed since he was a teenager, all lost. And no matter where he'd hide, Xavier would probably find him, as he did with Brett.

Not much better.

Xavier checked his watch.

Time to decide.

Luke's brain told him to turn himself in; it was the safest bet. Maybe this whole thing was a misunderstanding. Why jeopardise everything he'd worked so hard to achieve?

But something inside him decided otherwise. He left the coffee tucked behind a chair, crawled away and crossed a few empty rows of desks. Where were all those people? He reached an occupied desk, its owner typing on his keyboard while listening to loud music on his oversized earphones. The beat pulsed, fast and steady. His colleague was in the zone, detached from reality. Luke moved on and risked another look. Xavier hadn't moved.

Suddenly, the programmer spotted him. He jumped from his seat and screamed.

Luke's reptile brain took over. He jumped to his feet and ran. Head low, he raced as if the floor was on fire. He zigzagged through the open space towards the nearest corridor. Darting between rows of desks and meeting rooms, he never looked back.

Was Xavier following? Luke didn't waste any time finding out. His heart rate charged over triple figures.

He reached the nearest bank of elevators and pressed the up button. Then he entered the adjacent staircase and ran down.

On the ground floor, he saw the building's rear door. No, too easy.

He crossed the whole floor again, rushed through the lobby and opened the main door. His logic mode re-engaged, and he stopped. A swath of agony came over him. Receptors all over his body flashed warning lights, bright and urgent. He needed to think.

What were his chances of escaping unnoticed? In front of him, a parking lot the size of a football field had enough spots unoccupied to leave plenty of empty space. It'd take him more than a minute to cross it, maybe two. Too long without any cover. On the other side were a handful of Swoop buildings, each no doubt equipped with CCTV and facial recognition. The whole campus was wedged in a triangle of highways, each shielded by high noise protection walls. Apart from the main access road, closely monitored by security guards, there was no way out.

Nowhere to go. Nowhere to hide.

He looked back as Xavier's head popped through the rear door of the lobby, purple with anger. Luke ran.

Nowhere to go.

He couldn't outrun Xavier, who ran ultra-marathons as a hobby and no doubt knew how to corner an enemy. Even with his head start of maybe thirty seconds, Luke wouldn't last long.

Nowhere to hide.

A taxi pulled into one of the empty spots in front of him. Luke raced to it, opened the door and slid into the back seat. The car smelled like weed, its interior fitted with fluffy fabric in the colours of Jamaica.

The driver had dreadlocks and red eyes. 'Hello, friend. You Dave, eh?'

'What? Uhm, yes,' Luke lied. 'Please ... move ... can we move, please? I'm late.'

'Okeeeee.' The driver took off. He seemed more focused on his music than the traffic or whatever was happening behind his car. A good thing for Luke, because otherwise, he'd have noticed the man in black chasing the car.

Xavier was impossibly fast and closed the distance. Centimetres before he reached the trunk, Luke's new Jamaican friend found the gas pedal and moved out of reach.

Xavier's silhouette grew smaller and smaller in the back window and finally disappeared. Out of immediate danger, Luke realized what a mess he was. His clothes were drenched in sweat and coffee, his legs ached from his sprints, and his mouth tasted acidic. He desperately needed rest. Where was he even —

A new thought made his face flush cold. Ada.

With a shaking hand, he checked his phone and found a new voicemail from three minutes ago.

Ada spoke quickly, nervously. 'I know I wasn't supposed to call, but I have to get this out ... Shit ... I don't think I have much time ... a guy's snooping around my place, he already knocked at my door a bunch of times ... He's freakish big and looks scary ... And shit, now two other guys arrived ... I can see them from my window ... They're coming into the building.'

Luke didn't think he could feel any worse. Why had they messed with powers beyond their own? Why did he ever leave Belarus?

After a bit of rustling and shuffling on the other end, there was a short pause and a door slammed.

'I'm hiding in my closet,' Ada continued in a hushed voice. 'I think they're gonna find me ... Crap ... He killed him, Luke, Walter killed Clark. No doubt about it ... How can you do that? As a father, I mean ... His own son ... Fuck ... I found the recording ... damn right, it was Umesh and Walter ... he told ... ordered him to kill Clark.'

Even through the poor quality of the recording, he could hear her sobbing. He wanted to cry with her.

'He said it was all for the greater good, it had to be done ... at first, Walter pushed back ... I mean fuck, it's his son ... Umesh said it's either Clark or him ... the guy's insane, proper insane ... he told him to make it look like suicide, he should use what he learned in the army and —'

Another pause. There was noise in the distance, wood creaking and breaking. And footsteps.

Luke pictured her in her hideout. He saw three meat-packed maniacs pace through her apartment, obliterating anything in their way. They were getting closer to his friend. Any second, and it'd be over.

'Fuck, they're here. I got —'

The message ended. Luke stared at his screen. A wave of shock and fear ran through his whole body, crashing through every single cell.

He played the message again, his hands shaking, his legs quivering. He didn't have the slightest idea what to do. He didn't even know where he was going.

It was 11:15 am on the day that changed his life forever.

Chapter Twenty-Seven

Luke listened to the recording twice more before he believed what had happened. He was in a crazy dream, in one of the stories his parents had told him about the cruel old days in Belarus when a group of masked strangers broke into the apartment next door, took the neighbours away, and that was the last anybody ever saw of them. He felt the same terror his parents must have felt for years. The fear that tomorrow it could be him. He'd always believed in America, the great free country of the West, these things would never happen.

Yet here he was, listening to the recording of his friend's ... what exactly? Had she been kidnapped? Killed? He tried to steer his thoughts towards a happy place but failed miserably.

'Hey man, we're there ... Man? Helloooooo?' The driver's voice sounded distant and unreal. The car parked in front of an Italian restaurant.

Ada. Nothing else mattered. Luke couldn't lose another friend.

On his messenger app, she was still showing online. He resisted the temptation to call, afraid the ringtone would give her away.

'I changed my mind,' Luke said. 'Can we go somewhere else, please? Quick.' He gave Ada's apartment address.

'You got it, boss,' the driver said and turned the car around. He bobbed his head to a cover of 'I Shot the Sheriff' that was even more Reggae than the original.

Luke risked a message. *Ada, are you OK? I'm coming to your place. Call me if you can.*

He stared at his phone, waiting for a reply.

Five seconds, ten, twenty. No answer.

An email landed in his inbox from his manager letting him know he'd missed an important meeting. As if he cared.

He kept his eyes on his screen. Another minute went by, still no reply. An urge came over him to get out of the car and run there by himself. At least he'd be doing something.

He forced his gaze out of the window until the song was finished — a live version that took eight minutes.

11:35 am. Still no reply. Luke told the driver to speed up. He wanted to drag him from his steering wheel and take over.

'Relax, man. I'll get you there, no worries.'

Luke checked his phone again. Another email. A request from Swoop's HR department to stop by for a company survey. What was that about? Those surveys were usually conducted anonymously online. Surely, a trick. Was this Xavier trying to lure him back to work? He wasn't going to fall for it.

When he finally arrived, it was 11:39 am. As he got out of the car, he checked his messages once more. The icon next to Ada's avatar had changed to a green checkmark. A sign of life? Was this good news? All it meant was somebody had read the message.

She never called back.

When Luke knocked on Ada's apartment door, it opened by the touch of his hand. The wooden frame had been damaged and the metal piece holding the bolt was gone, leaving only splinters in its place. He found it inside, a few metres into the hallway. He'd never seen a door that'd been kicked in before but was sure he was looking at one now.

'Ada? Anybody here?' he shouted and immediately regretted it. What if the thugs were still there?

But he heard no answer, the silence was absolute.

He walked through the hallway into the living room. Would he find a dead body, just like before? With squinting eyes, he examined his surroundings. She wasn't there.

The kitchen and bathroom were empty.

He checked her bedroom. Nobody.

It took him a minute to find the closet, a narrow room concealed by the open bedroom door. How had he never seen it before? There were battered suitcases and stacks of old clothes, two of which had fallen over — a clever place to hide, but apparently not good enough. No Ada.

He allowed himself to breathe. The apartment was tiny, he'd seen every square centimetre of it. No corpse, no blood. So far, it seemed she was alive.

But somebody had taken her to God knows where. Silence returned. The only sound was the low hum of the refrigerator. It drilled through his skin into his bones.

Back in the kitchen, he searched for clues. If anything in this place could tell him what happened, it'd be there. And he was right. The coffee machine was on and a fresh pot was inside, about half full, an empty mug next to it. He poured himself a cup; an odd thing to do, but he hated waste and always thought better with caffeine.

On the table, he found an open notebook and a pen. The front page was full of scribbles about server addresses, ports, encryption algorithms and other technical details. As he flipped through the sheets, he noticed its position on the table was off. It wasn't directly in front of him, but about thirty centimetres to the right.

Her laptop. It'd been right here. They took it.

He tried to make sense of her notes but could barely read anything, her handwriting was terrible. Besides, he was pretty sure he couldn't reproduce her work even if he tried.

Ada was in grave danger. What was he supposed to do?

He listened to Ada's message again. The sound of her voice wrenched his gut. What in the world drove a father to kill his own son? Walter was a billionaire and by reputation a tough businessman. Not somebody to be messed with. Not somebody easily forced to do something against his will. But somehow, Umesh had done exactly that.

Something big, truly grand was going on. Something a bunch of powerful, misguided people thought was larger than life. What if Clark's death was just the tip of the iceberg?

Luke's phone vibrated, he almost dropped it. A message from Ada.

He clicked on a picture of her, held by a mountain of a man. His left hand covered her mouth and more or less her whole face. His right arm was wrapped around her torso. The guy was so tall his head wasn't even in the picture. He was almost twice as wide as her. Fear shone in her eyes.

Luke groaned. She didn't deserve that terror, but at least she was alive.

The phone vibrated again. A text message.

We have your friend. If you want to see her again, give up and turn yourself in. Go home and we'll pick you up. Nothing will happen to you and nothing will happen to her. We'll set you free in five days. If you refuse, we'll kill her. And then we'll kill you.

He stared at the letters. Each one an intimidating sword hanging over his head.

Blood drained from his face. In an automatic, almost comical movement, he tried to sip his coffee and spilled it on his shirt. The sensation kept him in the moment. His brain stem took over and switched into emergency mode.

They had Ada. The rest was probably a lie. They'd kill her anyway, and if he turned himself in, they'd kill him, too.

He checked his watch. Three minutes past noon. The countdown for their survival had begun.

Luke stepped out of Ada's apartment and listened hard. The corridor was buried in stillness, nothing moved or stirred. He went to the door to the left and knocked. No answer. He tried again. Nobody home.

He had more success with her neighbour on the right. A girl opened, about his age, blond and thin, in an oversized T-shirt from the University of Michigan. Her pants were so short it looked like they weren't there at all, the cliché of a cheerleader, at least from what Luke had seen in movies. Her right eye was black and swollen, her cheeks streaked with tears.

'Hello ... uhm, I'm Luke, a friend of Ada's. Are you ... are you OK?'

She slammed the door without saying a word.

Luke knocked again. No answer.

'I'm sorry, really sorry ... But I need your help,' he whispered through the door, knowing she was right there on the other side.

No reaction.

He put his ear on the door and listened. He made out the distant sound of an old Whitney Houston song and the not-so-distant sound of suppressed sobbing.

Time was running out. That girl knew something.

He went back to Ada's kitchen, tore an empty page out of her notebook and wrote a message on it.

I'm Ada's best friend, and I know she's been kidnapped. I have to help her. If you saw something, please talk to me. I'm in danger, too. Please!

He slid the note under the girl's door. This was all pretty primary school, but he didn't know what else to do. He sat down and waited.

The hand on his watch moved on relentlessly, each second a little tremor reminding him of his vulnerability.

He was about to give up when the door opened, and the girl stuck her head out. She sat down next to him.

'They said if I talk to anybody, they'd kill me. They'd know that I did. I don't know how, but ... but I don't want to find out,' she said and pointed at her eye. 'They made themselves pretty clear.'

It hurt just looking at it. Luke tried to give her a comforting smile, an awkward gesture, but he meant it.

She gave him an equally awkward smile back. 'It's not that bad, it'll pass.'

'They killed our friend,' Luke said. 'The police say it was suicide, but I know it wasn't. And now they have my other best friend. Clark and Ada were all I had. Something bad's going on here, and somebody has to stop it. I don't want to, but nobody else will. So it's on me. I need to know who I'm dealing with. Please help me.'

She wiped her tears with the bottom of her shirt. For a brief moment, Luke saw strength in her eyes. 'There were three guys, all tall and strong and mean. Their car had "Serious Security" written on it. And I heard someone call the big guy Butch. That's all I know. Not much to get a shiner for, huh?'

Luke's mind moved at high speed, examining his memory for any links to those names. He came up blank. But it was a start. 'This helps, you're doing well. Do you remember anything else?'

She shook her head.

Luke nodded. Time to move. 'Now go, buy yourself a stack of frozen pizzas and lock yourself in for the next five days. After that, you'll be safe. And … thanks.'

She went back inside. As she closed the door, she said, 'You know, I think Ada likes —'

She was interrupted by Luke's ringtone. He fumbled his phone out of his pocket. The number belonged to somebody in his phone book called Garth, but he didn't recall who that was. He declined the call.

'Sorry, what was that?' he said.

'Never mind,' she said with a tired grin and closed the door.

As he paced down the hallway, his phone rang again, the same number. This time, he took the call.

'Hello, Luke. This is Garth, remember me? Your neighbour. Haven't seen you in a while.'

Luke twigged. They'd exchanged numbers the day he moved in with Clark. Happier times.

'Garth, I can't talk right now.'

'Oh, sorry man. I'm calling because there was a super serious dude here looking for you. I thought I'd let you know, maybe it's a work thing.'

Now he had Luke's full attention.

'Serious dude? What was his name?'

'He didn't say. But I took a snap with my phone through the peephole. I always do, it's a habit. Give me a second, I'll send it over.'

The photo arrived, a blurry distorted fisheye shot. But it was clear who that person was.

Xavier.

'What did you tell him?' Luke said.

'He said he needed to talk to you about something urgently. Didn't mention what. I told him what I just told you, that I haven't seen you in a few weeks. Then he left. Didn't even say goodbye.'

Xavier's net around him grew tighter and tighter. He'd gotten away only because Ada had forced him to move to her place. Maybe she'd never know, but she'd saved his life.

But what now? Luke had no place to go. They were hunting him. Xavier, Umesh, Walter, Butch, Serious Security, whoever they were. They'd killed before and no doubt they'd kill again.

He had to disappear. Now.

Chapter Twenty-Eight

September 1997

Umesh was seventeen when he went back to India for the first time since they'd moved to the United States. His parents took him to visit his grandfather, his last living grandparent, whose health had been declining over the last year and who wished to see his gifted grandson one last time.

Umesh's parents were considered somewhat wealthy back in India, but the rest of his family was on the poor side, always had been. He didn't remember, however, what poor meant in this country that was home to four times as many people as the States but had only a tenth of its GDP. Most of his memories were about his house, everything else was blurry.

The facade of his grandfather's place looked reasonably solid, bricks painted bright pink, with thick green borders around the door and windows. Inside, the walls were bare stone, grey, rough and fractured. The corrugated metal roof had more holes than Umesh could count, and the floor was only raw flattened soil. In the bedroom, a dirty old rug separated the mattress from the ground, with all its insects, worms and whatever other animals inhabited this part of the world. The living room had no such luxury.

One corner hosted a small red brick structure with a sheet of metal on top. A fire burned in what turned out to be the oven; Naan bread stuck to its walls, cooking slowly. A bulimic-looking man with a shaved head sat cross-legged beside it, preparing the food, patiently checking on it every couple of minutes.

In the opposite corner, Umesh's grandfather, almost blind and with impaired hearing, rested on a green plastic chair with three legs. He looked two hundred years old. Umesh's parents insisted his mind was as good as in his best days. On the ground around him sat three other men and a woman, younger but probably not much — Umesh had trouble telling people's age in India, they all seemed sort of old to him.

'Let me touch you, young Umesh. That way I can see you,' his grandfather said with a thick Indian accent. He grabbed Umesh by his wrist and used both hands to feel his arm from hand to shoulder, then moved on to his chest and face.

Umesh bent down uncomfortably.

'Does he look healthy?' his grandfather asked. 'He feels healthy.'

'Yes, Dad, he does. Very healthy, very bright,' one of the other men said. And then, turning to Umesh, 'Remember me? I'm your Uncle Gaurav. This is your Uncle Sachin' — he gestured to the man sitting next to him, who nodded — 'and this is your Uncle Akshay with his wife. They don't speak English. Over there is your Uncle Varun. He speaks English very well.' The man at the oven waved and smiled.

'I remember your pictures on my dad's desk,' Umesh said. 'It's been a long time. I'm glad to meet you … again.'

Truth be told, Umesh had dreaded this visit. He loved his parents, but his opinion of the rest of his family — and the rest of India, for that matter — wasn't flash. He much preferred his new life in San Francisco: the technology, the lifestyle, the computer games he created. India was a closed chapter.

Still, knowing this visit meant a lot to his parents, he tried to stay on his best behaviour. Especially for his dad, who'd taken him aside a week earlier and told him about the importance of connecting with one's roots – an obvious lesson in modesty to show him where their family had come from and what they'd achieved. So Umesh politely answered questions about the Western world, their suburb, his grades, his friends and hobbies.

'Computer games, eh?' his Uncle Gaurav said. 'All the rich kids are playing them these days, I hear. It must be the future. You could become a very rich man.' And after a quick glance at Umesh's father, who was deep into a conversation with his other uncle, he added, 'Don't forget us when you are, eh?'

They ate their bread, which was plain but delicious. The five brothers talked about growing up together, their fights and achievements, friends and enemies. Varun spoke little and didn't eat anything at all. He refilled his water glass several times but otherwise didn't participate in their humble feast. After dinner, he went straight back to the oven and cleaned it.

In a moment of teenager's curiosity, Umesh joined him. 'Uncle Varun, are you sick? You didn't eat a single bite.'

His uncle's laugh came from deep in his heart. 'No, son, I'm fasting. It's part of my religion, I'm following the guidance of Jain. We live ascetic, which means we only possess three things: a set of plain clothes, a bowl for eating and begging, and this little book that contains our system of beliefs.'

He produced a leather-bound booklet that looked old and weathered, yet well cared for, as if it were his uncle's most valuable treasure. Umesh opened it and couldn't help but marvel at the exquisite calligraphy and the lush images. He didn't understand any of the words, but an unknown force drew his attention to it. 'What does it say?'

'Our teachings are powerful,' his uncle said with a smile. 'By foregoing any worldly pleasures, we reach ultimate enlightenment. Ask yourself, what are all these things good for?'

If somebody else had said this to him, a street preacher or a homeless in San Francisco, he'd have paid them no mind. But in this moment, coming from his own uncle with his fulfilled smile of crooked teeth, it simply made sense. What was the ultimate purpose of these things?

'And you don't even eat?' Umesh asked.

The old man smiled again. 'Most of the time, we eat, always modestly. But once a year, we fast for thirty days. Well, at least thirty days. Some of us endure the better part of the year without any food. As for me, I'm still far from enlightenment, but even so, thirty days isn't a big sacrifice.'

That thought fascinated Umesh. The human body needed food to function, the rules of biochemistry were pretty straightforward in this regard. Nutrients in our food were broken down by our gut and the energy released by this process powered bodily functions like heating, moving or thinking. Of course, the body had reserves, but in the long run, none of those things could work without a proper supply of energy. Yet, he didn't think his uncle was telling him lies.

'How do you ... not starve to death?'

'The body is stronger than you think, my son. Stronger than Western medicine wants you to believe. And your mind is more powerful still. With it, you can control everything. Even the need for food.' He gave a sly smile. 'Besides, we ascetics usually don't move much. We sit in silence and observe the world. We sit and think and learn. Until we reach enlightenment.'

In many ways, Umesh already considered himself a minimalist. He spent his days in front of his computer and wrote code, simple and clean. He didn't need many tools to enjoy his work, and agreed the mind was the most powerful device in the world. Imagination and discipline – one day, that's how he'd tell journalists he invented his games and became rich and famous.

But if everybody lived by these principles, who'd buy his products? He'd never thought about this dilemma before. He liked to create new worlds and ingenious characters, much more than he liked to consume these things. Yet he needed people to do exactly that. But why did they? Was there a deeper meaning behind pleasure? Would he ever find it? What about enlightenment?

His thoughts drifted to the hedonistic environment he called home. He'd been there for years, and yet he didn't fully understand what motivated people in California. He doubted they spent much time thinking about enlightenment or the higher sense of existence. That's when he realised he was still a boy at heart. A boy who hadn't thought about the meaning of life and who didn't have a goal. He wanted to be rich and famous, sure, but for what? What would he do with all this money? He needed guidance. He needed a plan.

'Why are you doing all this, uncle?' His initial politeness had turned into genuine interest. 'How did you decide to give up everything?'

The old man's face became serious. 'I was like your father once, you know. I wanted money, a family, to live a comfortable life. I was doing alright, I suppose, but the more I got, the less satisfied I was. There was always a hole in my heart. So I explored myself and talked to friends, priests of all sorts of religions, to people on the street. And I found true satisfaction doesn't come from any worldly goods. Possessions don't lead anywhere. I needed a goal, a goal for my soul. So now I'm searching for enlightenment, and even though I haven't found it yet, my heart is at peace.'

They ended up talking for more than two hours and, in a strange way, most of what his uncle said resonated with him. Umesh didn't want to be poor, and he didn't want to live on the street, but he realised money and power were not goals in themselves. They could only be the means to reach something else. But what?

When they left, his uncle gave him the little leather book as a gift. Umesh refused at first; he couldn't possibly accept the only thing of value his uncle possessed. But Varun insisted. 'I can always make a new copy.'

Umesh thanked him many times and they left.

On their way back, his father said, 'I hope your uncle didn't scare you. He's a bit of an odd bird, you know.'

Umesh nodded but didn't really listen. He was deep in his thoughts. Did he also have a hole in his heart? What was the meaning of his life?

Money and power, the means to reach a bigger goal, kept echoing in his head.

Chapter Twenty-Nine

Luke entered his motel room and instantly felt anonymous. As he inspected the interior, he realized most things in life differed from how they were commonly imagined. One of the core functions of the brain was to abstract from reality, to label experiences and store only generalised information. This process enabled humans to keep vast amounts of knowledge in the neural networks that make up their brains without going mad. But it formed clichés. It made people look better in the mirror, sights in foreign countries more glamorous, the great free country he lived in appear safer than it was. He lived in an exaggerated version of reality.

Except for motels. Motels always looked exactly like their cliché. There were slight variations between chains and locations, but somehow motels were always like everybody expects them to be: shabby.

This particular one was no exception. A single-story building, U-shaped around a parking lot and a pool, painted in a worn-out shade of green that was really closer to brown. The lights flickered, air conditioning units hummed, people sat outside their rooms in plastic chairs and smoked cigarettes.

Luke's room was reasonably clean but worn out by years and years of constant use. He'd been in there for more than an hour and could still smell the cleaning product from today's makeover. The sting was strong, but it barely covered the mixture of sweat and stale smoke from thousands of previous guests.

It wasn't luxury, not by a far stretch, but it was safety. And that's what mattered. His best friend was dead, alongside a number of random strangers connected by a string of events he didn't understand. Ada had been kidnapped. Two of the most powerful men in Silicon Valley were involved, as was a man trained by the French Legion. Even Shawn, of all people, was involved — Luke should've paid attention to his immediate grudge against him. And now they were after him.

Immediately after leaving Ada's place, he'd ditched his phone. Traceable and dangerous. Clauses in their contracts allowed Swoop to track them via their corporate phones, clauses he hadn't agreed with but had accepted anyway. Back then, he was convinced Swoop wouldn't use this data in any harmful way. Now he wasn't so sure. Truth be told, he wasn't sure about anything anymore.

He'd withdrawn a thousand dollars in cash and bought a second-hand phone, cheap enough to discard at any time but good enough for accessing the internet from wherever he needed. And a throwaway SIM card with unlimited calls and data for the next thirty days. He'd taken taxis everywhere, used cash for everything, picked a motel on the other end of town, and paid for a week in advance.

All in all, he'd done a good job becoming untraceable. He had six hundred dollars left, plenty of cash to get around for a week or two. No point thinking beyond that. He'd teleported himself into limbo, into a floating state on the apogee of his life, out of the confines of time and space, weightless and untouchable by any earthly being. Once he stepped out of this room, reality would reboot and he'd either live or die. He was Schrodinger's cat.

He sat on the squeaky bed and tried to wave away all thoughts: the events earlier that day, his worry about Ada, the fear for his life, the rush of adrenaline, all this had to go. His anxiety drain had to stop. He needed a break from life with all its wretched twists and turns.

He popped a Xanax in combination with an Aspirin and sat on his bed for another hour until the TV from his left neighbour and the sound of adult activity from his right neighbour became unbearable. He turned on his own TV, crept under his blanket and watched a show about home improvement. Novocaine for the soul. Within five minutes he was fast asleep.

He woke up to the drumroll of a large V8 engine. It was 9 am; he'd slept for almost twelve hours. He'd hit the reset button and was about to restart his life.

After a quick shower, he entered the breakfast room, equipped with a standard motel breakfast buffet: an old BUNN-O-Matic pouring out cheap strong filter coffee, a set of cereal silos holding Coco Pops and Corn Flakes, a belt toaster next to a stack of white and whole-wheat slices, a bowl containing an assortment of jams and marmalades, a food warmer with scrambled eggs and tiny sausages, and a broken juice machine. It looked disgusting, not appropriate for a new start. He went outside to search for something better.

He found a Denny's down the road, not a gourmet choice but passable, where he ordered bottomless coffee and a big breakfast. As he sipped, he evaluated his options.

The first priority was finding Ada. She'd disappeared less than twenty-four hours ago, so his chances with the police were zero; a person needed to be gone for several days to qualify for the use of their time. An in-person report was out of the question, it'd jeopardise his anonymity.

He called the California missing persons hotline and carefully stated as many details as possible without revealing anything about himself. Then he rang his old neighbour and told him his new number, just in case. When the waiter came back with his food, he asked for a top-up and started eating.

Now for the big decision. Part of him wanted to run back to Europe, away from this new world, its glamour and its troubles. He was no hero and there wasn't any shame in saving his own life. He'd thought about it before, several times. But now, it felt like the ultimate decision, the final go or no go before the rocket launch. There was nobody left who could advise him one way or the other. It was just him, his conscience and his survival instinct.

He longed to go. To leave this place behind and start over. But right in this moment, in his booth with his half-eaten breakfast, he couldn't. He couldn't abandon Ada, wherever she was, and he owed it to Clark to find out what happened.

But this choice meant he had to become active and stay ahead of those people in the real world, the physical world. No more research from the comfort of his home, no more data science, no more computers. He had to stop running and start chasing.

He took the Xanax out of his pocket, rubbed his thumb against the embossed letters of the package and nodded to a mental image of his fifty-year-old self. No, he wouldn't get hooked on this stuff. With all the energy of the universe channelled into his right arm, he threw them in the bin. No more pain. No more fear. No more Luke the victim.

Now back to Ada. She'd found the recordings, and with those tapes, they'd be able to get help. He didn't have the slightest idea where she was, but he had to start somewhere.

Umesh hadn't spent a lot of time at Swoop's campus recently, a fact that several tech magazines had noted, speculating he was working on a new idea. Luke was glad he'd memorised the address earlier. And since Umesh still had a company to manage, there would be a lot of comings and goings. Xavier most likely amongst them.

Going there was the logical choice, the place with the highest information density.

There was only one problem. It was exactly how their PI had disappeared.

Chapter Thirty

Crouching behind a hedge around a backyard in Palo Alto, Luke assured himself he was well hidden from the owner and any pedestrians passing by. It was dark and, apart from a few lonely crickets trying to find a mate, disturbingly quiet. Maybe this was a perk in a suburb where only those with an eight-digit net worth could afford a house. Luke was about four hundred metres away from the residence of Umesh Patel.

He'd arrived there after buying a drone in an electronics store on the other side of town. This kind of equipment was easy to find in an area where nerds ruled the world. There'd been a hundred options. He'd asked a salesperson for help and got what he figured was a reasonable deal, a so-called spy drone for two hundred dollars. The device had a camera with enhanced zoom, night vision, extra silent rotors, extended range and could be operated from a mobile phone. He'd studied the instructions on the way and then located a suitable base for his operation.

Tightness in his throat reminded him of the lurking danger. Was this a good idea? What if Umesh had security guards patrolling the area? Too late for second guesses now.

He unpacked the drone, checked the connection to his mobile phone and sent it upwards. The device had 45 minutes of battery to confirm two things: First, he needed to know whether Ada was held there or not. He assumed not; Umesh was surely smarter than that, but it was always good to verify the obvious. Second, search for possible points of entry.

Once the drone was in the air, he moved further into the hedge to maximise his cover. Scratches and bruises were a small price for extra safety.

Luke moved the drone up to 120 metres, the operational limit of the device. He listened hard for a couple of seconds to confirm he could no longer hear the sound of its rotors.

He bit his lip. So far, so good.

Luke manoeuvred over Umesh's neighbour to the west and observed Umesh's place using the drone's telephoto lens. The elegant building was big for a single person, but it seemed tiny compared to the other places in the street, all no doubt belonging to similarly rich but larger families.

There was nobody outside. No guards, no private army, no mean dogs ready to tear unwelcome strangers to pieces.

Using maximum zoom, he inspected each window and took pictures from different angles. He couldn't see anyone inside. Once he felt good about the western front, he moved the drone south and did the same, before repeating the same process on the eastern and northern sides.

No sign of Ada, Umesh or Xavier. A strange quietness lay over the whole place.

He flew closer to the single-story house and stopped in front of the garage. No cars in the driveway or on the street.

With half an hour of battery left, he lowered the drone, bit by bit. Only twenty metres separated his cameras from the walls. The house had large windows on three sides, and now he had an unobstructed view inside.

The closer he got, the bigger the place appeared. The living room spanned the whole eastern half. One side was connected to the main entrance by a hallway, the other opened onto a massive backyard terrace via a glass facade with a door in its centre. The western half was divided into four smaller rooms. The kitchen was next to the main entrance on the south and had an integrated dining area linked to the living room on the other side. After that, there was a small milk glass window, which Luke took for the bathroom. Then came the bedroom and a spacious home office, which connected to the living room on the northern side.

Nobody in sight, not even under close examination. The eeriness cast a disturbing shadow in Luke's mind. Was this a set-up?

He lowered the drone further and hovered less than five metres outside of each window. Details became clear — household items, furniture, books and magazines. No people. Could it be that easy?

The only part he couldn't see was the bathroom, but he figured nobody would stay in there for that long, especially with the lights off.

Luke brought the drone back up to maximum height and flew it back, where he landed in front of his feet and turned it off. Ten minutes of battery left.

Could he risk it?

Luke examined every photo, taking his time, painfully aware of the fate that'd befallen their poor PI. But there was nothing to see. The house was empty.

This was his chance to find those recordings, to figure out where his friend was, to learn more about this wretched conspiracy. He had to take it. For Ada and Clark.

Again, he flipped through the pictures to find the best approach. The backyard was huge, enclosed on three sides by tall trees with thick, leafy branches that resembled a proper hedge. He'd walk away with scratches but could make his way through. Then he could get into the house via the terrace door, which had some sort of keypad. A closer look revealed a Swoop logo on top and smaller writing below. It took him a while to decipher it on the grizzly picture, but when he was finally able to read it, he smiled.

Powered by CoreOS.

This was his way in. The steady drum of his heartbeat increased, rushing the blood through his body. For once, he'd gotten lucky. As long as the engineers at Swoop hadn't fixed Ada's bug. He searched his emails and found the one with her hack, sent several months ago. Months that had changed his life. Back then, Clark had been alive, Ada wasn't in danger, and their biggest worry had been where to eat for dinner.

As he tried to access the attachment, he realised he'd never asked for the password. Ada had said he'd know it anyway. He tried a few obvious choices, his name, birthday, home country and city. No luck.

Then Ada's birthday and the names of her parents. Nothing.

Clark's name and birthday. The file stayed locked. He clenched his teeth. He had virtually unlimited power in his mailbox but was unable to access it.

He tried the name of her old tech blog, her pseudonym as a hacker, the name of her neighbour. Nothing worked.

Was this a dead end? No. He needed to relax. The information was somewhere in his head.

He closed his eyes and remembered the day they talked about her hack, focussing on the details. They'd been in a Japanese restaurant, he had ramen then cake for dessert. They'd talked about the details of her exploit. The discussion was too much for Clark, but Luke had listened until the end. He replayed everything Ada had said as best as he could, entering every phrase from their conversation. That date, forwards and backwards. All incorrect.

Anguish grew in the back of his head, a demon of self-flagellation hammering on his brain. No. He could do it.

He read the email again.

That big brain of yours should be able to figure out the password, she'd written.

My brain, Luke thought. *Mine.*

Something only he would know. He thought about his strengths. Strengths Ada could rely on. His brain. Moments they shared.

He tried the day they met, their introduction at Swoop, forward and backward. It didn't work. But something told him he was getting closer.

Then he knew.

Society's a bitch. The first sentence Ada had ever said to him.

He typed it and saw a green checkmark on his screen. The file was unlocked.

Luke invaded Umesh's backyard through a narrow opening between the trees. For once, it paid to be skinny. He crossed the lawn and headed straight to the keypad. He fired up the drone and positioned it fifty metres over his head, switched to night vision. Still, nobody around; and now he'd know if any cars arrived.

Nine minutes of battery left.

The security device had a little screen that turned on automatically, displaying a login prompt for a username and password. Luke didn't know either of those, but he had Ada's program. He launched it and a little icon indicated it was searching for CoreOS devices within reach. It found eleven. The list contained UMESH_WIFI, UMESH_TV and

UMESH_WATCH. He wondered what he'd find on those. But now was not the time for that.

He selected a device at the bottom of the list called UMESH_SECUR. Its display flickered for a second and cryptic characters appeared in quick succession. Then the device reverted to its normal login screen.

A flash of a headache shook his skull, sending echoes throughout his whole body. Was that it? The hack didn't work?

But his phone now showed a different view: a panel with several security-related options. It had taken control over the device remotely. Ada was a genius.

He hit a button labelled SECURITY ADMIN. It enabled options to add and remove users, update the operating system, run a self-test, turn on panic mode and control individual locks.

Luke unlocked the door in front of him. It made no visible difference. He put his sweaty palm on the handle. If the alarm went off, they'd catch him, and everything would be over.

The moment of truth.

The door opened without any resistance. No alarm.

On his phone, the status of this door changed from UNLOCKED to OPEN. He stepped in and carefully closed behind him. He held his breath and listened. Not a sound.

Switching apps, he checked the view from his drone. Nothing had changed.

Seven more minutes of battery life.

He hurried into Umesh's office and found stacks of books about software engineering, management and public speaking. The same kind of literature they'd found in Umesh's Swoop office, except it was more chaotic and had a special corner dedicated to his hobby — old-fashioned computer games. A big whiteboard had a story outline, something fans and reporters would die to get their hands on. Below were torn-out notebook pages with scribbles and Post-it notes all over them.

Six more minutes.

He couldn't find anything about Ada and her location. He searched drawers, opened folders and read arbitrary notes. But apart from company paperwork and random gaming ideas, there was nothing. He sat at Umesh's desk, in Umesh's chair. He needed to think.

Where would a billionaire hide this type of information?

He looked up and down, right and left, tried to get inside Umesh's mind. A billionaire who embodied simplicity.

Simplicity.

There was a black plastic mat on the desk to cover the expensive wooden surface. He lifted it up.

And there it was, a single sheet of paper with 'Scaevola' written on top.

It stared as much at Luke as he stared at it.

The sheet contained about two hundred squares organised in rows of seven. Little numbers in each top left corner counted from one to thirty or thirty-one, starting again from one. A calendar of the last six months. It ended in four days.

All past days were crossed out. Half the boxes didn't contain anything, the others hosted short combinations of letters and numbers. R1 to R15 was spread more or less equally over the first three months, P1 to P22 scattered over the second half, C1 to C7 was randomly distributed over the entire time, and so on. Luke had seen similar calendars before, only less cryptic. He was looking at a project plan with timelines of different execution tracks, all culminating in one final deadline. That day was unmistakably marked with a red cross and a note: 8 pm.

As he tried to make sense of these codes, he heard the *clunk* of a closing door. Chaos swept through Luke's mind, paralysing his body.

A dim light filtered through from the main entrance.

Somebody was talking on the phone.

It was Xavier's voice. Without a doubt.

Luke needed to get out.

He took a photo of the project plan and switched apps to check what the drone saw. A black car had parked in front of the garage. Luke wanted to strangle himself for not noticing.

The drone had two more minutes of battery life. As if that mattered now.

Could he hide in Umesh's office? All furniture was placed firmly against the walls, and the table in the centre of the room was made of glass. Impossible.

Xavier's footsteps approached, every step pounding in Luke's temple.

Nowhere to hide.

Luke's lizard brain dropped him to the ground and made him crawl along the wall that separated the living room from the office.

He reached the far end and risked a look. Xavier, dressed all in black, stood in front of the glass façade and looked outside. His silhouette was the shape of Luke's nightmares.

He was still on the phone, listening quietly, less than five metres away from Luke. Could Xavier hear the drone humming outside? What was he looking at?

Abruptly, Xavier turned and strode towards Luke.

It was too late to move; the sound would give him away.

Luke had nowhere to go and no cover. He could only hope Xavier wouldn't see him in the dark. Not very likely.

Luke pressed his back against the wall and stopped breathing.

The steps came closer, slow but determined. Closer every second.

Xavier finished his call. He was almost next to Luke.

A faint sound came from outside. The muffled noise of tiny rotors spinning slower than they should, coming closer and closer, racing towards the ground. The battery of the drone had gone dead.

Xavier still moved on. One or two more steps and Luke would be found.

He closed his eyes.

Another sound ruptured the silence. *Thump*. The drone crash-landed in Umesh's backyard.

Stillness returned, absolute and manic.

Xavier stopped. He listened for a couple of seconds and walked slowly to the terrace door.

Luke's opportunity. He didn't have time to think, only a split second to run. Silently, he paced through the office and slid through the open door into Umesh's bedroom. For a second, he paused and listened. Was that his heartbeat or footsteps?

He tiptoed through a narrow hallway, past the bathroom to the kitchen.

He found cover behind the counter and peered around the corner. Xavier was in Umesh's office. The lights were on, and he was back on his phone.

Had Xavier discovered the drone? Was he calling reinforcements? His face was impossible to decode. Luke tried to make out the device in the grass. He couldn't see anything but darkness.

Luke fended off hyperventilation. The front door was less than five steps away. The perfect chance to escape.

But the clock was ticking for Ada, and he couldn't leave empty-handed. If he stayed, he could check again after Xavier left. Assuming he would leave. He had to try.

On closer inspection, the open space was more of an all-purpose area than an actual living room. It had one corner with a large couch and a TV set, an exercise bike and other gym equipment; another area with computers and gaming consoles; a third section with a shisha on a round coffee table and bean bags; shelves and other furniture all around. A decent place to hide.

Luke found a couch in the TV area that stood about an arm's length away from the wall. Narrow, but he'd fit. He'd tricked Xavier once before by hiding behind a couch, it might work a second time. He ran, and, when he reached it, pressed his body into the hole, legs first. He couldn't move anymore, but he was inside.

Just in time. Xavier came back from the office with a heavy tote bag in one hand. As he passed the terrace, he checked outside once again. Luke followed his gaze and tried to make out the drone in the grass. Still nothing. Black on black ground.

Xavier moved on. As he crossed the living room, he took out his phone again, dialled and waited a couple of seconds. 'I picked up the codes. I'll be there in ten minutes. How's the girl?'

There was a short break, enough to deliver a quick status report.

'OK. Let's keep it this way. He wants her to survive, but that doesn't mean she has to be comfortable. That's what you get for nosing around. Anything else?'

Another pause. Xavier frowned.

'It's a warehouse. Of course, it's big, that's the whole point. I'm aware this means you have to cover extra ground and be more alert … I know, a couple of additional bodies would be better, but I don't trust anybody else. That's why you get paid so much. End of story. If you and your guys can't do it, I have no more need for you.'

Xavier hung up and walked out the front door.

Luke's blood pressure finally dropped. He couldn't believe his luck. How many times could he get away from this guy?

Chapter Thirty-One

July 2003

The explosion was deafening. One second, the bustling marketplace was filled with the smell of spices, exotic fruits, sweat and donkey shit; wooden cartwheels creaked, merchants touted their goods, customers haggled and made jokes; everybody complained about the heat. A moment later, a shockwave pulsed through Xavier's body, throwing him off his feet and through the air.

Then came the sound, so loud his ears popped. His head crashed into the side of the merchant's cart, and he passed out. All this happened within a fraction of a second, but Xavier experienced it in slow motion. He observed the soundwaves expanding through the space in front of him. He actually saw them. Or was it his brain reliving the scene while he was out? Was this all a dream?

When he woke, the previous sounds were gone. All he heard was a high-pitched ringing that would stay in the back of his head for years. The comforting aromas of food and humanity had vanished, displaced by the scent of burned flesh, gunpowder and death. He opened his eyes. Black smoke encompassed everything around him. A woman held her dead child in her hands, screaming towards the sky. An old man wandered around aimlessly, his pants still burning. A boy lay on the ground with his bowels in his hand.

Xavier looked down and saw a piece of bone sticking out of his forearm. The pain was immense. But the shrill sound in his head hurt more. It numbed his mind.

Where were his wife and his daughter? They had been beside him, on their last holiday before their little girl would enter school. He held a mental picture of them in his inner eye. They were beautiful, the most amazing humans he'd ever seen. But for the life of him, he couldn't remember their names. Everything was blurry.

He looked around but didn't see either of them. Pulling himself up with his good arm, he struggled to his feet. His other arm dangled from his body like a foreign object. On unsteady legs, he limped back to where he thought he'd been standing a few minutes earlier. A blip of memory returned. They'd been waiting for freshly pressed orange juices at a makeshift bar made of wooden pallets. Now there was only debris.

Through a clearing in the smoke, he saw a crater about fifty metres out, the epicentre of the explosion. Within a perimeter of about ten metres, there was nothing left but gravel and burned soil. He'd later learn that the suicide bomber picked this location because the security around the common tourist spots was too tight. This place had been his second choice, the busiest corner of the busiest marketplace in Cairo. If the bomber had chosen a slightly different spot, or if the merchant carts between them had been arranged in a slightly different way, Xavier would be dead.

Instead, he was alive. He had bruises, scratches and a badly broken arm, but he'd survive—a few days in the hospital and a few months in a cast, no big deal. But he couldn't see his family, and that was way worse. They were more important than his life. The family he'd started so hesitantly, the wife he'd taken so reluctantly after giving up on his first true love. The love of his youth, the love that had never been returned, the love his Catholic parents would never have approved of. But eventually, he'd come to terms with his situation and found this beautiful woman. She was lovely in every imaginable way, and their child was born of pure love. The kid was smart and had heart. Xavier was a good father. All in all, he'd considered himself a lucky man.

Until he found their bodies. His wife lay on the ground, bloody, her neck twisted almost all the way around. Even in death, she held her arms around their lifeless baby girl. Xavier would experience a lot of misery in his life, but this was the most devastating picture he ever saw. It burned into his retina.

He collapsed. The world was black again.

A week later, in the hospital, when the pain was still too great to bear, he decided never to return to his old life. Instead, he joined the French Foreign Legion and became a ghost.

Chapter Thirty-Two

Back in his motel room, Luke rubbed his eyes. His drone was charging; he'd need it later that night. Coffee was brewing in the room's tiny machine. It was 2 am. Sleep was out of the question.

He'd made it back from Umesh's house without further trouble. He hadn't found any more information but left with the knowledge that Ada was still alive. It was all he needed. Somehow, he'd find his friend.

It hadn't taken him long to figure out where she was. Assuming a driving radius of ten minutes around Umesh's house—that's what Xavier had said on the phone—he pulled a list of buildings registered to Swoop or its subsidiaries from Palo Alto's online business directory. Only one matched the area, its footprint equal to a huge warehouse.

He had the address and knew what to expect. A large industrial place patrolled by security guards, but they'd be understaffed. He'd tackle it the same way as before—use his drone for reconnaissance and take it from there.

The mix of adrenaline and fatigue made him feel like Bruce Willis. It was unlike him to rush into a life-threatening undertaking without a detailed plan, but it had worked before, and he was learning to trust his instincts.

He'd arrive at 4 am to maximise his chances with the guards, precisely when the human circulatory system and level of attention were at their lowest. Enough time to finish charging the drone and drink a coffee or two. He needed to stay alert. Sleep could come later.

Three blocks away from the building, Luke got out of the taxi. His mouth was dry, his palms sweaty. The area was ghostly, not a soul in sight. He unpacked his drone on the sidewalk, checked the battery level one last time and sent it skywards.

Even in the darkness, he had no trouble identifying his target; all Swoop buildings had massive solar arrays on their roof, an attempt to offset the energy it took to operate their data centres.

He set course towards it, and as he came closer, spotted three human shapes in elevated positions on different sides of the building. They appeared to be walking around it on an exterior walkway. Their movements had clockwork precision. Probably ex-military.

There were no security cameras. Luke checked from multiple angles with different levels of zoom and different camera modes. Nothing. Whoever operated this warehouse didn't want anything on tape—no physical evidence of the comings and goings, only human memories. And humans could be silenced, at least that seemed to be Xavier's point of view. A fortress of anonymity.

This wasn't just for Ada; the building harboured a secret. What was in there? Adrenaline hustled through Luke's body with lightspeed. Would he finally get answers about Project Scaevola today?

Patience. He'd need all his wits to get past the guards.

After observing their rounds for a couple of minutes, he identified the pattern. They walked at exactly the same pace, each covering about 120 degrees of a virtual circle. Or, since the building was rectangular, one and a third of the building's four sides. Each guard had an unobstructed view along their current side, so at any given time, three sides were fully covered. The fourth one was the blind spot. His only way in.

He timed it with the stopwatch on his phone. The warehouse was about a hundred metres long and fifty metres wide, and it took each security guard about four minutes to do a full circle. Eighty seconds for each long side and forty for each short one. The blind spot was about twenty seconds for the long ones and forty for the short ones.

Was it possible to make it inside in forty seconds? The thirty-metre perimeter around the building had nothing but empty space. No cover whatsoever. Around the lot was a tall fence with barbed wire on top. It'd be a challenge to climb over the wires, cover the distance to the warehouse and slip inside unseen without any time pressure. No way he could do it in under forty seconds.

Luke's chest deflated. How could he outsmart seasoned soldiers?

If only they'd disappear.

He needed a diversion. That's how it could work. Luckily, he had exactly the right tool.

But first, he needed to get closer. He returned the drone and packed it in his backpack. Eighteen minutes of battery left; a good cushion.

Slowing his pace to a modest stroll—he didn't know who was watching—he covered the three blocks to the building, found a truck parked next to the fence and hid behind it. This new vantage point gave him a clear view of the building and the guards. He waited for the forty seconds of relative freedom, fired the drone up again and positioned it high over the building. The sentinels were still doing their rounds.

He opened Ada's hacker app, still connected to the security device in Umesh's house, still showing him its administrative options. All thanks to the cloud and its ability to log into any device from anywhere.

All doors in Umesh's house were locked, exactly as he'd left them. No activity. If Umesh was home, then he was fast asleep.

Pulling up the device's admin settings, he located panic mode. If Luke was right, besides making a hell of a noise and disturbing the whole neighbourhood, it'd issue an automated phone call to Umesh's security personnel with the quickest response time – the guards patrolling the warehouse in front of him.

His fingers trembled as he hit the button.

Luke watched the building through the drone. At first, nothing happened; the guard's movements didn't change. He checked the time. After a long minute, the guards took out their phones, listened for a few seconds, then briskly walked to the nearest entry. Another minute later, the automated gate of the warehouse opened, and a black Land Rover rushed through. Luke counted four tall men inside, two in the front and two in the back.

A smile lit Luke's face. It had worked.

Mostly. Just as Luke was about to run, a guard emerged onto the walkway and continued his rounds, looking more anxious and alert than before. It wouldn't be a walk in the park after all.

But Luke's odds had improved tremendously. The guard's blind spot was now three minutes and twenty seconds. Manageable.

One last time, he ran through the steps in his head: over the fence, towards the building, onto the walkway using a service ladder and inside. That's where his knowledge ended. But step by step.

Tensed like a sprinter in the starting blocks, he waited for the guard to pass. He ran to the fence. The mesh was easy to climb until he reached the barbed wire at the top. He threw his jacket over it and used his body weight to bend it down until there was a hole big enough for him to pass through. He swivelled over with too much momentum and fell down on the other side, trying to grab his jacket on the way. It got stuck in the wire and tore in two.

He landed on his face. His nose hurt like nothing had ever hurt before. There was blood, a lot of it. He'd probably walk away with a substantial scar on his forehead. Redirecting his scream into his T-shirt, he wanted to stay right there, curl up and die. But no. Think of Ada. The guard could be back any second.

He hid his torn jacket under the base of the fence and ran towards the ladder he'd spotted earlier. One foot after the other, he climbed up.

How much time did he have left? Seconds? A minute? It didn't matter. He couldn't go back, forward was the only way now.

On top of the walkway, he came to an abrupt stop. Which direction did the guard take? He'd better follow and not walk straight into his arms.

Right or left?

Should he check the drone? No time.

He picked right and ran. Luckily, after only a few metres, he came to a door. Unlocked. Luke took a deep breath and stepped inside.

He found himself on an internal version of the walkway. Same height, same width, same material, just on the inside. No guards.

The warehouse was nearly empty. Half was open space, the other half industrial-sized storage racks like the ones he'd seen in IKEA stores. As far as he could tell, all of them were empty.

The open space housed a few lonely pallets, about a metre wide, with white cubes on them. Wrapped in plastic, they were stacked neatly on top of each other in towers of five to eight. They seemed to contain smaller individual items, but from his standpoint, he couldn't make out what they were. A few forklifts stood next to them.

On the wall at the far end, three twenty-foot shipping containers looked tiny in the vast emptiness around them. Luke almost glossed over them, but then noticed their doors, windows and air conditioning units. Makeshift offices. Blinds covered the windows, but if Ada was indeed in this building, that's where she'd be.

Why didn't he see any people? Was this a trap? Should he do a quick sweep with his drone?

No time for doubts. The guards would be back soon, more angry and more alert than before. Time to take a risk.

He climbed down a ladder to the warehouse floor and raced across the open space, feeling acutely exposed and vulnerable. He stood out like Pennywise the Dancing Clown in a crowd full of people in black suits.

Curiosity got the better of him, and he slowed as he passed one of the stacks of cargo. They held boxes with mobile phones, hundreds of them in each cube, thousands in each stack — the newest line of Swoop devices, officially released a few weeks ago. The ones with the brain-machine interface. The whole warehouse had probably been full of them; what remained were likely the last of the first production wave. It seemed odd for stock to be at such a low level, but Luke guessed Swoop had similar warehouses all over the world, housing more contents.

He was only partly right. Swoop indeed owned dozens of almost identical warehouses at strategic locations. What he didn't know was they were all equally empty and that Swoop wasn't planning on making any more smartphones in the future.

As he reached the array of office containers, he headed for the left one, found the door unlocked and stepped inside. Two desks were covered with brown folders, stacks of dirty papers with signatures, pens, stamps and staplers. A large HP copying machine stood next to a water dispenser and a big filing cabinet. Ada wasn't there.

The second container wasn't locked either. There was only one desk, equally coated with paperwork. Next to it was a dark brown leather couch, so worn out the butt dents almost touched the ground, a surprisingly modern TV with a gaming console of the newest generation, and a dartboard, which had clearly seen better days. The fun zone. No Ada.

The last container had an external padlock on its door. If Luke was ever sure about anything, it was this: Ada was in there. He could almost feel her spirit.

Blood from his forehead dripped onto the lock as he examined it. It was hefty and locked tight. He hadn't seen a key rack or a lockbox in either of the other containers.

Standing in front of the door, the flow of time seemed relentless. How long had it been since the black Land Rover left? He figured he had around twenty minutes before the guards would be back, maybe less. Ten minutes to Umesh's house, a few minutes for the confusion to clear and probably less than ten to come back at full speed. How much had gone already?

Backing off from the container, he spotted a shelf with mechanical tools on an outer wall. Between an endless number of screwdrivers, wrenches, ratchets, hammers and clamps, he found a crowbar.

He slid one side through the shackle and jammed the tip against the aluminium doorframe. His arms hurt as he pulled back hard, but the lock didn't give. He tried again, putting his whole weight into it. The crowbar shrieked against the door frame, but the lock didn't budge.

Channelling his bottled-up frustration, he planted both his feet on the door frame while holding the crowbar with his hands. He pushed with his legs and pulled with his arms so hard he let out a primeval scream. A *crack* and a low metallic clank rang out and he flew through the air. A second later, he was on his back on the hard concrete floor.

Laying on the cold, dusty cement, he groaned and caught his breath before finding his bearings again. Pain chiselled into his backbone. He needed both arms to get to his feet.

The lock was, apart from a few scratches, still intact. But the metal sheet holding it to the door had split through its entire length. He took the crowbar out of the dangling padlock, threw it on the floor behind him and opened the door.

The container's interior walls were padded with old mattresses, two layers thick. A nasty smell came from a free-standing toilet in one corner and a heap of greasy paper plates in another. A rubber room.

In the centre, strapped to a metal chair, there she was. Ada.

Her face emitted a beam of relief as she recognized Luke. She seemed exhausted but unharmed. Her ankles and wrists were fixed with cable ties against the chair's legs; her mouth was covered with duct tape.

The agony in his back and his forehead eased by an order of magnitude. He'd found her. All he had to do was get her off this chair and bring her outside.

He ripped off the tape in one quick motion.

'Ouch,' she screeched. 'That's how you treat me, after everything I've been through? It's gonna look bad on your feedback form.'

Luke had to laugh. It was good to see her. 'Seriously? You're losing your edge. Thirty-six hours in captivity and that's all you could come up with?'

'Ha-ha, very damn funny, captain smarty-pants. Now get me the fuck out of here.'

'OK—' Luke was already out of the door again. 'Just a moment.'

'Wait, what—'

Thirty seconds later, he came back with a pair of scissors and cut the ties. She stood awkwardly, her legs quivering. 'What? I want to see you after a few days in this stupid tin. You helping me or what?'

All they had to do now was walk out.

He wrapped Ada's arm around his neck, and they hurried outside.

As they emerged from the container into the colossal warehouse, shock brought Luke's pain back into focus, amplified by the gun aimed at his face.

The security guard had found them. He stood right in their way.

'You again, missy? Still trying to escape? This time you actually made it out of your container, I guess we have to thank your boyfriend here for it.' He smiled grimly at Luke. 'Nice try, kid. Not sure how you did it, but the alarm was a pretty good trick. It almost worked. But I wasn't born yesterday.' He pointed his gun to a little black box on the edge of the container's roof. 'Motion sensors, cheap and easy to install. This one here notified me the second you entered the container.' His face had the smug grin of somebody looking forward to a nice fat bonus from his boss for delivering a long-lost treasure.

Disbelief paralysed Luke. How could he be so stupid? Everything had worked so well until this point. He had no plan B.

The barrel of the gun mocked him relentlessly. Would this be it?

No, at least not without a fight. 'What now?' he said with all the bravery he could muster. 'Are you going to shoot us?'

'Me?' the guard laughed. 'No, definitely not me and not now. That's somebody else's call. I'll wait here for my colleagues, they'll be back any minute. Then we'll tie you both up again, and that's it for today. Your sweetheart here, she's gonna be released when everything's over in a couple of days. Not sure about you, though. Your chances are about fifty-fifty. Sixty-forty to be precise.'

Luke didn't understand. But he wasn't going to fall into their plans.

Fighting off a stomach cramp, he took a deep breath and whispered to Ada, 'Sorry.' Then he drove his elbow into the side of her back and pushed her forward. She yelped and took a small step.

Another push and another step, then another, and another. Eyes wide, the guard moved backwards ever so slightly. Luke noticed the motion with a fleeting smile. That guard wasn't as comfortable with the situation as he tried to convey.

'Luke, what the hell—' Ada protested, confusion lining her face.

'That's what I get when I come to rescue you?' Luke shouted. 'I could've gone away and been done with you. But no, I have to be Mr Nice Guy, dumb enough to help you. See what happens?' Luke gave Ada a final push, much harder than before.

She stumbled towards the guard, couldn't keep her balance and landed on her knees right between his legs. He jumped backwards half a pace.

Luke grabbed the crowbar. He threw it at the guard with all the energy he had left.

It missed Ada by a few centimetres and hit the guard smack in the middle of his forehead. He went down like a sack of potatoes. His legs twitched as he lay on the ground, sobbing and groaning.

As Ada got back to her feet, Luke picked up the crowbar and bashed the guard on the head. With a final grunt, he turned himself into the foetal position and went silent.

Luke dropped the bar, took the guard's gun and reached out to Ada. 'Let's get out of here.'

With a satisfied grin, she delivered a final kick into the guard's groin. 'Fuck me blind. I didn't know I was friends with the Chuck Norris of Belarus.'

Supporting each other with their arms, they limped across the warehouse and climbed up to the interior walkway.

They slipped through the door outside, stumbled down the ladder, and half-ran, half-hobbled across the open space to the place where he'd crossed the fence earlier.

Luke grabbed his torn jacket, pushed himself up and wrapped it around the deformed rolls of barbed wire. This time, he took the last bit slower and stopped to sit on top with one leg hanging on each side. From this position, he reached down and helped Ada over. As he landed next to her, the force of the impact shot through his ankles and legs into his spine.

They hid behind the truck where his backpack was waiting for him just as the black Land Rover came rushing back through the warehouse's gate.

Chapter Thirty-Three

'This is a bit of a downward trend. Your living quarters I mean.' Ada sat on the squeaky bed in Luke's motel room and drank a Coke from the minibar. 'Although quite an improvement for me.'

'Funny,' said Luke while preparing another coffee with the room's tiny machine. It was 6 am. His whole body ached, having released a lifetime's supply of adrenaline in just twelve hours. The wound on his forehead pounded; coldness from the ice pack he held on it expanded into his brain. He didn't know it was possible to feel this exhausted.

But sleep wasn't an option. Too many questions. 'Beggars can't be choosers. We're both on Swoop's shit list now.'

Ada gave a tired smile. 'Profanity, really? How far has it come?'

Luke chuckled, took the mugs and sat down next to her. The motel coffee tasted like ashes, but it made up for it in strength.

Ada smelled it and made a face. 'Hey, Luke…'

'Yes?'

'Thanks for rescuing me.'

He tried to come up with something clever to say, but some things were better kept as they were.

'How'd you find me?' Ada asked after taking a long sip.

'Luck, I guess,' he said. 'I overheard a conversation between Xavier and one of his security guards when I was at Umesh's place.'

Ada almost spat out her coffee. 'What? Did you say Umesh? Evil billionaire asshole? *The* Umesh?'

Luke scratched himself behind his ear. 'Yeah, I guess. Long story.' He told her how he'd escaped Xavier at the office, covered his tracks and set up camp in this motel. How he'd broken into Umesh's house and finally discovered her inside the warehouse. 'You basically rescued yourself. All thanks to your hacker app.'

Ada laughed out aloud. Luke knew that in a different situation, a different time or a different place, she'd have boasted about her great skills, how she could get into any system and how everybody else sucked. But today, she didn't say a word. Today, she seemed happy and scared at the same time. Happy on the surface, an outer shell created by sarcasm and jokes others wouldn't be able to see beyond. But Luke knew his friend. Deep in her core was fright and panic.

'He's crazy, you know,' she said, looking down her empty mug. 'Absolutely nuts. He's obsessed with the Romans and has this completely twisted view of the world — which wouldn't matter if he was some random weirdo. But he's a gazillionaire and, shit, he has power, I mean real power. He can actually do it. He's gonna kill millions of people. Billions.'

'Umesh?' Luke said. 'I don't understand.'

'Yes, Luke. Umesh. Remember his arm? He told people he broke it during a skiing accident or some bullshit like that. It's all lies. You know what he did? He burned it. Himself. Son of a bitch. He burned his arm down to the stump of his elbow. Like that Roman guy Scaevola. He did it to prove his willpower and show the other lunatics what he's capable of. As proof he's gonna pull the trigger.'

'Ada, slow down. What trigger?' Luke tried to process, but her words didn't make sense. He'd assumed the story about Scaevola was only a myth, altered and amplified by thousands of years of storytelling and human imagination. The thought that somebody could scorch their own arm to make a point, suppressing reflexes that are hardwired into the human brain for millions of years, sent a shudder through his entire skeleton.

Ada looked up. 'Luke, he wants to kill five billion people. About sixty per cent of the human population. I'm not joking. The biggest fucking genocide the world has ever seen. And somehow, he thinks it's for the greater good.'

Luke's blood turned to ice. 'What? How? I don't understand. You don't make any —'

'Give me your phone. You need to see for yourself.' Luke reluctantly handed her his burner phone. 'I uploaded the video to a secure storage account before they got me.'

'What video?'

'This one,' said Ada and showed it to him.

The screen displayed Umesh sitting in his living room. Luke recognised the setting; he'd hidden behind the same couch less than twelve hours ago. The background was professionally blurred out, the focal point placed precisely on his face. He wore a grey suit with a Mandarin collar. His arm was in a black sling.

'By the time you're seeing this video,' he said, calm and focused, 'I'll have made the world a better place. I know not everybody, perhaps nobody will agree with me. But I know it's true. Over the last twenty years of my life, I've looked at it from many different angles and through many different lenses. I've assessed and reassessed and assured myself countless times. At first, I didn't want to believe it. But no matter how many times I checked, the facts were always the same. The truth was always the same. And so was the sad conclusion.

'All my life, I've been fascinated with the Roman Empire. And why not? It was the most successful enterprise in human history. No country, religion or organization was larger or existed longer. At its peak, it spanned almost the entire known world, and it lasted more than a thousand years. Their achievements can teach us many lessons is what I thought a long time ago.'

'I studied Roman history, mastered Latin and read countless old tomes to unveil their ancient truths. Some of these truths helped me to build my own little empire, the humble world called Swoop. To the rest of the world, this probably looked like my endgame. A company that makes billions of dollars, a glamorous life as its CEO. But I had bigger things in mind, things nobler than money or power. Swoop was just a step in the process, the one providing me with the means for my actual goal.'

'And why? Because I didn't just look at the success of the Roman Empire, I also looked at its downfall. What did I find? What brought down the most powerful nation in history? Not enemies, natural disasters or other uncontrollable forces. Their demise came from within. The Romans became content with their power. They became lazy and their interest shifted towards meaningless entertainment, hot baths, gladiators and orgies. They stopped caring about the things that matter. They became decadent and their great empire broke apart.'

'What can we learn from that? Well, look at Western society, how we devote our time, the things we do all day long. In the United States, the average adult spends five hours a day in front of the TV and four hours online. We are almost every waking minute in front of a screen. And for what? Entertainment.'

Luke didn't have any trouble believing those numbers. Social media had been on the rise everywhere, but people's addiction to it in America still bewildered him. And TV, of course. What was Umesh's point?

'All of this is completely inconsequential,' the video continued. 'Its only purpose is passing time in a society where we have everything. Where's our ambition? Why aren't we all working on making our present, our future better for our children? Why aren't we expanding our mindset, our horizons, our knowledge?'

Umesh's speech had gradually accelerated throughout the clip, and he became visibly more excited. But now he took a step back and paused.

'Because, like the Romans, we've become decadent. And like their Empire, we're at a turning point, right now. Only this time, the stakes are higher. This time, it's not about the fall of an empire, it's about the whole planet. We're doing everything we can to make it uninhabitable. We're polluting the oceans and the air; we're harvesting the last of our natural resources; we're tearing the whole place down and aren't even seriously exploring alternatives. Instead of funding space exploration, instead of pouring money into energy consumption research, our resources are spent on consumer products whose half-life is shorter than our attention span. Our decadence hinders us from taking the necessary steps to ensure our survival. If we don't act now, it'll be too late.'

Umesh's eyes radiated madness, yet he had a point. So far, they could be looking at a Greenpeace commercial and the message would be the same. Exaggerated, sure. Based on myth rather than reality, maybe. But not outright crazy.

Umesh took a deep breath and centred himself, as if he'd waited his whole life for this moment. 'So I decided to take action and save humanity. Many will say I'm crazy, a fanatic, or a terrorist. Depending on your point of view, it might look this way. And that's OK. I'm not doing this for fame or to be a hero. I'm doing this because it's the right thing. And because I'm willing to make this sacrifice for all of us.'

Umesh took his elbow, or what was left of it, out of the sling. His entire forearm was missing, only a stump remained. A chill made Luke's arm hair stand on end.

'This is a little taste of how serious I am,' Umesh said. 'I did this in honour of the great Gaius Mucius Scaevola to prove to my fellow conspirators how committed I am. About our future and about fixing this dreadful situation. Yes, I'm not the only one. I'm just the leader of a secret fellowship who believes humanity can survive and will survive in the long term. The other noble souls in our organization prefer anonymity, but I believe a revolution needs a face. And so I am this face, and I'm willing to give the ultimate sacrifice.'

'Together, we explored ideas for a better world. We searched for a way to optimise the world's use of resources and whether venturing into space can save humanity. We ran countless simulations to validate the future of our world, each one with different parameters. It's with great sadness that I must tell you, they all look very grim. We've regressed too far for any improvements to gain hold before we completely vanish. The clock has already moved past midnight.'

Luke's tongue was a sheet of sandpaper. He knew this was just a video, electrons on silicon activated to produce blips of light that formed an artificial image. But he couldn't look Umesh in the eyes.

'We figured out that only a radical step can save humanity. Our footprint needs to shrink dramatically. At the same time, we have to ensure those with the greatest potential survive. For progress. So we ran more simulations. We ran them again and again, using the world's most powerful supercomputers, to find out exactly how many of us have to perish and who needs to survive.'

'A band of researchers across the world validated these results from all possible angles, and I can assure you, there is no other way. Five billion people, more than half of us, have to go. The brightest minds on the planet in social engineering, environmental science and machine learning went over it again and again and confirmed this number. They also came up with a model to select the optimal subset of us for a brighter tomorrow. If you're seeing this video now, you're a part of this subset. Congratulations, you're alive and part of the planet's future.'

Umesh paused to let this sink in. Luke tried to swallow but couldn't, his throat closed, acidic. Umesh's words spun around his mind.

They were watching the tape of a madman, light-years away from the image of a benevolent genius, the way the media always portrayed him. On the surface, this man was a successful businessman, a charitable person, a man dedicated to humanity. Did he really believe this was the only way to save the world? No sane mind could come up with such a plan.

'You may think of this as genocide,' Umesh continued. 'Which it isn't. Genocide is the murder of a group of people based on race, colour, age, or other superficial criteria. I can assure you the factors we used for this decision were completely objective. They were defined not by people — arbitrary and error-prone — but by machines. By an AI whose only goal was to select the best of us, the least decadent of us. Nothing else mattered.'

'To prove this to you, let me tell you that the model also selected me to die. And I accept this decision. Even though all my actions and achievements in life have been centred around this moment, I indulged in entertainment and promoted decadence through the games I created and the products we sell at Swoop. To the world, I look like a decadent man, and maybe I've become one.'

The sickness in Luke's throat had reached his stomach. Why in the world had he thrown his pills away?

Umesh continued. 'But I decided to take my own life before it comes to that. I'm too afraid my human weakness could take over and hit the cancel button. This is too important to trust even my own self. At the same time, I'm aware of my actions. I deserve death for it. As you'll discover, I chose a particularly painful method to end my life, my own last punishment.'

'Rest assured, your loved ones had a better departure from this world. They barely suffered, we made sure of that. Months ago, I acquired a company specialised in brain-machine interaction and, together, we developed a painless way of disabling some of the core functions of the brain. Electromagnetic waves delivered by Swoop's smartphones and other CoreOS devices were the trigger and caused instant death. To a medical examiner, this will look like cancer in the brain stem, but I assure you, they didn't suffer.'

'I know this is of little comfort for you, but please let me tell you again: there was no other way. By all means, grieve for your friends and family. Grieve and be glad their sacrifice improved the world for you and your children. And in time, once you can detach from your hate, go and make the world a better place. Don't waste your time with hedonism and decadence, and remember why your friends had to die. Get to work. Work as hard as you can, rally behind research and save the planet. I know you can do it. And maybe, in a thousand years, think better of me.'

The video stopped and the picture of Umesh morphed into a black screen.

Chapter Thirty-Four

Umesh's eyes haunted Luke even after the video had finished. 'Do you think he's capable of doing this? I mean actually doing it?'

Ada's face was buried in her hands. 'Someone who burns his arm down to a fucking stump is capable of pretty much anything.'

Luke's eyes focused on a spot far outside the window. The first rays of sunlight appeared behind a small hill on the horizon, painting the otherwise perfectly blue sky in vivid shades of orange and red. A beautiful sight. A new day was about to start.

Logic rushed through his mind, and he went to throw away his phone. 'We need to ditch this thing and go completely offline.'

'Relax, Luke, you can keep it. Umesh said Swoop devices, and this phone's way too old. But as long as we're around modern tech, we're in danger. Hell, everybody is.'

She was right, Swoop controlled the majority of devices on the planet. But his burner phone was a no-name brand and wildly out of date. No way it had brain wave technology.

Luke nodded. 'I saw a project plan in Umesh's home office. It's going to happen tomorrow night at eight o'clock. All those deaths, all those people with brain cancer, they were just … I guess trials, equipment tests. And the acquisition of Whitefeed. All this is related, even Clark. It's all part of one massive project. And it ends tomorrow.'

Ada raised her head, her eyes wide open. 'Tomorrow? Seriously? We … we have to go to the police … the FBI … hell, the creeps from the NSA. What are we waiting for? We have proof now. Not for Clark, but a whole fucking genocide. Let's go … Like, now!'

Bitterness engulfed Luke, limiting his mental action radius. They were missing something. 'We don't know how he plans to do it. We need —'

'The fuck we do! *We* don't need anything. Not *us*. We're way over our heads on this one. I was kidnapped, Luke. And you rescued me only through sheer luck. We need to go to the professionals. Now. Fucking now!' Tears rolled down her cheeks. Luke had never seen her this serious, not even in that warehouse. All her cynicism, her sarcasm was gone, leaving only terror behind.

Luke closed his eyes, he needed to think. His rationality agreed with Ada; this was way too big for them. But there was a dark and heavy sensation he couldn't deny. A shadow of consequence, yelling at him from deep within his guts that he was about to make a mistake. What if Umesh had contacts in the police department? What if that's why they declared Clark's case a suicide? What if billions of lives would be annihilated because he made the wrong choice? Thoughts whirled around his mind.

His brain was about to crash. He needed time.

'OK,' he said, garnering all the calmness he had left. 'It's almost seven o'clock, breakfast is about to open. Let's get a coffee. We give ourselves ten minutes. If we still think the police is the best choice, we'll go and tell them everything. I'll call a taxi and we'll go. Ten minutes, Ada.'

'But Luke...' Ada wiped the tears off her face. She fixated on his eyes, serious and innocent at the same time. 'OK, fine. Let's have a coffee if that's what it takes.'

The breakfast room was empty. People who stayed in motels were, as a general rule, no early birds. Luke needed the space for his thoughts to expand.

This morning, the eggs and the bacon were fresh and smelled great. Somehow that made all the difference, releasing new energy into his body. The coffee machine was still running, the ancient BUNN-O-Matic, which probably predated the motel itself. They waited in front of it to finish. On the opposite side of the room, a wall-mounted screen showed the early morning news. A senator from Idaho and Republican presidential candidate for the race in two years had been caught in the middle of a large-scale money laundering scheme connected to the Russian mafia. Business as usual.

The machine finished with a friendly *bing* and they each took one of the many identical white mugs next to it. Luke grabbed the metal carafe and started filling his mug when he heard Ada's cup crash onto the grey tiles on the floor.

'Luke,' she yelled, pointing at the TV. 'What the fuck!'

He looked up to see a photograph of Walter Hamilton when he'd been younger. The caption read *Silicon Valley icon killed at 64.*

' – the preliminary police report leaves no doubt the successful businessman was murdered, only months after his son committed suicide,' the news anchor said. 'According to the autopsy, the founder and president of Hamilton Ventures was shot in the head with a stolen handgun from close range. Investigators conclude the killer and the victim knew each other well.'

Walter's picture faded into the blue-grey background of the TV studio. At the precise moment the screen focused on the reporter, her news desk and that soothing blue background, the world was still relatively clear-cut for Luke and Ada. The world was in colossal danger, the biggest mass murder in history a real short-term possibility. But if the universe had any perception of right or wrong, they were the good guys and Umesh, Xavier and whoever else were the bad guys.

This all changed a split second later when pictures of the two of them came up on the screen, right where Walter's photo had been. The tagline now read *Primary suspects: Lukasz Jankovic (24) Ada Fisher (28).*

The world stopped spinning. Luke's heartbeat suspended, countless processes in his body came to a halt. Just like that. The air around him stood still, preserving this moment for what seemed like an eternity.

He was vaguely aware of Ada muttering insults over and over. He didn't remember when he'd taken his last breath. The coffee had stopped dripping into his cup. The picture on the TV had frozen. It would show their images forever, branded as murderers until the end of time.

He looked around to see if anybody else was seeing what he saw right now. Still, nobody else had entered the room. But there'd be people in other parts of the state, maybe the whole nation, watching the same channel at this moment, and they'd soon point at him and scream, 'Look, it's that guy!'

A millennium of frozen time was about to pass, ruled by hatred and guilt.

Then the laws of physics fell back into place. His fingers felt an unpleasant sensation, the pain of boiling coffee on his skin. A reflex from deep inside his spinal cord made him drop the cup, while the more evolved neurons in his brain forced him to stay focused on the TV.

'—suspects are currently on the run. They're considered armed and dangerous. If you encounter one of these individuals, please don't engage. Instead, report any sightings or clues related to this crime to Santa Clara Police, who are offering a reward of up to $250,000 for information leading to their arrest. Please call 911 or your local police department if you have any —'

'Luke, Luuuuuuke', Ada screamed, yanking his shoulder so hard her nails pierced his T-shirt. 'What the hell?'

He couldn't think of anything. There were no viable options. Whoever had set them up had outmanoeuvred them.

He needed time, now more than ever. At least a few minutes to see the world a little clearer. 'Quick, back to the room, before anybody sees us.'

They ran outside and passed the clerk's office. Through its large window, Luke saw the receptionist, a fat man called Tony. An equally obese family stood in front of the counter, waiting to grab his attention. But instead of engaging with them, Tony was focused on his own screen on the other side of the room. It was on the same channel.

In a few moments, Tony would realize and call the police.

Luke turned to Ada, who said, 'Fuck!'

They rushed to their room. Luke shoved his belongings—the drone, the security guard's gun, his phone, the remaining cash—into his backpack.

Tony emerged from reception, already out of breath but with fire in his eyes.

They'd been discovered.

'Shit,' she said.

Tony closed the distance to their room as quickly as his body allowed, panting and sweating. Luke and Ada barely made it out of the room before he caught up with them. Failing to grab Luke's arm at full speed, Tony crashed into the plastic chair next to their door and let out a primeval grunt.

Luke and Ada ran along the side of the motel, towards the back.

Tony must have realised he had no chance of catching up, so he slowed to a trot and reached for his phone just as they disappeared behind the far corner of the building.

The need for survival pushed aside the looming catastrophe. Instinct led Luke around the motel onto the boardwalk on its left. He dragged Ada further away, into a petrol station that occupied the next lot. Once they reached the pumps, he forced himself to slow down.

'Luke, what are we —'

He didn't listen and pulled her behind one of the cars, an empty Chevrolet Impala, its owner probably at the counter. Ada understood. She hustled towards the passenger side as Luke jumped into the driver's seat.

Finally, some luck. The keys were in the lock.

He fired up the engine.

Ada's smile was mad with adrenaline. 'Man, I always wanted to play Bonnie and Clyde. Floor it!'

Before she could close her door, Luke took off with the sound of squealing tires.

For a few minutes, they flowed with the early morning traffic. The anonymity amongst the stream of cars provided a shield of relative safety. Wanted murderers shouldn't attract any attention.

But safety was something they couldn't afford. The end of the world was near. Luke took a sharp turn into an empty laneway, stopped the car and turned off the engine.

What the hell did I just do?

Ada seemed still out of breath, her face red as if she'd just finished a marathon. 'Well, that was fun. But why in the name of fuck did you steal this car? We could've easily outrun Mr motel fatso.'

'I don't care about that guy. We still need to get around, and this is safer than a taxi. They're already after us for murder — car theft doesn't change anything. And if Umesh's plan succeeds tomorrow, none of this matters.'

Ada stared at the dashboard. 'You badass, way to go! But what's the plan now? I need to know you have a plan.'

Luke's mind was engulfed by dilemma, the conflict between intuition and logic, the weight on his shoulders. 'Ada, there's no plan. I don't want this. I didn't prepare for this. It's just the two of us now. Even if we turn ourselves in, they won't care about our side of the story. I bet they won't even let us use our phones to show them the video. At least not until it's too late. Like it or not, we're on our own. You in?'

She took a deep breath. 'OK. I bet everybody we know is on Umesh's shit list. If it's the five billion most decadent people in the world, then fuck, most of California will be wiped out. If we don't do anything about it, we'll either be dead by tomorrow or the only ones left. Either way, we're screwed. So we might as well die trying to prevent all that shit. Where do we start?'

Chapter Thirty-Five

May 2011

When his squad arrived in the little village somewhere in the middle of Mali, Xavier was exhausted. It had been a long march, ten days through primeval rainforest, muddy ground and raging rivers. The sun blazed hot, but what killed him was the humidity. His clothes had been wet from the moment they'd gotten out of their helicopter, and they hadn't dried since.

Not that he didn't have experience with heat, humidity or long walks. After seven years of service in the Legion and six tours to Africa, he was used to all this, at least as much as anybody ever got used to it. Maybe he was finally getting old. Or maybe he just hated this whole place.

He appreciated, admired, the comradery in the Legion. It was entirely made up of people who'd fled a previous life for one reason or another, looking for anonymity and a new start. After three years of service, all Legionnaires were automatically granted French citizenship and a new life. Almost all of them became soldiers for that reason, but when the time came to move on, many stayed anyway. Xavier had done the same. Nobody forced him to talk about his previous life, and he had plenty of time to think in solitude. The work was hard, dangerous and often outright brutal. In his own way, he enjoyed it.

But he hated Mali. Of all his African assignments, this was the worst. People were in endless conflict. Rebels against the government, Tuareg against rebels, foreign soldiers against Tuareg, Al-Qaeda against everybody else. There were no rules and no end to it. People were killed in cold blood, and nobody wanted the troops sent to keep the peace.

'Sanchez, Müller, O'Neill, go and check the left. The rest comes with me to the right,' their commander said, a tall Frenchman called Antoine.

A cluster of twenty sandalwood huts around a common area with a massive fireplace made up the town. In other villages, the locals had greeted their group of heavily armed soldiers with raised arms and uncomfortable smiles. Universal signs for peace.

Not so in this town. The place was deserted, which meant one of two things. Either it was truly empty, and they'd all fled somewhere outside the war zone, or it was a trap, and their squad was about to be ambushed.

Xavier switched onto high alert. He led the two other soldiers to the last hut. If there was a trap, it'd be in the first or second hut, so they approached the other way, guns ready. Müller positioned himself in front of the entry door, Xavier and O'Neill went to cover the windows. They moved automatically, a practised pattern they'd executed many times in similar towns all over the continent.

Xavier pulled back the ragged window cloth with the tip of his gun. After the destruction caused by the bomb that killed his family, this was the other image he'd never forget.

He gave the 'all clear', and they sprinted to the next hut. The smell made him gag. But he had to move on. These huts could be a decoy, an ambush was still possible.

They repeated the procedure for all the remaining huts and the picture was the same everywhere. Once they finished their round, they waited for the other group. They showed up a minute later and had, based on Antoine's face, seen the same thing.

Antoine sent the remaining four men to scout the surroundings and quietly talked to Xavier. 'I don't think it's a trap, they'd have killed us by now.'

'Unless they're waiting for this exact moment,' said Xavier.

'Come on. You know as well as me they don't think that far … quite a mess here, huh?'

Xavier nodded and kept his eyes on the rainforest.

'Command will want pictures of this. Quite some next-level shit,' said Antoine and handed Xavier a camera. 'Here, we need every single hut.'

Xavier shook his head. He hated the thought of going back, but Antoine was the ranking officer and made the decisions. Reluctantly, he took it and went to work.

As he entered the first hut, he covered his mouth. The smell was unbearable. Flies were everywhere. Thousands, maybe millions of them feasting on the rotten flesh of the dead bodies. They'd been killed anywhere from a day to a week ago, hard to know in this climate. They'd been a family of four, father, mother, a boy and a girl. Both women had been chained to the ground, raped and killed. Their tormentors had used condoms, a smart move in AIDS-ridden areas like this, which they'd discarded next to their victims. To an outsider, it looked like carelessness, but Xavier knew they were trophies. He counted six next to the woman and nine next to the girl, who couldn't have been older than twelve. The boy and the father were chained to the corner posts of the hut. Their eyelids had been sliced off and their stomachs had a large cut. They'd been made to watch the defilement of their women, all while slowly dying themselves.

Xavier took ten pictures, then he'd seen enough. The other huts showed similar scenes. In some of them, the boys had been raped, too. None of the victims was marked with less than three condoms.

The last hut, the one he'd glimpsed first, was the worst. Xavier couldn't comprehend it. He took two pictures and stumbled back outside. He rested his arms on his legs, panting, deciding whether vomiting or holding it was a better choice. He'd seen a lot of misery in his life, a lot of death. He wasn't opposed to killing people for the right reasons. Or even for the wrong reasons, as long as things were ended in a civilised way.

But what he'd witnessed in those huts was not only insanely brutal, it was also wildly unnecessary. These people hadn't done anything wrong; they'd been simple farmers with almost no ties to the outside world. They'd been killed in the most brutal way only because of human cruelty. A cruelty he'd seen over and over again throughout his journeys through Africa. A cruelty that peaked in this moment.

As Xavier looked around, trying to keep his breakfast inside, he decided to quit. He'd enrolled to flee from life and to do a bit of good along the way. But there was no helping these people. They kept killing each other in unimaginably painful ways and despised those who only wanted to provide aid. Humanity couldn't be saved, not in this part of the world. Maybe nowhere.

Any minute, he could end up like one of these people. And what for? Helping those who didn't deserve it? To feel better about the life he fled? To distract himself from the lie he'd been telling himself for years?

No. Life was too short. He had to give in and go back to his first true love. A love that would never be answered, a love that couldn't exist anywhere but in his head. But it would be better to be around him than not.

Later that night, Xavier wrote his resignation letter and took the first plane back to San Francisco. Back to his old friend Umesh and his crazy ideas. He'd devote himself fully to the man who meant so much to him but who knew so little about his devotion.

Chapter Thirty-Six

The road was dull and the night was dark. They drove for six hours and had barely crossed the halfway mark. Traffic on the 101 during rush hour moved at a crawl. It took almost two full hours to get past San José before the cars thinned out and the drive became smoother. Their stolen car was old but well maintained, a comfortable ride.

Luke sat in the passenger seat and watched the centre strip blur into a continuous line. Exhaustion had become a permanent state, but sleep didn't come. Ada struggled to keep the car at a steady seventy miles per hour to stay inconspicuous. The cops were hunting for them and their car; her eyes were as much on the shoulder as on the street.

To make things worse, Ada didn't actually have a license, a climate change statement as she'd told Luke. But he'd drifted from his lane twice, so a few minutes earlier, she'd insisted on taking the wheel. Operating a car on the deserted highway wasn't much of a challenge, yet she had droplets of sweat on her forehead. Ironically, this could turn out to be a much more significant contribution towards saving the world than not driving had ever been.

Luke redirected his thoughts to the task ahead. He'd watched Umesh's video twice more, hoping to find further clues about his execution plan. Nothing. 'Shouldn't we upload this somewhere? At least we'll get attention. Don't you have thousands of followers?'

Ada scowled. 'Millions, actually. Don't you think I considered that? These assholes blocked my personal email address, too. I can't even log into my own blog. Everything's a Swoop account these days, so I'm completely locked out.'

'We could send it to a newspaper.'

'Don't bother, trust me, I tried. They receive so many whacky messages and videos every day, they don't look at them anymore. Besides, who's gonna watch this before it's too late? No, Luke. The shit has already hit the fan, it's on us now.'

At least they knew where they were going. It had taken them a few hours, but once they'd figured it out, the answer was crystal clear. Without their Swoop accounts, they had to rely on publicly available information, which made it harder but not impossible. The deadly code hidden in billions of devices would have to be triggered remotely from one of Swoop's data centres. Mass communication spanning the entire planet was not something that could be coordinated from somebody's basement, even if that somebody was Umesh Patel. The question was which data centre.

The online section on public tenders at the State Library of California provided the information they needed. Every security-related contract involving armed guards had to go through a publicly audited process, and Swoop operated about twenty data centres in the continental U.S. that needed to comply with these rules. These contracts made incredibly boring reading material, but they revealed that only one of them was subcontracted to a company called Serious Security.

Everything made sense. That particular data centre wasn't only Swoop's poster child, it was also their largest and naturally the most secure. It had been built right next to a source of virtually unlimited, clean energy that guaranteed maximum reliability.

But it was also the hardest one to access. This time, they wouldn't be able to spy on the building from a safe location. Things would be much more confined, and secrecy was off the table, so they'd spent two solid hours preparing their game plan. They'd investigated every satellite image, blueprint and photo they could find about the area. Ada had brushed up her knowledge about the security infrastructure of data centres, and Luke had found a way inside. An hour ago, they'd stopped to buy duct tape, rope, and other tools they might need.

But all that planning didn't overcome his lurking panic about the impossibility of their undertaking. Could he ever prepare enough? What if they weren't able to keep up with these criminal masterminds?

He took the gun he'd picked up from the security guard out of his backpack. The metal was cold and heavy in his hands. He checked the clip, it held eight bullets. Would he need them?

He took out his phone again and started typing. They had only had a few hours left, maybe he'd find a better way in. He'd just have to stay awake.

Chapter Thirty-Seven

Luke peered down Hoover Dam, one of the world's biggest man-made structures, once the highest dam and the largest hydroelectric power station on the planet. A plaque informed him it generated about 4 billion kilowatt-hours annually, enough to power the homes of 1.3 million people across Arizona, Nevada and California, plus the ever-glowing lights of Las Vegas. Lake Mead extended on the other side, the largest reservoir in the United States, covering about 642 square kilometres and holding some 35 trillion litres of water.

No wonder they chose this place. An unlimited supply of energy and maximum security.

Luke felt the enormous weight of the water pushing against the dam as he stood on it. In much the same way, the weight of billions of lives rested on his shoulders, a thought he desperately tried to evade.

His eyes itched as he registered the tourists passing by, taking pictures, laughing and eating ice cream. He imagined sixty per cent of them gone in an instant. Who would and who wouldn't survive? A couple of teenagers captured selfies from every possible angle. They probably wouldn't make the cut.

His heart suddenly stopped. Amongst a group of tourists, the silhouette of a tall man with a ponytail. Shawn. Instinctively, Luke closed his eyes.

When he forced them back open, Shawn was gone. Luke scanned the area but couldn't find anybody looking remotely similar. Fatigue was making him see ghosts. He rubbed his forehead and noticed a drop of fresh blood on his hand. A new crack had opened where he'd fallen off that warehouse fence. When this was over, one way or another, he'd need a doctor and a long sleep.

One way or another.

'I got the tickets,' Ada said. 'They almost closed their damn shop right in front of me. I got us the ultimate deluxe package, the longest, most expensive tour on offer. That should get us pretty close.'

Ten minutes later, they were amongst a group of seventeen Americans from twelve different states, six Germans, four French, three Australians and one man from Belgium. Their guide, grandson of the last resident of St. Thomas, an underwater ghost town created by the flooding of Lake Mead, had made them show hands. The act was a sting in Luke's gut. Why were they wasting time listening to this cretin?

Luke checked his watch—3:32 pm. Four and a half hours left.

The tour started on a platform that gave them a full view of the dam and the power plant below. If the clock weren't ticking, Luke would have marvelled at the eighty-five-year-old feat of engineering. But he barely listened. All he could think about was the one shot they had to get access to that data centre. Assuming they'd chosen the right place.

The group moved to the edge of the dam that joined the wall of the canyon, where their guide opened an inconspicuous metal door and led them into the bowels of the concrete and steel behemoth. They descended two hundred stairs down a narrow pathway and ended up inside a surprisingly large hall that looked like the control room of the early Apollo missions. Desks with built-in tube screens arranged around an enormous wireframe display with dozens of LEDs provided a full status report of the entire dam. Their guide told them it used to be the operational headquarters of the facility until everything had been digitised and moved above the surface a few years ago.

Luke's neck was so tight it cracked as he scanned his surroundings. They needed to get away from the group. Instead, they had to endure technical details nobody would ever care about if their plan failed. Why'd he been so naive to think they could just sneak off?

The room had only two doors, the one they'd entered from, and the one they'd exit through. The same for the next room, the head office for inspecting the static integrity of the dam, and the next, once a gigantic freezer that produced ice to cool the dam's concrete.

Luke failed to summon his happy place to distract himself from the pit in his stomach. His inner eye was blind.

They were almost an hour into the tour and still stuck. No opportunity. He glanced at Ada and saw her shifting her weight back and forth between her legs. The clock kept ticking.

Five more minutes … in five minutes he'd pull out the gun and force his way in there. Whatever happened, he'd stick to the plan. A plan he needed for his own sanity, a plan he could believe in, with options and fallbacks, no matter how unrealistic they were.

They descended one more set of stairs and found themselves inside a vast room aptly called 'the dome', the exact centre of the dam, functioning as the core of its nerve system where all tunnels met. Twenty corridors branched out in every direction, each marked by a metal plate with a numeric code on it.

'And behind this door is what we call' — their guide paused theatrically and continued in his best spooky voice—'the graveyard! No, this isn't where we buried all the workers who died during construction.' He chuckled. 'It's where we store our outdated equipment. You see, when the government awarded the contract to build all this, they demanded a hundred-year supply of tools, the same stuff they used during construction, to be stored inside the dam to make sure any problem could be fixed quickly and reliably. Of course, this is all obsolete now, and we don't need it anymore, but it has to stay here to honour that agreement. Everybody's already looking forward to getting rid of all this junk in 2036.'

With one of the many keys on his chain, he unlocked the door and let everybody peek inside. 'Take a good look. There's everything they could possibly need. Shovels, pikes, gloves, ropes, cement machines and so on. And the biggest chunk, two thousand carbide lamps, so workers can see what they're doing. Anybody remember carbide lamps?' A single hand went up, an old man from Australia. 'Hah, getting fewer every year. Well, for all the others, let me explain. These lamps use a chemical reaction with water to create a small flame, which produces a pretty bright light. That's how it was done in the times before electricity.'

As their group marvelled at technical relics, Luke finally saw their chance. It was now or never. Ada, examining the room with wide eyes, seemed like she'd reached the same conclusion. A set of vertical pipes ten metres away was wide enough to hide behind. They nodded at each other.

Stepping backwards, first carefully and then disregarding their group entirely, they accelerated until they reached the pipes. They hid behind just as the last batch of tourists peeked into the equipment room. Luke held his breath.

The guide checked the area one last time before moving on. He didn't notice them and turned off the lights. The door closed behind him with a low metallic clang.

Everything went dark and quiet, except for the low hum of generators below. Luke turned on his flashlight.

Ada walked from corridor to corridor, inspecting each number plate. 'Shit, they all look the same. Which one is it?' asked Ada.

Luke gulped. A wrong turn and they might never see daylight again. He cross-referenced each plate with the blueprints he'd memorised from the dam's Wikipedia page. The numbers had been in those plans, it'd been his responsibility to look them up. But they weren't in his brain anymore. He searched his mind and found the control room, the corridors, the junk, all these useless bits of information. But there was only grey static when it came to these labels. For the life of him, he couldn't remember.

Panic tightened around his throat like a too-short belt. He paced from one corridor to the next, trying to jog his memory.

Just as he was about to lose faith, he picked up a detail. 'This one,' he whispered. '76A, that's the one they recently added. The number plate is much newer than the others.'

They stepped through the door frame and stared into the dark narrow passage, too long for them to see the end, even using a flashlight.

No time for doubts.

After fifty metres or so — it was hard to know in this place where time and space seemed to stand still — Ada abruptly slammed her elbow into Luke's side.

He lost balance and fell onto the cold floor. 'Ada, what—'

'Ssh. There's something behind us. Turn off the damn light!'

They waited in absolute darkness. Luke's eyes and brain tried to latch onto a point of reference, anything. He couldn't see his own hand.

As his eyes adjusted, a shimmer of light appeared at the tunnel entrance. Almost too faint to make out, but it was there.

And then there was a distant rustling and a *thud*. Footsteps? Or was it his imagination again?

'No idea what or who this is,' Ada whispered. 'But I don't want to find out. We need to hurry.'

Luke closed his eyes. When he opened them again, the glimmer was gone. It was as quiet as a library at midnight. 'You're hallucinating. It's the darkness. I once read —'

'Cut the crap, Luke. I don't care about your stupid useless knowledge right now. Let's go!'

Luke left the flashlight off and used his phone instead. The screen's murky glow wasn't much, but it was enough to keep them going. They scuttled along for a minute and followed the tunnel as it turned left, right, and left again.

They reached a heavy steel door that looked like an old safe, with multiple levers and wheels on its front. A safety door, sealing off one area of the dam from another. After a few failed attempts, they figured out which levers to flip and how to turn the rusty wheels. Requiring their combined strength, it opened with a heavy metallic *creak*.

They entered a large vertical shaft, a metal staircase winding around its walls. The paint was fresher and the floor less worn than in the rest of the dam. Faint green exit signs illuminated the shaft and a loud hum made it almost impossible to speak. Luke could make out the floor through the narrow rectangular hole in the centre of the staircase — they were far from the top, only a couple of flights from the ground.

He checked the time. Less than three and a half hours left. Two hundred minutes.

They hurried down to the bottom floor. Luke peered around the corner and saw another steel door, a futuristic access panel next to it. And a security guard, a mountain of a man.

Luke swallowed. They were in the right place. Swoop's data centres were operated remotely without any intervention, needing only a constant input of energy to function. The company kept their inner workings so confidential they avoided humans on the premises at all costs.

But this wasn't a normal day, and it wasn't just any location. A single line of defence almost seemed too easy, given the stakes.

The guard didn't seem too concerned about imminent threats. A Kindle in his hands, he was immersed in his book.

Luke closed his eyes. Sweat ran over the wound on his forehead, making it itch.

This was a test. A test to see whether they could grow beyond curious nerds, to prove they were able to act. Not behind a computer screen, but in the real world. A test they couldn't fail. 'I'll make sure he doesn't move. You take his gun.'

Ada nodded but looked uncertain.

Hands trembling, he pulled out the gun, unlocked the safety and counted to three.

He leapt forward and shouted, 'HANDS UP!' It barely registered over the generator noise.

The guard looked up, frowning. He put down his reading device and raised his arms. His piercing eyes locked on Luke's, an invisible force amplifying Luke's insecurity. Ada grabbed the guard's weapon and phone.

Luke focussed on keeping the gun steady. The guard's face quivered; even in the dim green light, Luke could see the flush rising on his cheeks. The fear in his eyes. They'd just cornered an animal who was more afraid of disappointing his boss than of them.

Luke had never pointed a gun at somebody before. He despised weapons. If he pulled the trigger, the guard would be dead. But if he didn't, billions of people would die. A necessary evil, an acceptable means to an end.

But could he murder this man?

Please don't move.

The guard didn't.

Ada used duct tape to cover his mouth and then immobilised his wrists by taping multiple figure eights around them. She tried to move his hands but couldn't.

'Handcuffs,' she yelled. 'Saw it in a movie.'

The guard stayed quiet.

While she bent down to do the same with his ankles, Luke thought about their next steps. A small door under the staircase lay open, a key in its lock. It led to a room with cleaning equipment, the perfect place to lock the guard. They'd have to figure out how to get past the fingerprint reader on the access panel of the main door. It didn't look like a CoreOS device. Ada would have to fig —

A loud slap rang out. Then a high-pitched groan.

His confidence collapsed immediately. He'd allowed himself to get distracted.

Ada lay on the floor. The guard thrust forward, full speed, at Luke.

Luke still had the gun, his finger on the trigger. All he had to do was flex it, and the guard would drop. A motion he'd executed thousands of times before, just in a different context. Easy.

But he couldn't do it. He didn't have it in him.

And he didn't have a plan B. Armed but out of options.

The guard crashed into Luke, fists first and with inhuman momentum.

Luke's chest snapped. His lungs deflated. He stumbled backwards, reaching for something to hold on to. His hands found nothing, and he fell square on his back.

The guard clearly expected more resistance and tumbled forward. His beefy body sailed through the air. Helplessness ripped at Luke.

But this time, his reflexes worked. He swivelled aside before he was pinned down. The guard hit the ground hard, landing flat on his face. The crack of his nose cut through all that generator noise. Luke scrambled to his knees, trying to find the gun. But it had landed under the big guy, who now desperately tried to grab it with his tied hands.

The guard gripped it and rolled around. The muzzle trajectory led precisely to Luke's head. Was this it?

Ada appeared from behind and kicked the guard between his legs with immense force. With a loud cry, he dropped the gun and rolled onto his side.

Luke scrambled up. He pooled all his strength and slammed his foot into the guard's rib cage, before winding back and ramming his face.

The guard's face marbled with broken capillaries. Ada took the gun and gave him a final blow with its metal handle. His arms and legs flailed. Then he stopped moving.

Luke breathed hard, hands resting on his knees. Fire flowed through his veins.

Before the guard could regain consciousness, Luke used almost half the roll of tape to wrap his feet and again his hands. It had to hold now.

Meanwhile, Ada worked on the access panel. After typing on the little screen, she took out a screwdriver and removed the front cover. She fumbled with the cabling, her eyes jumping between the circuit board and her phone.

By the time Luke was done with the guard, she'd given up. 'Nothing I can do here. This shitbox isn't a Swoop device, it's custom-made by an independent security company. Their system's tight as fuck. And I don't have my equipment. It'll take me too long to find a weak spot.'

Luke pointed at the guard. 'We have something else.'

It took their combined strength to pull up the guard to press his thumb against the fingerprint reader. The display panel showed a white checkmark, and the door buzzer whirred.

They took one of the guard's shoes to block the door open, then dragged his motionless body into the storage room. Once more, Luke checked his tape cuffs were tight, then he locked the door behind him.

Luke and Ada exchanged a glance of hope and fear as they entered the world's largest, most modern and most secret data centre.

They hurried along a short corridor with four doors, two on each side, and descended a wide staircase into the biggest room they'd ever seen. After the smothering confines of the tunnels and shafts, it felt like the outdoors. The colossal space housed endless columns of servers, each too long to see its end.

Each column consisted of two arrays of server racks back-to-back. Each rack was half a metre wide and two metres tall, stacked with standard-sized servers flickering with green lights. Along the centre of each column, between the two racks, faintly illuminated transparent water tubes connected each server with bigger and bigger pipes. This network extended across each column and all the way to the top of the enormous hall, where iron pipelines ran from front to back, connected by larger, cross-cutting ones that finally disappeared into the ceiling. This weird subterranean world was cooled with water from the lake, there were no fans in any of the computers. It was remarkably quiet. The site also ran with clean, renewable power from the dam, fully self-sustained and completely independent from the outside world.

Luke was speechless. One of Swoop's best-kept company secrets was how many servers they operated to run all of its services globally; it was the subject of endless speculation by tech magazines. But nobody had imagined the enormity of this gargantuan machine, a complex array of metal, tubes and lights, interconnected by thousands of kilometres of cables, forming multiple layers of computing hierarchies that made up the world's most powerful supercomputer.

Market penetration was Umesh's big advantage. That's what all this was for, to make sure he could reach every device in the world and turn it into a killing machine. This room was a weapon of mass destruction, the most powerful the world had ever seen. The realisation ripped pain through Luke's chest.

Whatever it took to prevent these megalomaniacs from committing global mass murder, they had to do it. They had about three hours to sabotage this brilliant feat of engineering. Luke didn't have the faintest idea whether they stood a chance.

'Now it's over to you,' he said.

'We need to access a master terminal, crack the superuser password and get admin privileges,' Ada said. 'Then we can check what jobs are scheduled to run at eight o'clock and stop whatever the hell Umesh is about to do. Or you know what … screw it, we shut the whole damn system down. A total Swoop blackout. Serves them right. No problem from a master terminal.' She pointed to the doors they'd passed on their way in. 'I bet that's where we can find them.'

The first door turned out to be a restroom, and the second was a closet with all sorts of tools and cleaning utensils. Behind the third was an office with three rows of desks with four terminals in each row, labelled 'sysadmin1' to 'sysadmin12'.

'This is exactly what I need,' said Ada. 'Swoop has tactical admin teams twenty-four strong on standby around the world. They can be dispatched to any data centre to fix whatever the hell needs fixing. Thirteen to twenty-four must be in the other room.'

A creak echoed in the gigantic techno-crypt, vibrating all the way through Luke's bones. He gripped Ada's shoulder. 'Did you hear that? The sound?'

Ada froze and listened for a couple of seconds. 'You're hallucinating. There's nothing. Let me get to work.'

Was he losing his mind?

As Ada powered up one of the terminals, Luke went back into the hallway. He checked left and right, went into the other rooms, down the stairs into the server room. Not a soul in sight.

Back in the admin office, he found Ada with her head buried in her hands. 'They have a fucking hardware switch on all these terminals. We need an access card to activate them. There's no other way.'

Why couldn't anything ever be simple? 'I'll see if the guard has one,' said Luke.

'The guard? Cause he's such a great coder?'

But Luke was already back outside. He approached the storage room and saw the door open. Hadn't they closed it? Instinctively, he pulled out the gun.

He took another step. A cold sting bit his heart. The door frame was broken, exactly where the lock had been.

Pieces of metal stuck out, bent outward as if somebody had pulled the door open with a huge amount of force. He recognised the pattern from when he'd opened the container to free Ada in that warehouse. Someone had used a crowbar.

The guard lay motionless on the floor, his breathing shallow, his eyes closed. The zip on his jacket had been opened and a lanyard hung around his neck. It held a plastic cover about the size of a credit card, probably designed to hold a badge exactly like the one Ada needed. Except it was empty.

Luke wasn't hallucinating. They weren't alone.

Chapter Thirty-Eight

Luke found Ada in the middle of the staircase leading into the data centre. 'Somebody broke into the storage room and took the guard's badge. It must be Xavier. He's here.'

'Son of a bitch.' Ada stared into the stunning vastness of the room. 'No ... doesn't make any sense. Why would the head of security steal a fucking security badge? He'd have his own one with unlimited access to everything. Somebody else is down here.'

Would the bad news ever end? A thousand needles pierced Luke's brain, his mind was caught in a net of too many variables and unknowns. Who else could be after them?

His voice became monotone. 'Is there any way to access those terminals without a badge?'

'Without the badge, I can't do jack shit. No ... We need plan B. The only way to stop these servers from running that killer program is ... well, to shut them down.'

Luke closed his eyes. 'Are you sure there's no alternative? Didn't we say this is the worst idea? How do we even do it? Split up, go around and switch them off, one by one?'

Ada shook her head. 'We'll never be quick enough. There are over a million servers down here. Literally. Even if it only takes us a second to kill each one, we'll be way too late. They're load balancing, so if one goes down, another one takes over. As long as there's a single machine alive, it's going to fucking happen.'

'Then we cut the main power. Shut them down in one go. Come on!'

'It's not that easy, Luke. Shit, we're hooked into a dam that gives perpetual energy. That's the whole point of housing this thing down here. There's no way to nuke it unless you can drain that goddamn lake. Even if we could cut the main lines, there are backup generators. Everything's triple-secured in a data centre. Too expensive to have this thing offline.'

It was as if this place was built to intimidate him. Gazillions of individual transistors, working seamlessly together as one huge unit, fast and fail-proof. His mind searched left and right, probing for a weakness that wasn't there.

'Screw it. Let's blow it up,' Ada said. 'We blow the whole fucking thing up.'

They were wasting time. Every second was an opportunity not taken. A life not saved. 'What do you mean? We're under an enormous amount of water. And where can we get a bomb from? I don't have one with me today.'

'We have all we need, smartass. Have you ever read the Anarchist's Cookbook?'

Luke shook his head.

'No, of course you haven't. Well, if you were a bit more … uhm, free-spirited, you'd know you can build a pretty bad-ass bomb with carbide and water. When you mix them, it creates acetylene, a gas that explodes pretty fucking spectacularly. I once made a hell of a fireball like that. Anyway, we have both these things down here. Remember all those lamps we saw during the tour? The pre-electricity thingies? They're probably in a shitty shape, but there should be enough raw material to blow us to the moon. And as you said, there's tons of water.'

Her words came out faster and faster. 'So we spread a bunch of buckets across the room, fill them with carbide and pour water over them. Maybe we can pinch the smaller cooling pipes. Then we let them sit for a while to produce the gas. Obviously, we'd need to block that piece of shit ventilation system, so everything stays in here. But since all servers are water-cooled, it's probably not the most sophisticated machinery with annoying backups and stuff. Once we have enough acetylene in the air, boom! We only need a tiny spark and the whole place goes to hell.'

Luke shifted his weight. A self-made bomb? Based on shady instructions off the internet? That was their plan to save the world? Cold sweat broke out on his temples. So many things could go wrong. Too many or too few ingredients; they could blow themselves up; they could suffocate from the gas. Disaster upon disaster.

'There needs to be another —'

A piece of wall exploded right next to him. Concrete and paint filled the air, a cloud of dust and smoke spreading around them like wildfire. Luke had never heard a gunshot before, but when he saw the little crater in the wall, he instantly knew what it was.

A second bullet raced through the air above his shoulder, sending a shockwave of terror through his cerebral cortex. He didn't have any idea where the shots came from but knew the shooter wouldn't miss a third time. Grabbing Ada's arm, he dropped to the ground. She collapsed without any resistance.

The next seconds could be their last. Two more bullets passed over their heads.

They half-crawled, half-fell down the stairs. At the bottom, they raced towards the closest pair of server columns and took cover in the aisle between them. They got up, their backs pressed against the racks. Luke quivered with adrenaline.

The world stood still. Nothing moved, except the flickering green server LEDs illuminating their clothes. No more shots. No movement. All-encompassing silence.

Trembling, Ada whispered, 'Who the fuck —'

Luke shushed her. Footsteps came from the next aisle. Slowly but steadily, their assailant moved away from the staircase, closer to the end of the long column of servers. Closer to them.

Luke took Ada's hand and pulled her in the opposite direction, further into the labyrinth of computers and pipes. After thirty metres, they saw an opening in the never-ending line of racks, a cross-cutting corridor to move from column to column without having to travel to the end of the room.

They hurried to the next aisle and peeked around the corner. Nobody there. Where had the footsteps come from?

With his back against a wall of servers, Luke looked around the corner to where they'd come from. Luke was stunned, as if a dark abyss had appeared before him.

Xavier. He stood at the end of the aisle, dressed as always in black, a black that seemed to absorb the flickering lights around him. In his hand was a gun with a large silencer. He spotted Luke and fired.

It hit a metal handle close to Luke's head. The bullet shattered, spraying metal fragments. One piece hit a server on the opposite side. With a mechanical click and an electrical purr, the machine powered down. Another fragment scraped Luke's thigh, sending pain through his leg.

Luke stumbled backwards and ran for his life. Ada followed. At every intersection, he randomly turned right or left, trying to obscure his path, a rabbit on the run.

Despite the regular layout of columns and rows, the place was a maze. Everywhere looked the same.

Out of breath, he stopped close to the centre of the room. Ada pulled up beside him. He'd lost sight of walls on either side. No sign of Xavier.

They were safe for now. No way could Xavier have anticipated their erratic turns. Still, Luke shivered. He fought hard to suppress a panic attack.

Ada finally found her voice. 'Damn it, Luke, he's shooting at us. Like we're in a goddamn warzone … Shit … What now?'

The rhythm of one particular server light caught Luke's attention. Like the steady tick of a clock, it soothed his mind. 'Are you sure this carbide thing will work?'

'On this scale? Hell no. Look at this ginormous room. How can you be sure about anything in here? But in a small space, fuck yes, it did. Almost blew off my arm.'

It was dangerous, but it was their only chance. No time for contingencies or a safety net. Luke's eyes narrowed, and he looked deep into hers for an eye-to-eye sanity check. He trusted her.

'OK. We blow it up, like you said. We need to be fast, so we split up. You stay here and disable the ventilation. I'll go and get the carbide.'

'Sounds like a plan. Except for one fucking detail. I have vertigo, and ventilation units are usually pretty high up. We'll do it the other way around.'

'OK.'

They made their way back to the entry, never following a straight line, turning left and right, staying unpredictable. When they reached the staircase, he gave her his backpack.

'Throw away what you don't need and put the carbide in here.' Then he tossed her the gun. 'And take this, maybe you're more killer material than I am. When you're back, walk down the stairs, go straight and turn right on the fifth aisle. Then stop at the eighth column. I'll wait there for you. Be careful.'

Luke watched Ada go, hoping like hell this wasn't the last time he'd seen her. He liked her, really liked her, more than just a friend. He wasn't sure what that meant exactly, but he wanted to find out. And for that, he had to survive.

But time was working against them. It was 6:30 pm. Ninety minutes left.

The rudimentary ventilation system had shafts on the ceiling leading to air slits on the walls. Constantly checking over his shoulder, he returned to the janitor's closet and searched for material he could use — a large roll of trash bags, rags, string, tape and a staple gun.

He crept back into the main data centre like a panther on the hunt. Xavier stood twenty metres away, facing away from him, staring into the room, on high alert.

Luke had a sudden urge to cough. He swallowed hard and almost gagged. To control his deepest reflexes, he covered his mouth with his hand. As he concentrated on his breath, the door handle slipped out of his fingers.

The mechanical click of the lock sliding back into place betrayed him. Xavier spun around, his eyes firing a beam of rage into Luke's soul.

They both froze in almost comical poses — Luke holding the door handle, squinting and hoping an alien force would magically save him from his predicament, and Xavier, his eyes wide open, not believing his luck.

Then they both snapped back to reality. Xavier's hand jumped to the gun in his holster. Luke sprinted to the only place where he could hide. Down the wide staircase, into the data centre. Towards Xavier.

The first bullet smashed into the wall behind him. He ducked and changed direction, zigzagging across the full width of the stairs.

But Luke wasn't a gazelle, and his brain couldn't keep up with his feet down the steps. He had to slow down to avoid falling, making him an easier target.

The next bullet hit him in the left shoulder. He recoiled from the impact, surprised how little it hurt. At first. It wasn't the pain, but rather the shock that made him stumble on the last step.

His fall catapulted him out of Xavier's sightline. Luke rolled over twice and knocked his head hard on a server rack. Every cell in his body was on fire.

Xavier's footsteps approached.

No time to linger. Luke forced himself up. Instead of running down the aisle where he landed, he risked advancing further. He entered the next corridor.

It didn't pay off. As he turned into the first interconnecting pathway, he saw Xavier, his arm extended, ready to shoot.

This time, Luke ducked out of sight in time to avoid the bullet.

No reason to get comfortable. Xavier saw where he went. Luke covered the ground to the next column, and, in another attempt to masquerade his path, turned back towards the stairs.

But Xavier wasn't fooled so easily, not this time. He appeared a second later, his eyes locked on his target.

Luke willed away his misery. He ran back into the endless maze of servers, trying to outmanoeuvre Xavier. No success. Xavier followed closely. He anticipated Luke's turns and gained ground.

Luke's stamina approached his limit. The clock ticked on relentlessly. He needed an idea, and fast.

After yet another turn, Luke took the staple gun out of his pocket and threw it a few metres ahead of him, agony slapping his shoulder. The instant it left his hand, he dropped to the ground and crawled into the space between two columns of server racks. It was tight and dark, cables everywhere, but Luke squeezed his skinny body inside. As he disappeared into this no man's land, he heard a bang as the staple gun landed on the floor. He froze and held his breath.

Through a small opening between two servers, Luke saw Xavier running at full speed. No signs of exhaustion. As he approached, he slowed down and turned his head.

Luke's heart scrambled to keep up with the demand for fresh blood his cells required. His lungs screamed for air. But he couldn't allow himself a single breath. Too risky.

Barely an arm's length away, Xavier stopped. He turned a full 360 degrees, a human radar antenna in pursuit of prey. Luke saw the details of his face, the darkness under his eyes, the five-o'clock shadow, the lacklustre skin on his cheeks.

Droplets of sweat trickled down Luke's chin. He was out of air. Not a particle of oxygen left in his lungs. In a battle of willpower versus reflex, he kept his mouth closed.

Any second he wouldn't be able to control it anymore. Any second and this would all be over.

Just as Luke was about to faint, Xavier moved on. Within a few paces, he was in a full sprint, a light-footed marathon runner. He ran towards the staple gun and was soon out of Luke's field of vision.

Once Xavier was a couple of metres away, Luke allowed himself a quick breath. His hideout was hot and dusty, which didn't help to normalise his heartbeat. He took a few more shallow breaths, but his lungs couldn't draw enough oxygen from the stale air. He needed to get out before he passed out. The pain in his shoulder spread through his entire arm.

He was about to leave his hiding place when Xavier appeared again, creeping slowly, inspecting every rack he passed. Luke pushed himself further inside and closed his eyes using the logic of a five-year-old: if he couldn't see Xavier, Xavier wouldn't be able to see him.

When he opened them again, Xavier was gone.

As the space around him shrank, he was close to losing consciousness. Luke discarded every margin of safety. He had to get out.

When he emerged, he took a few deep breaths and his pulse dropped to a sustainable level. Where was Xavier? Luke strode to the next intersection and peered around the corner. In the distance, he saw one shadow chasing another. A fraction of a second later, they were gone.

The silhouette in pursuit matched Xavier's. But who was he hunting? Ada? No, the person was taller and probably male. Good. Whatever kept Xavier busy bought him time.

Luke had bruises and scratches all over his body. Checking his shoulder properly for the first time made it hurt even more. Blood ran down his chest; his shirt was soaked with it.

It was just a flesh wound. Nothing to worry about. The first aid course he'd taken more than ten years ago, a relic from the troubled past of his country, taught him to deal with it.

He took one of the janitor's rags, created a makeshift bandage and tightened it around his upper arm. It stopped the bleeding but limited the movement of his arm to a few degrees in either direction. It had to be good enough. He couldn't afford to slow down.

His watch told him seventy-four minutes to go. Too much time had passed. And the ventilation system was still running.

He'd lost all sense of direction. Turning in a circle, he found a wall about thirty metres to his left. As he got closer, he saw a ventilation slit a few centimetres from the floor. He sealed it with one of the trash bags and some tape. The draft stopped.

He moved on to the next one a few metres away and repeated the procedure. Two down.

He was cutting the tenth piece of tape when he realised he wouldn't have enough material for them all. Or time. Each opening was small, but there were many of them. Hundreds, maybe thousands. He'd never succeed.

Then, he had a much better idea.

Ten metres back into the enormous room, he saw a little white triangle mounted on an iron stick on top of one of the server racks. He recognised it from the office, where several of these were scattered throughout each building. The other engineers called them 'env boxes'; they contained sensors for measuring the temperature, the level of carbon dioxide, air pressure and other environmental indicators. With that data, a central control system adjusted the ventilation, heating and other machinery to achieve the optimal climate.

A few weeks ago, a particularly funny prankster had put a portable heater right under one of those boxes. The sensors picked up the heat and the air conditioning worked with full force, which created an Arctic climate on the entire floor.

Luke clumsily climbed up the rack. He couldn't make a sound; Xavier was out there somewhere. He wrapped the box in one of the trash bags and sealed the whole thing with duct tape.

Unlike his colleague, he didn't care about the temperature but the air composition. To save energy, modern climate systems only ran when necessary. A space like this was deserted most of the time, so all systems were usually on standby. When humans arrived, they changed the balance by converting oxygen into carbon dioxide with every breath. The sensor would detect these minuscule differences and power up the ventilation system, using fresh air from the outside to restore the balance. It had done that when they entered. By wrapping the box in its own microclimate, Luke created stable conditions around these sensors, which was the signal for the control unit to power down. The room would slowly fill up with carbon dioxide now, but nowhere fast enough to be a threat to them.

He climbed down and worked his way through the room in a large circle, halfway between the centre and its outer walls, the most effective distribution for measuring just about anything. He found seven more and treated them in the same way.

Then he paced back to the wall and checked one of the air vents. With his hand in front of it, he tried to detect a draft. No movement. He pressed his ear against the cold metal surface for a few seconds. The air stood still.

He allowed himself a brief smile. His task was accomplished.

He checked his watch — about fifty minutes to go. Time to find Ada.

Luke arrived at their prearranged meeting place and found nobody. Ada had a lot more ground to cover for her part of the job, so he'd expected to wait. He hated every second of it, the inability to do anything. Speculation was the only thing he had left: Where was she? Had she run into trouble? Where was Xavier? And who was the other mysterious stranger? Friend or foe? Was it the same person who had stolen the guard's pass?

He studied his watch, observing the movement of the hand, every tick triggering a tremor inside his spine.

Three minutes. He'd wait three minutes before looking for her. Could he afford that much?

He stared at his hands, unsteady and shaking, and thought about his options. If Ada didn't get the carbide, billions of people would be dead tomorrow. Plain and simple. Could he fetch the lamps from the storage room, run back, set up everything and light it in time? Probably not. But what alternatives did he have? Give up and hide down here, in Swoop's inner sanctum? Get out and run to the most remote place he could find? With fifty minutes left? Even if he survived the mass murder that was about to happen, Xavier probably would go the extra mile to find and kill him afterwards.

Twenty seconds before his deadline, Ada showed up.

'What took you so long?' he asked.

She stared at his bandage and the blood on it. Her face paled. 'Fuck, what happened?'

'I'm fine,' Luke lied. 'I got shot. But it doesn't hurt that much.'

'Xavier?'

Luke nodded. 'We'll fix it later. All that matters is that we hurry up.' The pain in his shoulder was excruciating, but responsibility drove him on. He closed his eyes to conjure his childhood home. Only crude shapes came to him, all details and colours were gone.

Ada's voice interrupted his attempt to escape. 'That manic asshole, I'll fucking shoot him to the moon when I see him. Where's he now?'

'Chasing somebody else.' Luke shook his head. 'I don't care who, we're running out of time. I disabled the ventilation. We need to get going with the carbide.'

Ada smiled, the colour returning to her face. 'I'm way ahead of you. I got eight buckets full of carbide, probably five kilos each. Eight little acetylene factories. With forty kilos of carbide, we should get a decent amount of gas if we spread them evenly across this place.' Her smile grew wider. 'And I've already set up six of them. Look!'

She pointed between the backsides of two racks, similar to the place where Luke had hidden earlier. Pushing a bunch of cables away, she showed Luke three big black buckets. Two were filled with dry carbide, a yellow, powder-like substance. The contents of the third one looked muddy, like a thick yellow soup. A steady trickle of water from one of the cooling pipes fed into it.

'The wet one is already producing. We have to hurry to set up the other two.'

Luke grabbed one of the dry buckets. 'So there's already acetylene in the air? Right here around us?'

'Yes, Captain Obvious. It's completely transparent and harmless. Unless of course the concentration is high enough and someone blows it up. But we're not there yet.'

Luke couldn't help but hold his breath for a couple of seconds until his brain took control. He couldn't abandon logic. They had work to do. 'OK, let's set up the other two.'

'First, take this son of a bitch back' — Ada handed him the gun — 'I almost shot myself in the foot.'

Each with a bucket in their hands, they proceeded to the next spot, watching out for Xavier. They'd come too far to risk being discovered now.

'Shit.' Ada came to a halt. 'Stop,' she mouthed, pressing her right finger on her lips.

Luke didn't see anything. 'Ada, what's —'

She pressed her hand against his mouth and pointed to a distant corridor. The silhouette of a person stood in the shadows about fifty metres ahead. Not Xavier. The person was male, tall and relatively thin from what Luke could make out. He had long hair and was wearing jeans and a sweater. Was that the mysterious stranger who'd stolen the guard's badge?

Quietly, they backtracked to the next interconnecting pathway, moved a couple of columns sideways and forward again. The manoeuvre placed them a little off their original spot, but out of sight. While Ada set up the two last buckets, Luke tried to get a better look at the stranger through a narrow opening between two racks. He was gone.

'You sure you're looking in the right place?' whispered Ada.

'Positive. Maybe he went somewhere else. The further the better. Let's get out of here.'

Ada had already hidden a bucket behind a stack of servers and was pinching a hole into a cooling tube. 'Done.' She shifted a few dangling cables to hide the carbide.

A voice boomed. 'Lukasz ... Ada ... stop!'

Luke squeezed his eyes shut. The voice was vaguely familiar. It didn't belong to Xavier or Umesh. But Luke had heard it before.

'Fuck,' Ada said.

They turned around slowly and instinctively raised their arms. Pain flared from Luke's shoulder wound. It was all over.

He placed the voice—he'd heard it months ago on their first day at Swoop and had developed a distaste for it ever since. Luke hadn't been dreaming; it was Shawn after all. Of course. Who else would follow Umesh's insane orders no matter what? Luke hated his guts.

Shawn was breathing hard, sweat ran down his cheeks. His long hair was a mess. He held a crowbar in one hand and a phone in the other.

'We need to talk,' Shawn said, a grave expression on his face. He moved closer, one step at a time. Despite his apparent state of exhaustion, he looked reasonably fit. Too fit to outrun.

He came to a halt an arm's length away. His face was red, the crowbar high in his right hand, shaking but ready to release. 'You should —'

No time for this, whatever it was. Using his good arm, Luke hit him hard in the face with the last bucket of carbide. He produced enough force to keep the contents inside and reach his target before Shawn could react. The element of surprise caught him unprepared. It sent him staggering backwards.

Ada stepped back, but Luke pushed forward. Swinging the bucket a second time, circling up, then looping down, he completed a full figure eight around his body. With the increased momentum, the second smack into Shawn's face was even harder. It sent him to the ground.

Luke yelled, 'RUN!'

They raced away as hard as their tired legs allowed them.

After a few turns, Luke's thigh cramped, and they stopped.

'Screw distribution, we're putting the last one right here,' Ada said.

Forty-three minutes left.

'What now?' asked Luke. 'How long? How long until we have enough gas?'

'I can't say for sure how long the reaction takes. But based on my first attempt at home, taking into account the total volume of the room, distribution of the buckets over time —'

'Ada!'

'OK, OK. About half an hour.'

Luke checked his watch again. Forty-one minutes left. How did they waste two full minutes just now? His heartbeat raged in his temples, fuelling his ever-growing headache. 'How do we set it off?'

Ada grinned. 'I know a way to blow up your phone.'

'What?'

'Remember those Samsung phones a couple of years back? The ones that were banned from planes?'

'Yeah,' Luke answered. 'Their batteries exploded, right?'

'Correct. But here's the thing, the root cause wasn't their shitty batteries, it was in their equally shitty code. They had a bad loop somewhere that called the self-check functionality of the power supply over and over again until it overheated. The battery wasn't protected against that, so it nuked.'

The itching inside Luke's skull became stronger. He had no patience left for nerdiness. 'Ada, get to the fucking point. How does that help us?'

'Relax. We can replicate the whole damn thing on your phone. I'll write an app doing exactly that.'

Disbelief flooded Luke's face. 'That's your plan? Are you nuts? You want to start coding now? We don't even have a computer.'

'I can do all the coding directly on the phone, it's old but apps are just apps. I'll have to use a plain text editor, but we're only talking about a few lines, probably less than fifty. If I add a timer, we can get out of here before everything gets fucked up.'

'Who says this battery will blow as well? People must've learned from Samsung's mistakes.'

'Not really. They fixed the bug in the software, sure, but on the hardware side, all they ever did was increase the safety margins. I mean a battery is still just a stupid battery, not a spaceship. If we disable the auto-shutdown and put it on something that's already pretty warm, that should do the trick.'

This was all too much for Luke. 'Should do the trick? You're crazy. The time, Ada! Look at the time.'

Ada took a deep breath. 'If it doesn't work…' She fumbled in the pocket of her pants and produced a small metallic bit that looked like a button with nothing attached. The trigger mechanism from one of the carbide lamps. 'Well, then I'll do it myself.'

Luke felt his jaw drop. The heartbeat in his temples came to a stop.

'Ada…'

'Stop talking and let me get to work.'

Ada sat cross-legged on the cold floor of the janitor's closet and typed frantically on her phone, her eyes squinting on the tiny screen. Luke stood next to her, trying not to watch what she was doing. He aimed the gun at the door, shaking enough to make the metallic bits clatter. He still wasn't sure he could kill somebody, but he had to do something.

'How much longer?' he asked for the tenth time.

'You're annoying, you know that? Anyway … let me just … I only have to… Ha, there we go! Now I only have to deploy it.' Ada raised her arm theatrically and let her index finger fall on the miniature ENTER key on the phone's display.

A command window with cryptic output popped up and a second later, a new icon appeared on the phone's home screen. The stylised version of a mushroom cloud was titled 'Screw you Swoop'.

'Subtle. How do we know there are no bugs?'

'Oh please, Luke, give me a damn break. I don't do bugs. It was only a couple of lines. Besides, there's no way to test-blow something up, OK?'

Luke almost dropped the gun. 'It's too risky. Billions of people, Ada.'

Ada shook her head. 'Trust me. It's gonna blow in five minutes, and we have nine left. Four minutes buffer. If it doesn't work, I'll come back and do it myself. Now let's hide this thing and get the fuck out of here.'

Never in his life had Luke heard a sentence that made more sense. Leaving everything else behind, they exited the closet and ran to the staircase.

Maybe it was his mind playing tricks on him, but he was sure there was a weird smell in the air. He gagged and coughed but kept going. No time to worry about his health. He only hoped none of these servers would generate a spark.

Out of nowhere, Xavier stepped into their path.

They had to break hard to avoid crashing into him. Where did he come from?

They'd been so close.

Xavier aimed his gun at Luke's forehead. Its silencer almost reached his skin. Nobody in the world would miss that shot. 'You've been lucky today, Lukasz, very lucky. But let me assure you, I won't miss again. Now tell me, what did you do? If you stop it now, I might let you live. Or at least make you suffer less.'

Luke felt the gun in his pocket. Like a deadly metal siren, it sang to him. It begged him to pull it out and shoot.

His fingers tensed.

Now or never.

Time to act.

'Please, please ... don't shoot!' he cried out. A tear rolled down his cheek. 'I'll tell you every —'

In one quick motion, he took the gun out of his pocket and aimed it at Xavier's face. Luke closed his eyes in a mix of fear and to convince himself his actions were not his own.

Then he squeezed the trigger.

The gun's firing mechanism started to click, but it never completed the movement. Sharp pain struck his hand. His arm swung upwards in a motion he didn't initiate.

He opened his eyes to see Xavier's arm completing a slap that had hit his hand with incredible force. The gun flew in a high arc and landed a few metres behind Luke.

Now Ada punched Xavier's hands.

He handled the blow better and kept his grip on his gun. But the evasive move left his upper body exposed.

All this happened within a fraction of a second. Mists of Xavier's sweat vapoured through the air in slow motion.

Luke gathered his remaining strength and charged headfirst at Xavier. Ada did the same. Together, they crashed into him with everything they had. Xavier was no wrestler; he shouldn't have been able to stand his ground.

But he did.

They crashed into Xavier's chest, who struggled to fight off both of them at the same time. Luke's arms flailed, trying to grab Xavier's gun. Ada gripped his throat in an attempt to choke him.

Xavier's red face turned darker and darker. Why didn't he pass out?

Xavier let out a roar and sent them both staggering backwards in an explosion of force.

'ENOUGH!' he screamed, waving the gun, his hand shaking. 'Whatever you did, I'll figure it out myself. You two had your chance!'

Luke sat on the ground, panting and gasping. He was done with the world. Pain was everywhere. His arm had gone completely numb. The acetylene smell was overwhelming, scratching his throat from the inside. He could barely breathe.

Ada lay still on the floor next to him. She'd fallen backwards and hit her head on the hard floor. Was she even conscious?

They'd tried their best, they'd mustered all their strength and they'd come all the way here. But it wasn't far enough. Everything was lost. They'd been defeated.

Xavier pointed his gun at Luke.

He was about to be executed.

He closed his eyes and flashed a bitter smile. They'd probably succeed in their mission; the shot would set off the explosion. If only he'd be around to see whether it actually worked.

He thought about the people he was trying to save. Dying was a small price for saving the world.

But this was no consolation. He was young and had his whole life ahead of him. He didn't want to die.

His parents. He'd give everything to tell them everything would be alright. Tears rolled down his cheeks.

Xavier's trigger finger started flexing. Time slowed.

Will I hear the shot before the bullet hits me? How odd it was to think about physics in this moment.

He heard a soft *thump*. Not the short, powerful bang of a gunshot. No pain.

Luke looked up. Shawn stood behind Xavier, a bloody crowbar in his hand. Xavier's face was loaded with terror and pain. But that wasn't all. Rage and determination blasted from his eyes. He'd taken a hit, but it hadn't been enough.

Xavier's gun swung around. A bullet escaped and missed Luke's head by a hair.

Shawn's arm prepared for another punch. It'd be too late. Xavier's gun was nearly there.

Now, Luke. Time to show the world.

Harvesting energy from the last of his resolve, he launched himself into Xavier. Head first, no regard for limits or safety. They crashed into a server rack, metal splinters everywhere.

A sharp *crack* came from Xavier's temple. His eyes went blank. Blood streamed down his cheeks. A splinter of white bone stuck out from his skull. His body deflated between them.

Luke collapsed onto the floor, his system drained to the last bit. An arm extended towards him. He followed it and saw Shawn's bruised face.

'I told you I just wanted to talk.' He helped Luke back up. 'I'm on your side, guys. Always was. I found out about Umesh's plan ... and about you trying to prevent it. I tried to get in touch, over and over, but Xavier was always there ... I came to help.'

Luke didn't know what to say. If there were any sides in this game, he'd have placed Shawn on Umesh's team.

Ada found her words first. 'I ... I'm deeply sorry. We thought you'd —'

'Don't ... No need to explain. Let's talk later.' He checked his watch. 'We have seven minutes.'

'This phone's going to trigger an explosion. We need to get the hell out of —' Ada picked the device up from the floor. Its display was cracked. The screen was completely black. She pressed every key but nothing happened.

The phone was gone. Completely useless.

'Fuck.' She took out the carbide lamp trigger from her pocket and stared at it.

Luke took a deep breath. 'One of us has to do it manually. Should we draw —'

'I'll do it,' Shawn said in a voice that didn't leave any room for doubt.

Luke frowned. 'Are you—'

'I'm sure, yes. You're young, you have so much ahead of you. I'm...' He lowered his head. 'I'm corrupted. For years I followed them blindly. I did everything they said. No more. It's time to pay the price.'

Luke saw nothing but truth in Shawn's eyes and pushed away his doubts. Shawn was going to push that button no matter what. Luke exchanged a look with Ada and nodded respectfully.

'I'm sorry,' Ada said. 'We underestimated you.'

'Engineers always do,' Shawn said with a last smile. He waved them off.

They ran as fast as their hurting bodies would let them. Up the staircase and out of the server room, through the narrow corridor with the admin offices, up the long vertical shaft. One flight of stairs after another, out of breath but pushing through.

Luke tried to check the time. In his hurry, he broke his watch on the metallic handrail. His ties with time and reality were severed. It didn't matter. All he could do was run and hope for the best.

The staircase seemed endless. Luke's calves felt like bricks after four flights, followed by his hamstrings, quads and the remaining muscles in his legs.

Ada sweated, muttering insults under her breath. Their pace decreased to a trot, then into a desperate scramble.

How much time did they have? No point in estimating anymore. They moved as fast as they could. Maybe it was enough, maybe it wasn't.

At the top of the staircase, they reached another corridor leading away from the shaft. Luke stumbled along, his heart pattering.

Finally, they reached a door with a pale shimmer of light shining through the crack at its bottom. They'd reached the surface.

The door was locked.

Ada pushed the handle with all her strength, moving it up and down.

Luke groaned. How could this simple metal door be their demise?

A low rumble came from below.

The explosion.

In a way, Luke was relieved. Until this moment, he wasn't entirely sure whether the acetylene, produced by eighty-year-old chemicals and triggered by an equally old mechanical button, would really ignite.

But it did. Spectacularly. The ground shook under their feet, the rumble grew louder and louder.

No. This couldn't be the end. Luke wouldn't let a door stand between his life and death.

Harnessing the last of his energy, he stepped back two paces and charged. Shoulder first, ignoring his injury. A spasm rumbled through his body as he crashed into it.

The door snapped open.

He fell through and landed on the ground. Ada emerged and collapsed next to him.

A hot wave of fire passed over their heads, expanding from the narrow corridor into the open air. Luke felt the enormous energy release and covered his ears with both hands. The roar was deafening. Heat scorched their clothes and their hair.

The wave turned into a round fireball and shot into the sky.

Half a second later, a flood of invisible pressure passed over them in the opposite direction, as air from the outside was sucked back into the bowels of the dam to replace the gas that'd been set free.

Then everything fell quiet.

They'd done it.

Luke and Ada lay motionless on the ground.

She poked him in his good arm and smiled. No need to say anything.

He smiled back.

Chapter Thirty-Nine

Luke sat in front of his laptop in a tiny room in a nameless office building in Menlo Park and typed on his keyboard. A few last tweaks to the model, a few optimizations here and there, and he'd be done.

'What the hell are you doing? We're going live in' — Ada checked at her watch— 'damn, in less than an hour. And you're still messing around with one of the core components. If you fuck this up, it'll be beyond embarrassing. We'll never hear the end of it.'

Luke turned his head to crack his neck. A trace of discomfort ran through his shoulder, where he'd been shot three months ago. He thought back and smiled. They were going to be alright.

'A couple more lines and I'm done for the day,' he promised. 'I'm ninety-nine per cent sure this won't break anything. Well, maybe ninety per cent. And it'll make a difference, believe me.' He paused a second and grinned. 'You know what, eighty per cent. Yes, that's probably accurate. I'm eighty per cent sure this is fine.'

'You're fucking unbelievable,' Ada said. 'But you know what, it's OK. I'll tell everyone it was you who single-handedly butchered our promising startup and burned the three million we got in funding. I used to be a blogger, you know, a successful one. People believe me. I have followers.'

'Oh, come on, please … By the way, while you were complaining like a little baby, I ran the tests and everything's still green, thank you very much.'

He hit the ENTER key to start the rollout of their first official deployment and saw lines of output in a little window on his screen. While version 1.0 uploaded to their servers, he recollected the last few months.

Their decision not to return to Swoop, despite a personal apology from the new CEO, a substantial raise and a huge equity packet in exchange for their silence.

Their agreement to use their skills to make the world a better place—actually doing so, not just throwing the phrase around.

The long nights brainstorming.

The realization that Umesh's premise was right—the world had indeed become decadent—but the understanding that his methods had been utterly wrong.

The decision to fight decadence in their own humble way.

The fun nights hashing out the technical details.

The countless dreadful meetings with stakeholders, trying to convince them to invest.

All this seemed far in the past now. After a lot of hard work, today was the day their app would go live. Their little startup would finally be on the map. In the app store.

Digital wellbeing was still a young field, nobody else did what they were about to offer. No other app used state-of-the-art machine learning to monitor the habits of each user and determine when it was psychologically safe for them to use their phone. And when it was better not to. Nobody else had the guts to turn off the user's phone when that was the case.

They had great technology, and their chances were pretty good. At least if people truly wanted to become happier versions of themselves.

Ada jolted him out of his dreams. 'Son of a bitch … Look, they finally busted those bastards.'

She pointed at their TV and turned up the volume. They had the news on day and night, a habit they'd established on day one of their new venture.

'…were arrested by the IRS for tax evasion,' the news anchor declared. 'The twenty-four top managers allegedly engaged in a coordinated group effort to game the tax system and escape prosecution. The list reads like the who is who in the tech business and contains C-level executives from companies like Google, Apple, Facebook, Amazon, Swoop, Microsoft and several startups. Most of the accused individuals work in fields related to artificial intelligence and brain-computer interfaces, a fact that could be related to the case or purely coincidental, as a spokesperson from the IRS has told us.'

'It remains unclear whether this case is related to the mysterious deaths of Umesh Patel, former CEO and founder of Swoop, and Walter Hamilton, president of venture capital fund Hamilton Ventures. Given the amount of uncertainty and the potentially connected string of tech employee fatalities a few weeks earlier, conspiracy theorists suggest there's something larger going on behind the scenes of the Valley. Some go as far as linking these cases to the legendary society of the Illuminati. Representatives from all companies declined to comment on the matter.'

'Twenty-four … tax evasion … Illuminati … interesting,' Luke muttered and took a long sip from his mug. They'd waited for such an announcement, but now that it was out, it sounded surprisingly unspectacular.

He looked at Ada, their eyes met, and they smiled, the comforting smile of two people sharing a secret they knew was better hidden from the public. It'd taken him a full week to convince her the world wasn't ready for their story, no matter how wrong it was. In the end, she'd trusted him.

It was the smile of two people who'd gone through hell and back, a journey that had changed them, made them more aware of themselves and humanity. The smile of two friends.

He pondered that thought for a minute. An idea popped into his head. 'What if we cross-reference behavioural patterns across different apps and use that to improve our accuracy? I bet I could get a proto—'

'Luke, no … No, no, no, no, no. For fuck's sake, stop it, no more changes. We're shipping as is.'

They released their brand-new app thirty minutes later, and just like that, a new chapter in their lives began.